I0700770

MIDNIGHT WANDERINGS

GRANT BUTLER

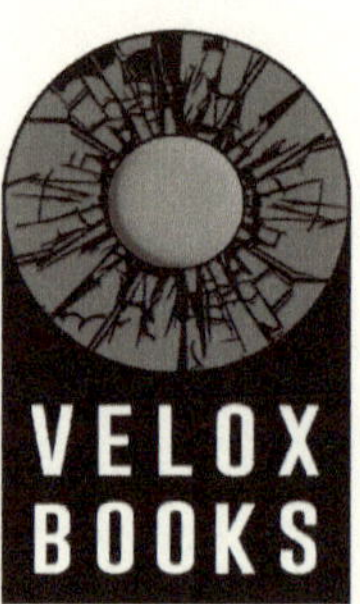

Published by arrangement with the author.

Copyright © 2025 by Grant Butler.

All rights reserved.

No part of this publication may be reproduced, distributed, or transmitted in any form or by any means, including photocopying, recording, or other electronic or mechanical methods, without the prior written permission of the publisher, except as permitted by U.S. copyright law.

The story, all names, characters, and incidents portrayed in this production are fictitious. No identification with actual persons (living or deceased), places, buildings, and products is intended or should be inferred.

YOU'RE READING ANOTHER TERRIFYING COLLECTION FROM

**FOLLOW VELOX TO KEEP
THE NIGHTMARES COMING:**

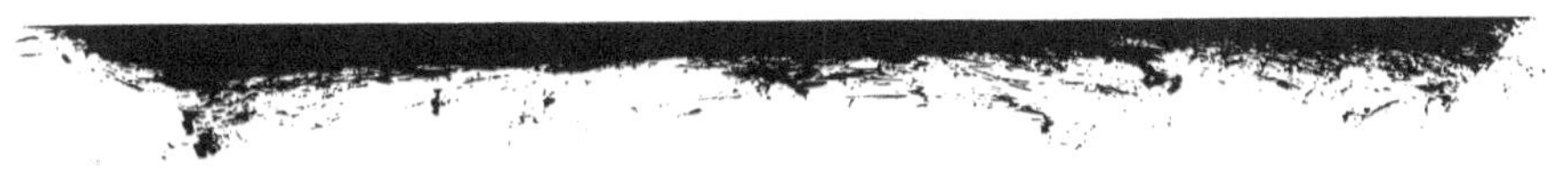

CONTENTS

FORTUNE COOKIES

CHINESE FOOD HAS ALWAYS been a favorite of mine. There's nothing else quite like it. The combination of flavors and dishes are beyond unique. While I try not to eat it too often, I do love to treat myself to it about once a month at the most.

A few months ago, it had been a while since I brought home the iconic white containers with the red pagoda and matching letters on it. And having just finished a particularly long week at work, that meant Chinese takeout was on the menu for dinner. So as soon as 5 pm came, I was out the door and walking towards my car. Once inside, I placed a call to The Roaring Dragon, a new place in town for Chinese takeout. I went with my standard order of General Tso's Chicken, vegetable fried rice, and a few egg rolls. The woman taking my order said it would be ready in fifteen minutes.

I arrived at the restaurant right on time and hustled inside. The place looked like most other Chinese restaurants. A huge fish tank near the front, lanterns hanging from the ceiling, golden cat statues located in various places, and red banners with Chinese calligraphy hung from the walls.

"Hi, order for pickup. The name is Archer," I said when I spotted the waitress on duty.

She took all of five seconds to walk to the back and return with my order.

"Here you are Mr. Archer, anything else I can get for you?"

"No, that will be all."

"23.95 please."

I gave her 29 and told her to keep the change before I headed home. The smell of the food immediately took over my car and by the time I arrived at my house, I was starving. I wasted no time in ripping through the brown paper bag and taking out the white paper cartons, which were warm in my hands. Once I had filled a plate, I walked to the living room and turned on the TV before I chowed down. It was all delicious. The Dragon's egg rolls are some of the best I've ever had. Perfectly fried and crunchy, they go good with either spicy mustard or duck sauce, which were both included.

After I had cleaned my plate, I walked back to the kitchen and cracked open a fortune cookie. I don't usually care for the cookies themselves, I much prefer the almond cookies with chocolate frosting, but the fortunes are mildly amusing.

Opening the tiny strip of paper, I read what was written in small blue letters.

"She who has wronged you will reap what she sowed."

Looking at it, I was mildly surprised. That was a bit different than the usual philosophical quote about knowledge, wealth, or happiness. Well, whatever, the rest of my egg rolls weren't going to eat themselves. So I went back to the living room and finished my dinner. When I was done, I packed everything away and put it in the fridge. Another great thing about Chinese food is that it always heats up amazingly well, fried rice in particular.

The next day, I got up late since it was Saturday and tossed some eggs on the stove to scramble for breakfast. After washing it down with some orange juice, I grabbed my phone to see what was going on. It turned out that earlier this morning a friend of mine had sent me a news article.

"Two dead in late night car accident," the local headline blared before I scrolled down further. "At approximately 2:30 am, an accident took place at the intersection of Hilliard Drive and Oak Avenue. A 2018 Ford Escape was flipped over and two of the three passengers died on impact. The driver of the car, Brooke Carlton, was unconscious at the scene and was determined to have been driving while intoxicated. The other two passengers, Zack Thompson and Eric Hollings, were pronounced dead at the scene. Ms. Carlton is being arraigned on Monday in connection with the two deaths."

I sat there silently for a moment. Brooke really did it this time. It wasn't bad enough she got caught drunk driving; her drunk driving killed the two guys she was with. I had no idea who Hollings was, but Zack Thompson, oh, I could never forget him or his obnoxious sneering face. Well jokes on you buddy, you may have been the guy my ex-girlfriend cheated on me with, but now you're nothing but a statistic and a sob story to be told in court.

But then I remembered the fortune cookie from last night. That had to just be a coincidence. Brooke winding up this way was a surprise to no one who knew her and had a brain. Without thinking, I found myself walking to the kitchen, the smell of my breakfast still in the air. I grabbed the other fortune cookie that came with my meal and ripped open the plastic before I broke open the cookie and unfurled the small scrap of paper.

"An alarm is a handy thing to have for one's house. But an alarm is only as good as the person who turns it on."

That one made me chuckle. I had recently gotten a home security system on account of a rise in local burglaries, but since it was new to me, I kept forgetting to turn it on. I tossed the cookie into the garbage and hopped in the shower so I could officially begin my Saturday. I did the usual errands before I went to a movie and met some friends for dinner at a bistro. But before I left, I made sure to set the alarm before locking up.

When I came home a few hours later, I was shocked to find a squad car in front of my house with its lights flashing.

"Can I help you?" I asked the officer as soon as I parked in my driveway.

"Hi, we were responding to an alarm that was activated at this residence about fifteen minutes ago. When we arrived, we saw someone dressed in a sweat suit running down the street. Then we did a quick check, and it looks like he was in the middle of breaking in through the front door when the alarm went off. We did a secondary search of the perimeter, and it looks like everything else is shut. I also checked your front door, which is still working as it should be. You'll want to do a quick look and make sure everything is accounted for, but apart from that you should be ok. Let us know if you need anything else."

"Thank you so much. You have a good night now."

I did as was recommended and everything was indeed accounted for. But when that was done, I sat at the kitchen table and stared at the fortune from earlier. This couldn't be happening. It had to be a coincidence. Out of all the thousands of fortune cookies that get handed out each day, some were bound to be accurate. Even a broken clock is right twice a day.

To get my mind off it, I spent the rest of the evening watching *The Crown* on Netflix before going to bed. When I woke up the following day, I managed to have a normal afternoon and didn't think too much about the weird coincidences. The work week followed in the same fashion, and I carried on as usual. But something began to nag at me. What would happen if I got another fortune cookie? Maybe this time I would get the winning lottery numbers. All that had happened so far was that it had predicted my train wreck of an ex-girlfriend would meet a sticky end and having a home security system is no good if you don't turn it on. Not exactly stretches of the imagination.

So that meant Thursday night's dinner was Chinese.

This time, my order from The Roaring Dragon was Orange Chicken, white rice, and Crab Rangoon. I paid for my order and brought the food home, the usually short drive now seeming to take an eternity. But in what was a first for me, I ignored the food and went straight for the fortune cookie, wasting no time in ripping through the wrapper and cookie before staring at the fortune in my now sweaty hands.

"Beware people who wear red. They are up to no good."

I stared down at the fortune in disbelief. What the hell did that mean? That didn't even make sense. How was I supposed to beware people who wear red? You pass people who wear that every day. I wore it regularly myself. But then I remembered there was another fortune in there. So I grabbed the other cookie and tore through it.

"Someone with a drawing of a tiger will try to kill you."

I immediately crumpled the paper up in my fist. This was definitely not funny anymore. I don't know what I was thinking, but this was ridiculous. Tossing the fortune aside, I grabbed the food I ordered and headed towards the TV. The Crab Rangoon turned out to be the best I've ever had in my life. Unlike most other places, the filling was perfect. The Orange Chicken was also delicious, the sauce sweet but not overpowering. The next few days came and went and before too long, my mind was onto other matters besides weird utterances concealed inside cookies. That's the great thing about life. No matter what happens, time marches on and eventually you move on to other things.

One night when I went out with an old friend from college, I met this girl he knew in passing. Isabelle was stunning. Beautiful hazel eyes, long black hair, and perfect skin. It had been a long time since I had been truly interested in someone, and I was very happy the two of us hit it off. We made plans to go to dinner at this fancy Italian place and when the night came, I was both super excited and super nervous. I picked her up right on time and we had a lot of fun at dinner. Then I drove back to her house, and we hung out for a while.

Eventually Isabelle told me she wanted to change into something more comfortable and she came back looking great in a red t-shirt and shorts. But after the initial thought of how good she looked, my brain flashed back to the fortune about someone wearing red. I tried to brush it away, but the memory wasn't going anywhere.

"You look great," I offered with a smile.

"Thanks," she said before cuddling up next to me. After sitting there for a while, she leaned back, and I noticed for the first time she had a tattoo on her back, just beneath her neck.

"You never said you had a tattoo," I said teasingly.

"I do. Maybe if you're lucky, I'll show the whole thing to you."

"The whole thing?"

"Yeah, it takes up almost all of my back."

"That's hardcore."

We didn't say anything else after that, and after a little while, I noticed she had nodded off. When she shifted in her sleep, her shirt hitched up and I got a good look at the splash of color across her back.

A roaring tiger crouched on all fours.

My jaw almost hit the floor. This couldn't be happening. But one way or another, it was time to leave because Isabelle was asleep. I made a hasty note on a scrap of paper that I had a great time, and I left because she nodded off and I'd talk to her soon.

On the drive home, my mind was a mess. What was I supposed to do? Almost without thinking, I realized I was a bit hungry, and The Roaring Dragon was open late. But when I picked up my order of Egg Drop Soup and Sweet and Sour Chicken, I didn't even wait to get home to open the fortune cookies.

"The basement of a house is where the secrets are." said the first one. Gripping it in hand while sitting in the restaurant parking lot, I nervously opened the other one, terrified of what I may find.

"You have all the tools you need to make things happen," was all it said. That was oddly reassuring. Ok, so what did that mean? There were secrets in Isabelle's basement?

Right on cue, my phone rang, the caller ID confirming that it was Isabelle herself. I took a deep breath before answering.

"Hey sleepyhead."

"Hey you. I got your note and I'm sorry you left."

"Me too, but I couldn't take your snoring."

"Lies, I don't snore. But maybe next time if I fall asleep, you can join me."

"That'd be fun. I'll look forward to it."

So we made plans to hang out the following weekend, the thought of which both unnerved and excited me. When I arrived at Isabelle's house a few minutes early that Saturday, I stood on the front porch and looked at the white ranch house with dread. What secrets were inside? But before I could ponder further, Isabelle answered the front door and immediately greeted me with a kiss on the lips.

"Hey handsome, come on in," she added once the kiss was over. "I'm so sorry I have to do this, but I need to run a quick errand. Do you mind just waiting here while I go take care of it? You can watch TV while I'm out."

This was music to my ears.

"I guess I can manage," I said, offering my best nonchalant face. "Gonna be a while?"

"Not too long I hope. Should be half an hour tops."

"I think I can stand that long without you. Barely."

"Awe, well don't miss me too bad. Behave yourself while I'm gone!" She shot over her shoulder while walking towards her car, which was parked next to mine.

"Never!" I said as Isabelle got in the car and started it. When I saw it pull down the road, I knew it was safe to do what I came here for and headed inside.

Once I found the basement door, I carefully opened it. I had no idea what to expect, but I was greeted by a few wooden steps and a dark staircase. Once I flipped the light switch located just inside the basement door, I slowly followed the creaky stairs. With each step I glanced around, unsure of where to begin. There were boxes, knickknacks, and trinkets everywhere, the overhead light casting shadows on the walls. Ignoring my heart thudding in my chest and the fear clawing at me, I took a deep breath and tried to focus. I switched on one of the bulbs dangling from the ceiling and got another look at the room. Then I saw it. An expensive painting of a sunset sitting face up on a box.

I knew that painting. It belonged to my neighbor Jocelyn and had been stolen from her house not too long ago during one of the break-ins that caused me to get my alarm system. Casting another look around, I saw something else I recognized. An antique silver tea set, which had once sat in the dining room of James Cutler, who lived down the street from me.

That was all I needed to see before calling the police, who managed to arrive before Isabelle came home. When they confronted her, she muttered a few lame excuses before they took her in for questioning. Shortly after that, the fact that she had participated in the break-ins came out. But that was only part of the story. Break-ins were the least of the things Isabelle had participated in, as she turned out to be wanted in connection with several missing person cases from out of state. She eventually admitted that she and several others were planning to kidnap several people from well off families and hold them for ransom. I was one of those people. The matter is currently a legal mess, but Isabelle and several of her associates are now in jail.

Once I was free to go, I was on my way home when I realized I hadn't eaten all day. With a wry laugh, I decided that nothing else but Chinese food would be fitting. When I picked up my regular order of General Tso's Chicken, Fried Rice, and Spring Rolls, I paid for it with a 100-dollar bill and told them to keep the change. The expression on the woman's face was priceless.

As she stammered out a thank you, I headed back to my car to see what the fortune said. This time, there was just a single cookie.

"Laughter is both the best medicine and the happiest companion."

Well played fortune cookie. Well played indeed.

Halloween Spirit

I'M THE KIND OF person who starts counting down to Halloween on November 1. Always have been. I could never get enough of the holiday when I was younger, and that's stayed with me as I've gotten older. So you better believe every October I make it a point to have that house on the block. The one that you can barely see the lawn from how many Halloween decorations there are. Once the leaves start turning, that's my cue to put out the decorations. And considering how people are always stopping by to take pictures or drive past my house, I wouldn't have it any other way. Although the one thing I can't put out until shortly before Halloween itself are the jack-o'-lanterns.

Of course, that moment is always a bit bittersweet for me. Because on one hand, carving the pumpkins means Halloween is almost here. But on the other hand, before we know it, Halloween will be over.

But I recently got an idea. Why don't I carve some pumpkins early? It could be a fun little quirky tradition. Christmas in July is a thing, so why not jack-o'-lanterns when summer is in full swing? I saw no reason to not try it, so I went off to get some pumpkins. Finding them in the summer isn't as easy as other times in the year, but in the modern era, finding stuff out of season has never been easier. So once I was able to find some pumpkins, it was just a question of how many I wanted.

I decided on five. Then I paid for the pumpkins, bought some candles to go with them, and brought the stuff home. All that was left was to decide when to carve them and then get down to work. I decided to do it that weekend because we were due for a nasty storm.

Sure enough, the weekend came, and the storm arrived right on schedule, and it was intense. This was no quick summer downpour that lasts 10 minutes and then it's over. It rained all day, and it didn't take long for there to be flooding in the area. The sky was an overcast grey, and I didn't feel like going anywhere, so that was my cue to start carving pumpkins.

By now I've done it a million times, so I'm well practiced at it. Which means it wasn't long before I had hollowed out the first one and was working on etching a face into the pumpkin's surface. This part was definitely way harder than hollowing out a pumpkin, but I've practiced this enough as well to the point where I'm not horrible at carving a face, but I'm still nowhere near the amazing artist that some people are at this. That's the one Halloween thing I haven't mastered. Yet.

So, my first one turned into a generic spooky face with a twisted grin. It's simple, but a classic. Then I got started on the second one. This one I turned into a happy face with a genuine smile. The other three I tried different things with, but they just ended up being variations of the first two. But that didn't bother me a bit. I always enjoyed the process, and they all truly become something special once you light the candles.

Which is exactly what I did after that. Then I placed them inside the pumpkins, turned off the light in my kitchen, and stood back to admire the effect. It made me smile. As it always does. So now all that was left was for me to take them outside one by one and arrange them.

My house is a small two-story building, but it comes with a comfortable front porch. That's where I put some of the pumpkins once I've turned them into jack-o'-lanterns, along with on the three stone steps leading up to my porch. So I arranged them and stood back to admire my handiwork as the rain thudded on the roof and filled the streets. It was a nice effect, because the pumpkins and the candles within them stood out starkly amongst the grey, wet atmosphere. And thanks to my porch roof, which extended all the way to the first stone step, it kept me dry, and gave me a great view of the entire street.

With that done, I went inside to enjoy the rest of my evening. I had some ravioli with tomato sauce and salad for dinner and treated myself to some red velvet cake for dessert. Then I watched a movie on TV. Just before I went to bed, I stepped back outside to blow out the candles inside the pumpkins. The clouds in the sky made it seem extra dark outside, and after the intense rain, the air was muggy and humid. As a result, the candles in the jack-o'-lanterns seemed to shimmer in the intense humidity, and the orange glow seemed incredibly pronounced. For just a moment, I was briefly transported to a crisp October night.

But just as I was about to extinguish the candles, I noticed something. My porch light and the candles revealed what looked like footprints leading to and away from my front door. The heavy rain and the water it left standing everywhere meant that if you went walking tonight, you'd be leaving wet footprints everywhere, and thanks to the intense humidity, those footprints wouldn't immediately dry.

So there I was, staring at a set of footprints that arrived at my door, then went away. I just shrugged it off and chuckled. No doubt someone wanted to come for a closer look at my jack-o'-lanterns. Probably to take a picture or two. Well, they got a look just in time because I extinguished the candles, went back inside, and headed to bed without a moment's hesitation.

I got up the next morning, had some breakfast, then went about my day. After spending time with my family, I came home, put away the leftovers from our meal together, and read a book on the couch. After a while, I had a snack and since it was dark enough out, I went out on my front porch and lit the candles in the jack-o'-lanterns. Then I stood back to admire the sight for a moment until I went back inside and returned to my book. The intense humidity had lessened a bit, but was still high, so I stayed indoors to read instead of sitting on the porch like I often did.

When it was time for me to head to bed, I went back out to extinguish the candles. The sight of candles inside the jack-o'-lanterns flickering away against the thick night sky was striking. I took it in for a moment before, one by one, the candles were out, and all that was left was a tiny wave of smoke billowing from each one.

I was just about to turn around and go back inside when I looked down the street and saw someone. Despite all the bright streetlamps positioned at every interval, I couldn't see quite as clearly as usual, as the person was standing far away, and the humidity still lingered in the air and gave everything a haze. But even from that distance, I could've sworn that whoever was there was watching me. And I couldn't be sure, but I thought the person was wearing some kind of costume.

But then a car drove down the street, and when the car passed the spot where the person had been standing, there was no one there. So I went back in the house, turned off the lights, and went to sleep. The next day went by without incident, and I arrived home from work at my usual time. It was a bright sunny day, but not quite as humid as it was, so that was nice.

After I lit all the candles in the jack-o'-lanterns, I ordered some pizza for dinner. Then I watched some TV until it arrived. Right on schedule, my doorbell rang.

My pizza had been delivered by a guy in his mid-20s. When he told me the price, I handed him the money with a nice tip, told him to keep the change, and he gave me my pizza.

"Love the jack-o'-lanterns by the way," he told me just as I was about to close the door.

"Thanks."

"And I don't think I'm the only one who likes them. I saw a few people running by just as I was about to pull up. They were in costume too, so I think you started a trend."

I laughed. "Maybe. We'll see if it lasts. Thanks again for the pizza."

"Sure. You have a good night."

Then I went inside, put on a movie, and had my pizza and some ice cream for dessert. I didn't feel tired, but at some point, I nodded off and woke up to the sound of knocking at my front door. I quickly checked my phone and saw it was 10:15. Then I headed to my front door.

Whoever was at my door knocked again just as I was about to answer it. But just before I did, I looked through the peephole and saw someone dressed as a vampire standing on the other side of the door.

The sight made me chuckle.

I was still chuckling when I unlocked the door and opened it. I have a screen door that also locks, so it provided another barrier between me and the guy in a vampire costume. Now I could see it was a guy in his early 20s. And his costume looked more elaborate than the typical one you get in a bag at the costume store, and his makeup looked carefully done. And he was holding a candy bag in front of him.

"Trick or Treat!" He called out enthusiastically a moment after I opened the door.

I didn't answer at first, but I laughed.

"I love it!" I said as I took in the sight of the costume. I had to laugh at the initiative. If I could carve pumpkins and put them outside this time of year, I couldn't help but admire someone doing this.

The guy in the vampire costume hadn't said anything else, but he looked at me expectantly, the bag held out in front of him.

"Please give me one minute, I'll be right back. I promise." I said sincerely before I closed the main door and went to the kitchen. I always had plenty of candy, so it wasn't hard for me to get some miniature chocolate bars, some individually wrapped mints, and some peanut butter chocolates and get back to the door in a minute.

When I opened the door again, the guy in the vampire costume hadn't moved an inch, but he held his bag up expectantly as he saw me with the candy in hand. He stood back as I opened the screen door and placed all the candy in his bag. I thought he deserved a lot of candy for effort.

"Here you are," I said as I placed the candy in the plastic bag. "You look great!"

"Thank you." He nodded respectfully as the last piece of candy fell into the bag. "Happy Halloween."

"You too!"

Then he turned around, walked off my porch, and headed down the block and out of sight without saying a word. I took the opportunity to blow out the Jack-o'-Lantern candles before I went back inside. I was still laughing at the guy asking for candy. In all honesty, I was surprised more people hadn't done that.

The rest of the week passed without anything noteworthy happening. In fact, I was so busy at work I didn't have time to think about much of anything. I had been staying late, and I hadn't had time to light the jack-o'-lanterns by the time I got home. It was Friday afternoon by the time I could think about something other than work, and I immediately kicked myself mentally when I looked at my house and saw the pumpkins. Thanks to the summer heat, the pumpkins, which never lasted that long when carved to begin with, were not doing well at all, and this would probably be the last night before I had to throw them out. But it was fun while it lasted. So I went inside to get the lighter to light the candles, and just managed to get them all lit.

Then I went back inside and made myself some dinner. Exhausted from my long week, I fell asleep on the couch and woke up later to knocking on my door. I briefly checked the time, saw it was past nine, and went to see who it was.

A look out the peephole told me it was more people in Halloween costumes, but this time, the sight gave me a shiver. There were five of them, and when I opened the door, I immediately felt uneasy. They were dressed as a clown, a witch, a skeleton, a doctor, and a ghost. They looked to be about the same age as the guy in the vampire costume, but that was where the similarities stopped. The entire mood was different from last time. There was a feeling of tenseness in the air that I could sense the moment I saw them through the locked screen door. The guy in the vampire costume was quiet but I could tell he had a sense of fun. I could feel the five of them intently studying me. I had no idea what they were looking for, but I didn't like it.

The clown had his face painted in a wide, eerie grin that looked right at me as I looked at them through the screen door. I stood there silently for a moment, watching them watching me.

"Trick or treat!" They all called out in unison from my front porch.

"Hi," I smiled at them with what I hoped was a convincing smile. "I'll be right back with some candy for you all."

Then I immediately closed the door again. I could still feel their presence on the other side, their gaze still looking at me. Despite my best efforts, I could feel myself start to panic. The vampire costume had been good, but these costumes were creepy good. Too good to have been picked up on a whim from a store or put together at the last minute as a simple joke on me. I tried to convince myself it was all in good fun, but it all felt off. I knew something was up. I just didn't know what to do about it.

I was halfway to the kitchen when I looked out the window overlooking the street and saw the clown and the ghost had moved off the porch and were watching me from the kitchen window. I almost shouted out loud in shock, but immediately tried to play it off with a smile, like I knew they were just joking and pointed for them to go back to the porch so I could give them their candy. After what felt like an eternity, I watched them go back around to the front of the house.

That made me feel a bit better. But just a bit. Because inside, I was now in full-blown panic mode. What were the other three doing? Were they lurking in my backyard, waiting for me? Or were they trying to sneak in the back of my house? My stomach lurched as I thought this might all be a diversion, and that while the five of them distracted me, someone might be trying to break in my house another way. What was I supposed to do? What would I tell people if I called for help? Despite the fear, I felt myself take a bowl from the cabinet and stuff it with plenty of candy. Then, I went to the counter and took a knife out of the drawer. I was just about to start walking back to the front door when I heard two dull thuds come from the porch in quick succession.

I willed myself to go to the front door, and after I took a deep breath, I looked out the peephole.

There was nothing there.

I slowly opened the door, still holding the knife, and braced myself.

Everything was quiet, and the five people in costume were gone. And the entire mood felt different. So I took another deep breath, unlocked the screen door, and slowly set foot on my porch.

After a moment, I noticed something. Two of my jack-o'-lanterns had finally reached the end and had crumpled to the ground. The candles inside had been extinguished, and the smell of smoke lingered in the air. Meanwhile, the candles in two of the others had finally burnt out, so only one candle remained illuminated.

Or at least it did until I extinguished it a moment later. Then, after I checked my whole house and yard to make sure there was no one in a costume waiting to surprise me, I scooped up the remains of the pumpkins and tossed them in the garbage.

I slept horribly, but nothing happened. And the people in costume didn't come back. I still love Halloween, but I'll definitely hold off on carving pumpkins until fall gets here.

Artists

I HAVE THREE OF the best friends anyone could ever ask for. Phillip, Greg, Nate, and I have been through a lot together. After we all turned 28, we decided to get matching tattoos to commemorate us being friends ever since we'd first met at school all those years ago. So we did our homework and researched all the local tattoo parlors. Near the end, I found one simply named Artists.

While it was a new place in town, the prices at Artists were considerably higher than those at the average tattoo parlor. But the customer reviews explained why, because Artists had universal rave reviews, and the work of two people named Holly and Jay was constantly being praised as amazing and beyond worth the price. It didn't take me long to find out that Jay and Holly were the place's owners and operators, that Artists was a family business, and the designs there were truly beautiful. I also saw that Holly and Jay both had impressive degrees in fine arts and design.

So with that, there was no doubt we were going to Artists. Once Thursday was the day we decided on, all that was left to do was wait. When the day arrived, we all got there on time and strolled over to the place.

A fashionable townhouse style building in a calming shade of purple, Artists was printed on a sign above the front door in elegant black letters.

As I eagerly pushed the front door open, I heard a small bell chime somewhere within the building. The place smelled clean and fresh, and the massive drawings on every inch of wall space were stunning. Each one was a showcase for lavish colors, bold designs, and unique styles. Even the most routine drawings were made up of varying shapes and sizes that caught your attention. If you didn't know better, you might mistake this place for an art gallery or boutique had it not been for the reclining black leather chairs stationed at odd intervals.

The man behind the counter at the front of Artists looked nothing like your typical tattoo artist. Dressed in a black suit coat, red t-shirt, and plain black jeans, he had closely cropped blond hair and piercing blue eyes.

"Good evening, how may I help you?" He greeted us politely.

"We'd all like to get tattoos." Nate said.

"Very good. Please check out some of the designs and let me know which ones interest you."

"It's hard to pick one. They're all stunning." I said after looking for a minute or two.

His lips curled into what I felt was an uncommon smile.

"Thank you. I take great pride in my work. You may have noticed this isn't your typical tattoo establishment and I'm not someone just trying to earn a quick buck. I emphasize the artist part of tattoo artist and to me, someone getting a tattoo is like someone paying me to paint a portrait for them. A tattoo here isn't just an image or words, it's a story."

"I'm guessing you're Jay?" I asked.

"I am." He nodded. "Glad to have you all here."

"You're definitely talented." Phillip said. "Did you design all these yourself?"

"The color scheme and contrasting styles are mostly mine, but the original designs are much older than that. My great grandfather was involved in calligraphy and somehow got involved in tattooing and found he had a talent for it. I'm assuming you've taken a look at our website?"

"Yes." I nodded. "We all have."

"Then you know it's a family business. This is our first establishment here, but my family has operated them for generations."

"It shows." Greg added while he wandered around and looked at the designs. "They're incredible. Somehow they manage to be calming and mysterious at the same time."

"We get that a lot." I looked up from the drawing I was looking at and saw a young woman had joined us. It only took me a few seconds to notice that with her blue eyes and blond hair, she looked very similar to Jay.

"This is Holly, my sister." Jay briefly took a step over towards her. "The only other artist on site."

"There's absolutely no rush." She smiled at us. "We want you to take your time and choose the design that speaks to you."

"You're certainly not like the average tattoo place." Phillip observed while eyeing one picture.

"That's for sure." Jay nodded with a faint smile.

As I walked around, a drawing near the front of the tattoo parlor caught my eye. I had never seen a drawing like it before. It used alternating colors, lines, and patterns to create a design that looked more like a finished art canvas than a tattoo. The contrasting waves of color created an effect that made it hard to look away. I had never seen anything like it before. I also knew immediately that it was my choice of tattoo, and I decided to place it on my right upper arm. Once the others decided what they wanted, Jay and Holly went through the process of getting their equipment ready to do their best work. When Jay took off his jacket, I noticed that he didn't have a single tattoo.

With that, we all took turns in the chair. Phillip and Nate went to Holly, while Greg and I were in Jay's chair. Greg went first, and I watched him with a mix of anticipation and slight nerves. When it was my turn, I felt nervous when Jay started, but it didn't hurt as much as I thought it would, and I began to relax as Jay meticulously focused. Eventually we were all done and once we were all paid up and ready to go, Jay and Holly gave us a brief list of instructions for how to take care of our new tattoos before they thanked us for stopping in and we all walked out. I can't speak for the others, but I was trying not to think about the warm and itchy feeling where their equipment had been.

But after we all parted ways for the evening, those sensations started to fade, and the bold colors and designs started to come in. None of us wasted an opportunity to text each other pictures of how they looked, but eventually our conversation moved onto other matters. One of those was our annual camping trip, which we took every spring for a week.

After we all settled on a date, we each went out to pick up the food and stuff we'd need to bring along in addition to packing the right clothes and bringing the necessary camping supplies. Then, when the date came, we packed into Greg's SUV and drove to the campground we'd been to before.

It was a perfect spot and had a beautiful view overlooking a valley. The air was crisp, and the scent of pine made everything feel refreshing and invigorating. So we all unpacked in good spirits and settled in for a great time. The first day was exactly that; filled with walks on the trails in the woods and ending with a campfire at night that included making s'mores.

The second day of camping started just like the first. After a breakfast consisting of pancakes made over an open fire from the remnants of the previous night's campfire, we went canoeing on the local lake and hiked some more on some different paths that led us up the valley and gave us a stunning view of the whole area. I made sure to take plenty of pictures.

Once the sun started to set, we all headed back to camp to cook dinner. We had a great meal, and we were just unwinding in front of the fire when we heard it.

The sound of a twig snapping out in the woods.

It should have been just another sound. The woods were full of them, and up until that point I'd found the sounds of nature calming and something to enjoy. But for some reason, this time it made me sit up a little straighter in front of the fire. It was probably nothing, but it's always good to stay alert. But when I looked around the fire, I saw that my three friends had done the exact same thing as me. None of us had said a word to each other, but I could see the look in their eyes. Not worried, just watchful.

Then another sound came from the woods a few moments later. But instead of the sound of a twig snapping, this was the crunch of a footstep as it made an impact on the ground. The sound of someone being slow, steady, and deliberate.

I began to get nervous. We had been camping and hiking on numerous occasions, and there was no mistaking the sounds of a human walking around in the woods.

By now my three friends were looking around warily just like I was. Someone was out there. Someone we couldn't see, but someone who could certainly see us.

"Don't panic." Greg whispered to the three of us. "If we need to run for it, we all head for my car."

"What do we do if we can't just run?" Nate whispered back.

Before he could say a word, there were more footsteps coming from somewhere in the woods just beyond our campsite. I tried to ignore the tightening feeling in my chest and took a deep breath. We all sat there and waited silently for whatever and whoever was out there to appear.

But nothing happened. The air was still, and a chill hung over the area as we all sat silently. The tension was unbearable as we all sat there, unsure of what was going on. I was just about to say something when a piercing human shriek came from the woods.

All four of us jumped up from where we were sitting and frantically looked around for the source of the noise that came from the far end of the trees away from our campsite.

All of us stood there, looking around and unsure of what was going on, but not daring to try to investigate ourselves. The area was now eerily silent, and I listened intently for every possible sound and looked for the slightest hint of movement out in the trees. But there was nothing. Not a hint about who or what made that noise. Not even when another scream came out of the woods about a minute later. It was a far different sounding scream than the first one, and it sounded much closer to us than the first one.

"Run for the car." Greg whispered.

We did just that. Our feet thudded on the dense ground as we sprinted to the car and hopped in the seats. As we did that, a third scream tore through the woods to the left of us. This one sounded the worst of all. It made chills run down my back.

The final scream ended just as Greg hopped in the driver's seat, started the engine, and took care to ease out of there without panicking. As we pulled out of the campsite, the headlights illuminated a section of the woods, and I could faintly make out several figures watching us before Greg hit the gas and we were speeding away.

As our campsite and the area in general receded into the distance, I tried to take a deep breath in the hopes that my heart rate might slow down a tad. Nate and Phillip were also panting slightly from running.

"Can someone call for help?" Greg asked. His hands were tightly gripping the steering wheel.

"I'm on it." Nate nodded.

The police came quickly after Nate called, but that didn't prepare any of us for what they found. When they arrived at our campsite, the police arrested three men who had been seen in the general area several days before. It turns out our campsite had not been the first one they visited, because before visiting us, the men had attacked three other sites a few miles away from us. Using recordings of screams, they lured people out into the woods to ambush them. The four of us were the only survivors.

We eventually retrieved our gear and went back home to process what had happened. I thought about it for several weeks, but it eventually began to fade into the background when one day I stumbled upon the news of an attempted burglary.

A news crew was interviewing a local man who lived in a flat above a store he owned. One night, he had woken up late to hear a sound coming from downstairs. After calling the police, he went down to investigate. When he did, the man found himself face to face with an armed burglar who held him at gunpoint. But as the intruder was barking orders at the store owner, he slipped on the floor and accidentally shot himself in the head.

As the store owner was finishing the story, he stretched out his arm to emphasize a point, and I saw a flash of color and realized immediately what I was looking at. The store owner had several tattoos on his arm that looked just like the ones my friends and I had recently gotten.

I sat there stunned. This couldn't be just a coincidence. So I walked over to my computer, turned it on, and looked up a few keywords connected to my tattoo. It only took a few seconds for me to find a match. A variation of my tattoo was an ancient design that was said to be a sign of luck and good fortune. And my friends' tattoos matched designs said to bring health and protection from harm.

I sat there dumbfounded. But after I sat there for a while and processed everything, there was only one thing I could do. Once I was on the website for Artists, I put in the necessary information confirming I was a customer, and I wasted no time in leaving yet another rave review about my experience there.

Storage Unit 34

I JUST MOVED IN with my girlfriend about a month ago. After discussing it, she agreed that she would move into my place, because it's closer to our work and stuff. We're so happy together, but we had to put a lot of our furniture and stuff away because there just wasn't a lot of space.

To make things easier, I rented a storage unit. It seemed simple enough. We could just use it to keep the excess stuff until we moved somewhere with more space or sold some of our things. I found a place just outside of Minneapolis that rented units and got a good deal. The owner, a pretty chill older guy named Larry, asked if we wanted management to clean the unit out before we got there. According to him, since they had no readily available empty units, the one he was offering to us had been used in the past and had never been cleaned out since. Records showed that there had been no contact from the owner or account activity regarding said storage unit in over twenty years. The existing agreement on the unit had expired 15 years ago, so he had no problem renting it to us.

As there was a fee charged for them cleaning it for us, I told Larry no thanks. My friends and I wouldn't mind cleaning out the unit. Especially since any items found inside would legally belong to whoever held the current lease. Not gonna lie, I was pretty excited to be playing treasure hunter and see what was inside.

What would we find inside? The possibilities were endless. It could be some jewelry we could pawn or maybe want to keep. Rare baseball cards of Babe Ruth that would be worth a fortune. Millions perhaps? Some old forgotten sketch that was actually an original Picasso? Even if it was just some furniture, we could still sell that and earn some cash. No wonder people got so excited about this sort of thing. It was really like gambling.

My girlfriend and I got our unit paid for and everything, and we went one Saturday morning to clean it out. We made sure to bring a bunch of our friends with us in case we needed their help. To ensure their participation, I made sure to bribe them with pizza, which always works. Right when we arrived, Larry Fields, the owner, was there to greet us.

"Right this way ladies and gentlemen," he said as he walked us to the unit, number 34. Larry was a short, squatter guy who sort of waddled across the pavement. He had the keys in hand to open the unit for us, as well as keys that were ours. A short walk later we were in front of the metal door to Unit 34. Larry unlocked it without much trouble and the door opened easily for us. I could feel myself getting excited to see what we might find. Christine, my girlfriend, squeezed my hand in excitement.

He flipped on the lights as we took a look inside. At first, it looked to be a perfectly ordinary unit. A lot of whitewashed out cement walls and everything. A light bulb or two hanging over-head. Tons of room for stuff. The only things taking up any space were a few duffel bags scattered around, an antique style desk, two large cedar chests, and score, a small car! It was a small black sedan, an 80's Ford model. Christine immediately pulled me in for a kiss, which I was thrilled to receive.

"Nice choice, baby," she smiled happily.

"Like I ever make anything else." She rolled her eyes at this, but didn't say a word.

"I'll leave you all to it. In case you need anything, you can find me in the office," Larry said cheerily as he walked off. That was like firing the starting gun at the race for us.

We immediately jumped into it. From the outside, the car's interior looked absolutely filthy. A ton of old fast-food garbage and rags were everywhere. It also smelled a bit, which didn't surprise me at all. I decided to save the car for last, since it probably required the most effort. I grabbed one of the duffle bags carefully and began opening it. It wasn't real heavy. Just before I could unzip it, my girlfriend called to me.

"Ben, I think you should come take a look at this," she said, sounding concerned. I immediately went over to see what she was talking about.

"What's up? Are we rich?" I said with a smile, but she didn't return it. Christine had just opened one of the two cedar chests. Inside, there was a small collection of pistols and rifles. Also in the chest were a few serrated knives, the kind usually used for hunting.

"Oh, so whoever owned this must have been a hunter or something. No big deal. Maybe we can find a store or something who collects them." But there was this look on her face that said she wasn't exactly convinced. Before we could discuss it further, my friend Billy spoke up.

"Dude, no way, come see this! You should be able to make some cash off these!" Good man. I quickly went over to Billy, who was standing by the old desk. "Watches are worth big bucks, man!"

I high fived him as I saw what he was talking about. In one of the open drawers, there were probably about 20 different watches. Some of them looked pretty expensive, the old school kind. Most of them were wrist watches, with two or three pocket watches thrown in. Two of them were even Rolexes according to the label. I was psyched. I began taking them out of the drawer and placing them on the top of the desk so I could take them with us. Then I began going through the other drawers to see what else I could find.

Opening the next drawer, I got a bit confused. No watches or valuables here. Just a bunch of old driver's licenses. According to the dates on them, they were at least 20 years old. The people they belonged to were pretty diverse; young, old, men, women, white, black, and from a bunch of different states. Why would someone need or keep these?

"Babe?" Christine called out. Her voice seemed much more afraid than it had last time. "What are these?"

As I walked over to her, I couldn't help but feel a bit tense. Something felt wrong. She was standing by the duffel bag I was about to open. She had beaten me to it, but looked genuinely afraid of something. I immediately gave her a kiss and a hug to make her feel better, which she gladly accepted. When I kissed her, I could feel how uneasy she was.

"What is it?" I asked. Now she was really starting to concern me. Christine looked pale and so terrified. She didn't say a word, but reached down and pulled something out of the red and faded duffel bag. It looked like a stack of trading cards or something.

"Here," was all she said as I looked at whatever it was. They were a stack of old pictures. Polaroid brand, the kind that automatically developed back in the day. As I looked through the pictures, I felt like I had just taken a cold shower.

At first, the pictures were of just random things. A camp site, a house, a minivan, a trailer, stuff like that. One of the pictures was of the same car that was in our unit. Except in the picture it was way cleaner. Then, random people began to show up; people outside walking, fishing, and in an even creepier twist, some of them looked like they were sleeping.

Then the pictures got weirder. Pictures of men in orange ski masks began to pop up. In most pictures, they were flashing some of the knives and guns that I had seen in the chest. I could feel my heart rate beginning to pick up, but I tried to take a deep breath to calm myself down. This had to just be a joke, right? Only one way to find out. So I kept going.

Some of the people who had been photographed unknowingly were appearing again. But believe me, they weren't unknowingly being photographed now. This time, they knew someone was taking their picture, and it absolutely terrified them. You didn't need to say it, but I felt that they were all being held at gunpoint or something. You could almost feel the fear in their eyes. Some of them looked like they had been shaken awake or caught in the middle of something. I tried telling myself this was just more of a sick joke, but that didn't seem to be working. Something within me didn't buy it.

Just when I thought it could not get any worse, it did. Now there were pictures of countless people; men, women, entire families, looking like they were being held hostage or something. They were all tied up with rope and everything. It was without a doubt the scariest thing I had ever seen. Three guys in orange ski masks were back to pose with these people, the same way a fisherman or hunter might pose with a piece of game they caught. As I kept going, it was undeniable these pictures were no joke. I won't tell you what exactly the last few pictures showed, but I truly hope the only time any of you has seen anything like it was during a movie. With a sinking feeling in the pit of my stomach, I realized something.

I had seen some of these people before. Just moments ago. On their driver's license pictures.

Immediately, I dropped the photos. They scattered all over the floor, but I didn't even notice. My hands suddenly felt dirty. I looked at them as if they were contaminated or something.

"Don't touch another thing," I said to everyone in the unit without even looking up. "Look at those pictures. Christine and I will be right back." Then I grabbed her hand and stormed across the lot to Larry's office. Without knocking or anything, I barged inside.

"No deal, we want our money back. We did not pay for whatever freak show is in there."

"What?" He just sat there, stunned.

"Call the cops and then go look at the pictures we found." Christine stood beside me silently, her hand in mine. He immediately called the police and told them what was up. Then Larry followed us to the unit. His reaction was about the same as mine.

When the police arrived, we told them what we found. Larry gave them all the records he had for that account, and that was it. Because of confidentiality agreements, he honestly had no idea what was in any of his units. The cops told us they would be in touch with anything they found. Christine and I promptly got our money back and left. Needless to say, we would be using a different place to keep our stuff.

A few days ago, we got an update. A few of the old driver's licenses matched up to some decades old missing person cases. While I doubt they will be able to, I hope they find out who had that unit before I did, and what happened to the people whose stuff we found.

Campground Policy

I'D ALWAYS LOVED THE outdoors, so when Clay, my best friend and college roommate, invited me and a few others to spend a week during summer at his family's cabin, I didn't hesitate to say yes. Nor did the others. So once we had the week picked out, all that was left was to pack and look forward to it.

It was the early 2000s, so it was both very similar and very different from today in many respects. The most obvious was technology. Any pictures of the trip were taken on an actual camera, which in our case was handled by Stephanie, Clay's girlfriend and our resident photographer and camera operator. The others he invited were Lydia, Nolan, and Bailey. Lydia was Stephanie's best friend, Nolan was a good friend of both of us, and Bailey was Clay's cousin. We'd all hung out before and had gotten along fine.

It had been a long time since I'd been on a trip out in the woods, and I was looking forward to it. I was looking forward to this summer in general, and boy was this one beautiful. It was everything you hope for during the rest of the year while you're counting down the days until it arrives. The mornings and afternoons were soaked with warmth and light, and the nights were alternately balmy or crisp and cool. It had been a rainy spring, so the grass was thick and green.

By the time the day finally came, I was beyond excited. Once I was done with breakfast, I tossed my stuff in my car and hit the road. I'd been to Clay's cabin before, so I knew what to expect and where to go. I got there just on time about two hours later. But to my surprise, everyone else had already gotten there ahead of me.

The cabin looked just like I remembered. All sturdy wooden beams and comfortable furniture. It had a master bedroom, two guest bedrooms, two bathrooms, a large sitting room, dining room, and a full kitchen. The only occasional problem was sometimes the shower would run out of hot water, so we'd have to heat some up in the kitchen. But of all the potential problems, that was nothing. The air conditioner always worked perfectly, and the power never went out. The cabin itself was charmingly rustic, but had all the basics. My favorite feature was the screened in back porch that offered a perfect view of the backyard.

I felt instantly at home the moment I drove up the cabin's gravel driveway. The surrounding pine trees were dotted around at random intervals, and they varied from small to towering in size. It was no surprise when all six of us were immediately swept up in the outdoor vacation atmosphere of sleeping late and having s'mores out by the campfire. Lydia and Nolan tried to deliberately toast their marshmallows, but half of the time they burnt anyways. And instead of using just plain chocolate bars every time, we mixed it up and used other types of candy bars. This was all done in my second favorite feature of the cabin, which was the fire pit and the area that had been specifically arranged for people to sit around an open fire. It was an amazing time, filled with many small memories that never fail to make me smile.

After we were all settled in for a few days, we went to a local video store in the nearest town to check out some movies to rent for the short time we were there. But on the way, we made a brief stop at the ice cream shop just down the street. It was one of a handful of stores nearby, along with a grocery store and hardware store. Past that was a strip mall that held a clothing boutique, a laundromat, and a store specializing in camping and outdoor gear.

The video store was a local joint located next door to a pizzeria, and you could smell it the moment you walked inside. I had no doubt that the pizza place got great business from the video store and vice versa.

We browsed through the aisles, checking out the latest releases as the smell of homemade pizza filled the air. I never failed to enjoy browsing through the latest selections.. Clay and I had spent many an evening debating and arguing over what movies to rent or watch. Today was no exception. But since there was no shortage of available TVs at the cabin, that meant we could all watch what we wanted. So we all picked out a few selections and went to the checkout. Once we were done with that, we went next door for our pizza order to go, then headed back to the cabin to watch some movies and eat our lunch. When we watched one that didn't exactly appeal to Stephanie or Lydia, the two of them went out to shoot some pictures of the local scenery. They returned about two hours later, which was just in time for our hike before dinner. The insects were noisily buzzing around, so we took care to cover ourselves in plenty of bug spray.

Then we headed off the local trails and had a great time exploring. We were just about to head back when Stephanie padded her pocket and looked worried before she sighed.

"I'm such an idiot." Stephanie shook her head. "I misplaced my car keys. I know exactly where I left them too, on the wooden table outside the main office at the campground nearby. I remember sitting there to check the film in my camera. Do you all mind if we go swing by there on the way?"

"Fine by me." Clay said. "What about the rest of you?"

There was a murmur of agreement as everyone stood up and headed to the trail that led to the campground. It was only about a mile from our present location, so we were there in no time. I'd passed it on the way over here but had never been inside. By now night had fallen, and the heat had faded from the air. We rounded the corner that led to the campground, and there the front office stood there right inside an open gate. The table in question was right in front of it.

But then we all took a few steps forward, and that's when things got weird.

The campground looked like any other campground, but apart from that, it couldn't have been more different from anything I'd seen before. At nighttime during summer, campgrounds are filled with sounds. The pulse of music, the crackle of fires and grills, and the din of conversation. Here, all was silent. Not a single person was outside, and every single camper was quiet, with the doors shut. There were no campers sitting out there by a crackling fire, and there were no people throwing footballs or frisbees back and forth. If you didn't know better, you'd swear the place had turned into a ghost town, since it felt so lifeless and quiet. But the strangest part was that in front of each camper, there was a black candle in a holder. The candles were large, and each camper had one lit and situated directly in front of the door on the camper steps. I wasn't sure, but I thought I could smell one from the nearest camper, and the smell was odd. Not bad, but odd. Like nothing I had ever smelled before.

I had no idea what was going on, but it gave me the creeps. As I looked around at the others, it was clear they were having the same reaction as me.

"Is this some kind of a joke?" Lydia eventually whispered to no one in particular. "Or some weird campground policy?"

"I don't know," Clay answered. "It's possible, but something feels off."

"I agree," I said. "Get your keys, and let's get out of here."

"Slowly." Clay whispered so quietly I could barely hear him. "We don't want anyone to know we were here."

Good point. Everything was too orderly and quiet for this to be a coincidence. I stood there with the others as Stephanie and Clay slowly crept towards the table as silently as possible. It wasn't real far, but it felt like miles away.

After what seemed like an hour, she grabbed her keys and the two of them started slowly walking back towards us. I felt a faint sense of relief wash over me, and with each step that they got closer, I felt better. Once the two of them were back with us, we all quietly turned and started back down the road, with each of us all looking in a different direction to keep an eye out. The evening's humidity was stifling, but even that couldn't prevent an icy chill from settling over everything.

We had just reached the road when there came a loud crash of something falling in the woods behind the campground, which was immediately followed by the loudest roar I had ever heard in my life.

That was when we gave up all pretense of silence and sprinted out of there as fast as we could. We ran for what felt like a painful distance until the cabin was in sight. We were all already tired from the hike, so this was really pushing it. I felt some relief as the cabin came into view, but I didn't truly feel calm until we were back inside with the door locked.

The cabin was soon filled with the sound of all six of us panting for breath. I had never felt so out of breath in my life, and it took several minutes for everyone to calm down and relax. Then we all gulped down several glasses of water in record time.

Then we all huddled inside, made some pasta for dinner, and stayed there behind locked doors for the evening. I felt simultaneously wired and exhausted from the experience. The sky was clear, so that meant the moon was clearly visible and loomed out of the horizon in the way only the moon can when you're on edge at night. Almost as if on cue, from somewhere deep within the woods, I heard howling. You could feel the tension in the room, as it sounded like the animal was right outside our door. From far out in the trees, I momentarily thought I saw a giant shadow that looked like a wolf before it immediately vanished.

At some point, we decided to play a few board games to try to relax for the evening. We were discussing which one to go with when I heard it, the sound of thick and heavy footsteps on the front porch. Immediately, all six of us went silent as we listened for the sound. The footsteps went back and forth briefly across the porch before they stopped.

Clay didn't dare get up and see who was there. He just stood there and listened like the rest of us, which was smart. It felt unnaturally silent as we all sat there, waiting for whatever was going to happen. Then, after what must've been a few minutes, came the sound of footsteps walking back down the porch's steps and away from the cabin.

This time, Clay did get up and go to the front door's peephole to see outside. But when he turned back around, he shook his head.

"Nothing there."

With all thoughts of a board game over, we turned on the TV and found some sitcom to watch. I eventually dozed off on the couch like everyone else, and we woke up to a rainy day. Since it did nothing but rain, and we didn't want to go outside anyways, we spent the entire day indoors watching the movies we rented. The following day was also the final day of our time in the cabin, so we all packed up and got ready to leave. The only thing left to do was return our movie rentals to the store.

We all got in our respective cars and headed to town, with plans to head back home from there. Everything looked just as it had been the last time, and the video store smelled just like pizza again. Even the guy who ran the place was the same, a middle-aged guy of average height with blond hair and a beard to match.

"Enjoy the movies?" He asked with a smile.

"Always." Clay smiled back. "I was wondering something, though. I've stayed around here for years, and I've never gone in the campground close by before. What's it like?"

He paused. "Never had much cause to go there myself. Not much of a camper here, but a friend of mine was there once. He didn't have much to say one way or the other."

Clay nodded. "I get it."

"But my uncle did tell me something once, years ago. My uncle is who technically owns this place. I help run it for him when he needs me. He's been around here his whole life, so he knows all the stories. Apparently the land the campground is on used to be a private estate or something, and there was some kind of accident. Someone vanished and was never found, a cousin of whoever owned it if I recall correctly. They never had a clue about what might have happened either, so of course, life went on and the property was sold to some kind of developer to turn into a big hotel or some kind of resort. Everything went well, until someone disappeared one night. In this case, it was someone working the late shift at the hotel's front desk. By all appearances, the person seemed to have just gotten up and left. And just like last time, there was no sign that anything had happened. So business at the hotel went on until it was eventually converted into the campground that still exists to this day. According to my uncle, the campground office used to be part of the original estate that was converted into the hotel building. Most of the other campground buildings date back from the old days, too."

"Nice," Clay said. "And that's it?"

"Not quite." The man's face slightly frowned, and he leaned in closer. "Nothing like that has happened since it became a campground, but I won't lie, I've heard stories. People who swear they saw or heard something lurking in the woods by there. One couple who owned a massive RV came in to rent a few movies, and they swore that one night while they were staying on a friend's property, they woke up to find a pair of eyes watching them from a window in the RV's kitchen. And the next morning, they woke up to what looked like handprints all over their vehicle. Needless to say, they packed up and headed out later that day."

"Wow." Stephanie muttered.

"Uh huh." The man at the counter nodded. "How true it is, I don't know. But one thing I know for sure is that stories or not, I don't mess around in these woods. Or any woods, for that matter."

"It's a good rule." I nodded.

"I think so."

"I think so too," Clay agreed. "And thank you for everything."

"My pleasure. You all be safe out there."

Then we all left the video store and got on the road. I didn't realize it, but I didn't feel truly better until we were away from there. Years later, Clay's parents decided to sell the cabin and get a different one by the beach. Can't say I blame them.

A Personal Silver Bullet

I've worked in a jewelry store for several years, and it's a pretty routine job. One of the best parts of the job is when you work with a customer who is celebrating something, and you get to be part of their excitement and happiness. That's a big part of the experience of buying jewelry. Someone isn't just buying a ring or a watch, they are commemorating a moment, and the jewelry is simply a tangible symbol of that. And sometimes those tangible reminders of timeless moments need to be repaired for one reason or another. That was what started my strangest experience on the job.

It was a Wednesday afternoon when the first customer came in. An older gentleman wearing a flawlessly tailored three-piece suit, he had slicked back grey hair and eyes that seemed to study everything they encountered.

"Hello, how may I assist you?" I asked him with a friendly nod when he approached me while I was at the counter.

"Yes, I'd like to have my watch repaired."

"Of course. What is the issue?"

"The clasp isn't working." He took the watch out of his suit pocket and placed it on the counter. It was an expensive gold wristwatch with a small diamond in the center. To demonstrate, he tried to fasten it shut and it wouldn't.

"I see. We can certainly fix that."

Then I launched into our rates and prices, which he agreed to. Once he'd signed all the paperwork, his watch was taken to the back, where it was properly cataloged and stored away until one of our professionals would fix the clasp. Once that was done, I went back to work, and that was it.

I didn't see the gentleman in the suit until a week later, and the watch was ready to be picked up. He came dressed in a different, but equally expensive suit. Then he gave his name, and I hustled to the back to pick up his now fixed watch.

Once he signed the paperwork confirming he'd picked up his order and paid the bill, he took the watch, placed it on his wrist, and closed the clasp, where it shut with a satisfying click. The gesture made him smile.

"Good job Michael," he said to me.

"Thank you. Our staff are the best."

"I know, that's why I've always come here. There's no chance I would go anywhere else for this. It means the world to me. I had a nasty spill at home, and the clasp was probably broken in the fall."

"I'm very sorry to hear that."

"That's very kind of you. But I was fine. Lucky too. But anyhow, you have a wonderful day."

"You do the same." I smiled as he turned around and left the store.

I didn't think anything more about him until about two weeks later when I saw on the news, he had been in a car accident close to where he lived. He was unharmed, but his car was completely totaled. No one would be able to fix that.

Since I was about to leave for work when I saw that, I shut off the TV and headed out. My day at work was uneventful until the end when a young woman in her late 20s walked into the store. By that time of day it was quiet, and she was the only customer. She was casually dressed in jeans and a sweatshirt, and she looked like she felt a little out of place in the store.

"Hello, how may I assist you?" I asked, as I gave her my most welcoming smile.

"Hi," she smiled in return as she hesitantly walked to the counter. "I'd like to get a bracelet repaired."

"Of course. And what bracelet would we be working on?"

"This one." She reached in her sweatshirt pocket and took out a black velvet box. She opened it, took out the bracelet inside, and placed it gently on the counter. It was a beautiful gold bracelet dotted with sapphires. Right in the middle, there was an empty space where a sapphire should have been.

"It's beautiful."

"Thank you." She nodded solemnly. "And here's the sapphire that fell out."

She reached into her pocket and took out a small plastic bag. The missing sapphire was inside.

"Very good." I took the bag in hand, set it on the counter, and got to work with the paperwork. Once she had her pickup time in hand, she left the store, and I went to put both the bracelet and the bag with the sapphire away. I had just put both away when I got a very odd feeling. The best thing I can describe it as is unease. But I shrugged it off, reminding myself that the customer was obviously going through something. It happens a lot, as jewelry can be inherited for sad reasons, or just bring a lot of emotions to the surface. So I finished logging the order and returned to the counter.

I was there a week later when she returned for her repaired bracelet. This time, she seemed slightly more at ease, and when she saw the repaired bracelet, her eyes lit up.

"Thank you so much," she said with a wide smile. "I feel so much better now that it's back to normal."

"That's terrific. That's what we're here for."

"This bracelet means the world to me, so I was beyond upset to see it get damaged."

"Completely understandable."

"It was a gift from my husband. For our wedding anniversary. We took a vacation together, and it was a disaster. Our luggage got stolen, and it was downhill from there."

"I'm truly sorry to hear that."

"Thank you. And I'm sorry for rambling in the middle of your store."

"No, it's ok. That's what we're here for. Jewelry tells a story, and no two pieces tell the same story."

"That makes a lot of sense." She nodded. "Thanks again for your help."

"Of course. Have a great day."

"You too."

She turned away from the counter and walked back outside. Then I went on with the rest of my day.

The rest of the month went by without anything noteworthy until one day, a woman with long grey hair came in towards the middle of my shift. She was dressed in a black business suit, wore glasses over intelligent green eyes, and carried a small black purse.

"Hello, how may I assist you?"

"Good afternoon, I was hoping to get a locket engraved."

"We can certainly do that. Which locket would we be engraving?"

"This one." She reached into her purse and took out an elegant gold locket, which she carefully placed on the counter.

"And what are we engraving on it?"

"For Marissa."

I wrote that carefully on the order.

"And where do you want that?"

"Inside the locket."

"And what script would you like?" I asked before I presented her with a list of the various options she could go with.

She studied it for a moment before she pointed to an option halfway down the list.

"That one."

"Good choice." I nodded approvingly before I wrote that into the order as well. "Is there anything else you would like to incorporate? Or that we should know before we file this order?"

"No, that's it. It's for my niece. She's getting married."

"Congratulations to her."

"Thank you. We've always been very close, so I'm very happy for her."

"That's great."

Then she finished signing the paperwork, and once she was able to leave the store, I filed away the order and the locket for our experts. The rest of the day passed by, until I was left to close the place up. I went through the end of shift routine, closed up, and headed to my car. As I was walking towards it, I suddenly got the feeling I was being watched. So I immediately looked around to check the area.

Nobody was watching me, and there was nothing going on. Still, I carefully walked to my car, got inside, and quickly left once I had locked the doors. I immediately felt better as I drove away.

I didn't see the woman with the locket again, but she picked up her order, and my boss told me she was thrilled with it. I wasn't surprised I wasn't there, because I was on vacation that week. I'd long been looking forward to seeing my best friend Craig's new cabin out in the woods, so the first chance I got, I'd made plans with him to go see it.

It didn't disappoint. It was like something out of a painting with its log structure and stone fireplace. And it had all the modern conveniences you could want, and plenty of room for guests. Craig's parents and his sister Christina were also going to be there, so I was looking forward to seeing them as well.

"There he is." Craig greeted me with a grin before he and his whole family took turns hugging me and saying it had been too long. Then I took my bags inside, got settled in my room, and we had some dinner. Then we all headed out to the backyard, where Craig and his dad built a fire that we all sat around for hours. After we all had our fill of s'mores and it had gotten late, we all went inside, said goodnight, and headed to our respective rooms. I was tired from the long drive out of the city, so I fell asleep quickly.

It felt like moments later when I was shaken awake by Craig.

"Mike, wake up."

"Huh?" I mumbled out.

"Wake up," he whispered intently.

"What's going on?"

"There's someone outside."

That woke me up immediately.

"Someone outside?"

He nodded. "And we think there's more than one. You weren't followed here, were you?"

"No," I said quietly.

I quietly got out of bed and crouched by Craig on the floor. My heart was thudding loudly in my chest, and I had no idea what to do. Not only was I in an unfamiliar area, I was in a house I had never been in before. But I took a deep breath and tried to stay calm.

"Did you call the police?" I asked after what felt like an eternity.

"Yeah. They said they'd be out here as soon as they could, but out here, who knows what that means. At least we have an alarm system. And you know my dad."

I did. Craig's dad was the kind of guy you wanted to have with you in a situation like this. That was the one thing that kept me at least relatively calm, aside from the fact I wasn't alone.

"Did he send you in here?"

Craig nodded. "Told me to stay here until he told me otherwise."

Time seemed to stop as the two of us sat there, silently watching each other while I tried my best to ignore the fear creeping in the back of my mind.

It seemed like we'd been sitting there for hours when suddenly, there was a loud crash from downstairs that was immediately followed by the sound of an alarm screaming to life. Then came several loud bangs in rapid succession that were followed by the much quieter sound of footsteps fleeing from the cabin. Then, I heard Craig's dad yelling at whoever was running away. I couldn't quite make out what he said, but I didn't blame whoever had been fleeing.

Craig and I had bolted upright at the commotion, but we stayed inside as Craig's dad had said. Moments later, the alarm was shut off and there was a gentle knock on the door.

"Come on out guys," Craig's dad instructed us.

He didn't need to tell us twice. We immediately bolted out of my room while Craig's mom came out of Christina's room, where the two of them had been during this time.

"Everything's fine. They're gone," Craig's dad said before he walked back to the living room where he'd been keeping watch with his gun.

We all quietly sat there until the police arrived and took statements about what had happened. They agreed to put a car outside the cabin for the night and keep watch on the area. By the time they left, I felt exhausted. So I fell asleep even quicker than before. Fortunately, no one interrupted my sleep this time, and I woke up late the next morning.

Craig's mom made pancakes for breakfast, and since we were all starving, we were happy to dig in.

Once we all had our fill and were sipping coffee, the conversation drifted to other matters. At some point, I noticed Christina was wearing a necklace I hadn't noticed before. It was a simple but elegant gold hoop on a chain.

"Nice necklace Christina," I said before I took another sip of coffee.

"Oh thanks. It was a birthday gift from Aunt Helen."

"Nice."

"She didn't get it from your store, but it's still nice."

I chuckled. "No doubt."

Then Craig's dad, who had been reading the morning paper, turned the page. As he did, I saw the front page and saw there was a headline about some company declaring bankruptcy. The company didn't sound familiar to me at all, but there was a photo of the family that owned it. In the middle of the photo was the woman who had come in to get the locket engraved.

My stomach sank and the pancakes I'd just eaten now felt uncomfortably heavy. Craig must've sensed something because he immediately asked, "Mike? What's wrong?"

I managed to explain the story of the customers who'd recently come into the store and the unfortunate incidents that seemed to have happened to them. Craig and his family quietly listened to the story until I finished, then added that nothing like last night had happened to them before. Once we all got back to the city, Christina gave me the paperwork her Aunt Helen had given her with the necklace, and I did a little research. Since jewelry stores keep tons of information on file, it didn't take me long to find out the scoop on Christina's necklace.

The gold in it had come from a local mine in California. It had been doing quite well until one day there was a cave in, and a ton of workers died in the accident. The mine was eventually shut down, but not until all the gold that could be retrieved was obtained. And I didn't need to look up the mine to know that the rumor was, the place was considered cursed or haunted by locals. I'd been to the area years ago on a vacation, and the place had given me the creeps. But even I got chills when I looked later through the store's records and saw documents that the man in the suit and the other two customers had all brought in items containing gold mined from the area.

Christina wasted no time in trading in her necklace for a ring made of silver. When she did, I got a text from her that had a picture of the ring next to a joke about it being a personal silver bullet to ward off monsters. It made me laugh.

School Projects

I HAVE BEEN A 3rd grade teacher for about 15 years. By now, I thought I had become used to anything and everything kids could pull. Times change, but kids don't. One of the assignments in my class is to have a week or two where my students bring in reports of their parents and their jobs. For five minutes or so, the students take turns and stand in front of the class to talk a little bit about what their parents do for a living. You get your fill of doctors, lawyers, police officers, accountants, and even the occasional homemaker.

Of course, since there are always students who like to exaggerate what their parents do this can be quite entertaining. Most of the time, you can tell they have no clue about what their parents' actual job involves. But they have the rest of their lives to learn about that.

We were over halfway through the exercise when Hunter began to give his report. He went through his mom's job, everything was normal, nothing out of the ordinary there. But then he started talking about his dad.

"Dad is a really cool guy," he began, squinting to read what he wrote. "He works as a lawyer. This is a real cool job where you get to do things like go to court and argue with another lawyer in a big room in front of some guy in black. His office is the coolest. Super big, and with an awesome chair and a lot of books. Sometimes, if I am really lucky, he lets me carry his briefcase." Hunter struggled a little on pronouncing the final word, but he figured it out.

"But he also told me he has a secret job." At this point, the whole class began to whisper amongst themselves excitedly. I, on the other hand, was rather puzzled. Was this a stunt? Or some daydream.

"At night, my dad has to sneak out of the house. I didn't know about this for a long time. But when I did, he told me my mom and my sister Jayne both knew and were ok with it. Because once everyone in my family is asleep, my dad goes out to fight the bad guys."

Ah, this finally made sense. It was the whole, 'my dad is a secret superhero' daydream. You'd be surprised how many kids try to pull this. Hunter admired his dad, I knew that well enough.

"Dad always has to take care that no one sees him, because he told me if they did, the bad guys would come get him. But my dad is amazing! Not once have the bad guys caught him!"

Now the other kids in class began to full on scream and yell in excitement.

"Quiet down!" I instructed them firmly. "Go ahead Hunter." Best to get this over with. Hunter did always have a fantastic imagination.

"My dad does his secret job because he says it needs to be done. He told me that sometimes people do bad things and need to pay for what they've done. He always brings the coolest things home after. Gold things, silver things, things that look real expensive. Sometimes he comes home with lots of money. But he always has to do something with them, otherwise people will try to take them away from him. My dad is always so nice."

He said this with the widest smile. Unfortunately, he wasn't quite done yet.

"One time I saw him come home just before it got light out and his truck had some big sheet in the backseat that got red all over it.

When I asked him about it, Dad told me he had to take care of a bad guy and then move him so he couldn't hurt anyone else. He then told me if I went inside and did my homework, he'd take me out for ice cream. Which he did. I got cookie dough, my favorite."

Ok, this daydream had officially crossed into crazy territory. Hunter's favorite ice cream really was cookie dough. Or was it an actual dream he had? I began to feel uneasy. Either way, this couldn't be real. Sadly enough, I have heard of daydreams far more insane than this one. Thankfully, Hunter was almost done.

"The last time I saw him come home at night was a few days ago. I saw him playing in the backyard like he was digging in the sandbox. I saw him put something big wrapped in that same red sheet in the hole and cover it with dirt. When I asked him what it was, he said it was the bad pirate's treasure, and he was gonna give it back to the people he stole it from as soon as he could. Then he told me to go back inside and watch TV. I did, but when I got inside I looked out the window, and saw that he had started a big fire outside. My dad is the best at building fires, too. Sometimes he has to use clothes that don't belong to any of us. Dad always says they are the best to start a good fire with. Sometimes they also look like the big sheet I saw from the backseat, too."

I felt like I had just been punched in the stomach at this point. What the hell was going on? There was no way Hunter was making this up. This was real.

"So yeah, that's what my parents do!" he finished excitedly. The other students seemed to think it was as cool as what Hunter said, as they murmured their approval.

"Alright class, give Hunter a round of applause," I said hastily. They did as I asked. The rest of the students took their turn for the period, then class was dismissed for the day.

Once class let out and the other students were gone, Hunter came up to my desk with an eager look on his face.

"Hi Mom, did I do good on my project about what you and Dad do?" he asked happily.

"You did great sweetie," I told Hunter as I ruffled his hair fondly, doing everything I could to act normal in front of him. "Ready to go home?" He nodded excitedly. I grabbed my bag and followed him out of the classroom, locking it behind me.

My mind was spinning as I walked with my son across the parking lot. What. The. Hell. Hunter was an incredibly smart kid, and an honest one at that.

I must confess, for a little while now I've thought something was up with his dad. He had been very withdrawn for a few weeks now. My husband, Hunter's Dad, is usually a very gregarious, upbeat guy, so when something is up you can tell. He's recently been in the habit of going up to his office and sitting in silence for a while. I know he's been frustrated at work, so I just chalked it up to that.

For a brief moment, I wondered if he was having an affair before putting it out of my mind. Funny, now I wish that was all I was worried about him doing. As Hunter got in the passenger seat and buckled in, I put the car in gear and took off down the road. One of the benefits of driving a car is that it gives you time to think. Focusing on the road is an amazing time to reflect on whatever is on your mind.

Hunter's report was being played endlessly on a loop in my brain. The most troubling part being the "pirate treasure" buried in the backyard. Fortunately, Hunter was playing a game on my phone as we drove home. The drive seemed to take no time at all. Looking up at my house, I didn't know what to think. I loved our house, a beautiful white colonial with black shutters. As I parked in our driveway, I decided what I would do about Kyle, my husband.

When I got out of the car and unlocked the door, Hunter ran inside with his backpack, tossing it on the bench in the hallway as he usually did on the way up to his room. I couldn't blame him; one of the happiest feelings when you are a kid is that moment you get home from school. And it never really goes away when you are an adult. You just substitute work for school.

"Hey guys, how was your day?" Kyle walked up with a smile on his face. I almost froze when he did. One of the worst things about getting dirt, gossip, or inside info is that it forces you to rethink everything you believe about someone, whether it's true or not.

"Good," I replied politely. His face fell slightly at my cool answer. I had decided to not out and out accuse him of what was in Hunter's report. Because if he really was a murdering lunatic, the last thing I wanted to do was to make him feel cornered. I was going with a tried-and-true method to get information out of someone voluntarily. Make them feel as uncomfortable and nervous as possible, so they inadvertently blurt out something they think you know, but don't. If he wasn't sure of what I knew, there was no telling what secrets he would blurt out in an attempt to find out why I wasn't happy. It's basically the equivalent of saying to someone 'I know what you did,' so they feel free to talk about it with you.

"Something wrong babe?" he asked, stopping abruptly as he walked towards me.

"Nothing, I'm fine, just a little tired is all." I said with a smile, extending my cheek towards him for a kiss. He obliged, but he still looked unconvinced. Good.

"How was your day?"

"Fine, how was yours?" No reason to panic, I was just fishing for information. Or at least that was what I was telling myself.

"Good, the Simmons meeting went well," he looked incredibly pleased.

"Wonderful. I know you were working hard on it. How about we celebrate tonight with pizza? I don't feel like cooking." Stupid question, really. Like most people, including me, my husband will always say yes to pizza. He's not the only one who can use a favorite food as a distraction.

"Like I would ever say no. Our regular from Giorgio's?" Now Kyle looked truly happy.

"You know it, order and pick it up for us?" Our regular order consisted of two large pizzas, peperoni for the kids, green peppers and black olives for Kyle and Me, plus an order of cheesy bread.

"Will do. I'll get right on it," he agreed as he took his phone out of his pocket and promptly dialed Giorgio's while walking into the kitchen. I heard him place the order, then promptly walk back out in the living room where I had settled on the couch.

"It'll be ready in 30 minutes, heading out now to go get it!" he called out as he walked towards the front door.

"See you later, hon."

The door closed shut behind him. I took care of a few things I had been thinking of on the ride back home. School stuff and whatnot. When this was done and after making sure Hunter was in his room watching TV, I went downstairs into Kyle's office. I went through all his desk drawers, and there was nothing out of the ordinary there. Then I went to the garage, and it was the same story.

Finally, I went to the backyard, the place where "the pirate's treasure" allegedly was. I stared at the ground for a while, trying to figure out where Hunter said my husband had been digging. Since it had been raining a lot recently, the grass was very lush and green. No spot looked recently disturbed, so it was hard to say. It was at that moment I heard the sound of Kyle's car coming up the driveway, so I hastily walked back inside the house through the porch.

"Pizza's here!" he called out as Hunter ran down the stairs excitedly. Our older daughter, Jayne, was at a friend's house for the weekend since it was Friday night, so it was just us three. And there is nothing like the smell of hot pizza. We got the plates out, sat down at the table, and dug right in. I may have just been paranoid, but I made sure Kyle ate a slice of pizza before I did. But my husband had no problem with chowing down. We all ate quietly, little bits of ordinary conversation occasionally breaking the silence.

After dinner, Hunter returned to his room, and I cleaned up the dining room.

"Want to watch a movie?" Kyle asked when I was almost done.

"Sure. Oh and by the way, Hunter did a great job on his project on us," I added as if an afterthought.

"Yeah?"

"Yes, despite his including some fantasy he had about you having a secret job," I managed a pretend chuckle at this. Kyle on the other hand stood quietly on the spot, with a neutral expression on his face.

"That boy has some imagination," he was pretending it was a joke, but his smile was too wide. It was stretched tightly over his face. The look didn't suit him.

"I know, he claimed you were a secret superhero who goes out at night to fight bad guys. Crazy right?" I was impressed at how I managed to pretend I thought it was all a joke.

"Yeah," he began chuckling too. But it wasn't his usual laugh. It was a nervous 'something is up' laugh.

"I wonder where he would get that idea though? Especially since he claimed you told me and Jayne about it and swore us to secrecy."

"It's a mystery," he shrugged. My husband was doing a pretty good job acting like he wasn't on edge. He was a good lawyer after all. But I know him. He was tense. The pursed lips are a giveaway every time.

"Yup. So what movie you want to watch?"

I felt sickened, Hunter's story was true. Or part of it was. I've known that he has had some shady clients in the past. People you wouldn't want to be seen with in public and shake their hand. But I always told myself what lawyer hasn't? Well, most lawyers don't have suspicious jewelry or burn clothes and bury bloody sheet covered things in the backyard. What exactly did he get into at work? That had to be it. But I used my teacher abilities to act like I was completely nonchalant.

"How about *The Wolf of Wall Street*?"

"Good choice." I did have a soft spot for Scorsese and we both had yet to see that one. He also looked happy and surprised I dropped the matter so easily.

"Want me to go get it from Redbox?" Kyle offered.

"If you don't mind?"

"Sure, I'll be back in a few. Love you, Vanessa."

"Love you too."

He got back with the movie in what seemed like no time at all. Honestly, part of me was expecting him to run and never come back. But we watched the movie, and it was terrific. I didn't mention anything about Hunter's project for the rest of the night, but right before we went to bed, I suggested a new project while we were watching the news.

"Hey babe, how about we think about putting in a swimming pool for the kids?" Not one of those cheap things, but a real one. Hire a pro to come and work on the yard and install it in time for summer?" I could practically feel him thinking on the couch beside me before he answered.

"Sure, sounds great."

That was all he said about my suggestion. After a few more minutes of watching the news, we called it a night and went through our usual nighttime routines before getting into bed. I was just about to fall asleep when an idea came to me. I thought of the last place he could be hiding something here. The attic. No one ever goes up there but him. We also keep it locked so that Hunter can't get inside and hurt himself. Or at least that's what I always thought.

As soon as Kyle was asleep, I silently got out of bed and walked into the hallway. I can always tell when he is out cold. His breathing gets super deep. Plus, he tosses and turns a lot when he is in a deep sleep. But still, I took care not to make a sound as I inched down the hallway. First, I had to go down to the kitchen to get the key to the attic. We stored it in the one place we knew Hunter would never look, which was where we keep the vegetables. The kitchen, along with the rest of the house, was dark and silent.

Once I grabbed the key, I made my way back upstairs. Our attic was accessed by a trapdoor with a ladder that folded down. Taking great care to make as little noise as possible, I undid the padlock and slowly ascended the ladder. I could feel the air getting heavier as the ladder steps creaked under my body weight. As I quietly climbed the steps to the trapdoor, I thought about Hunter. There was no way he was lying.

Most people don't think about this, but teachers have to be keen observers of people. Kids will try to pull a fast one over you any chance they get, especially in matters relating to school. But the trick is kids are terrible liars and have no idea they are. So it's quite simple to watch them.

When it comes to kids in a classroom, you are in arguably the greatest possible vantage point to observe basic human nature. When dealing with kids at a young age and you have the chance to see them in their prime, you can see where they come from and where they are going. It's a perfect opportunity to learn how to observe and read people. Not to mention it is part of what makes an effective teacher.

Because either you get with the program and adapt accordingly, or you fail. Not just yourself, but the students as well, since what you observe could be a matter of grave importance. Sadly enough, there have been cases where I've had to contact social services because of what I observed from a student. Not in words, oh no. But in a gesture, a look in their eye, a mannerism. The interaction with their parent or parents is also key.

Allow me to let you in on another little secret; at parent-teacher conferences we analyze parents just as much, if not more, as they analyze the teacher. Abuse, especially child abuse, is like a bad blemish on the wall. You can try to pretend it doesn't exist by covering it up on the surface as much as you like, but it's still there. It's just a matter of who can discern it. It saddens me to say it, but if a child is being abused, odds are good that a teacher will be the one to spot it.

By nature, teachers see their students every day for hours on end, so we have a large window to see into their lives. We see the ups and downs. When a student who was always so happy turns glum, or one of the best students' grades suddenly tank, that's a sign for concern, and the cause isn't too hard to figure out.

Kids are more perceptive than people care to admit. At that age, children have a sense for anything that is out of place, out of the ordinary, or just plain different. Kids are so cruel to each other because they can sense something is unusual but can't process the reason why and comprehend it. Abuse is no different. The child instinctively knows something is amiss, they just can't quite understand it. So their behavior changes in some fashion.

When a student's behavior at school starts to change, it's usually for the following reasons: problems at home, problems with peers, drugs, or dating issues. When it comes to the students I teach, the last two usually aren't an issue; so that just leaves problems at home or with peers. It's why when there is a conference and some issue comes up, we inadvertently ask "Are there any problems at home?" The reaction of both student and parent is always quite telling. That's how I know Hunter truly believed what he was saying about his dad, that was never in doubt. It was just a matter of the source he was getting it from. Hunter hadn't been acting out or anything, so there was that to consider as well.

With that thought, I switched the attic light on and took a look around. Cardboard boxes scattered around here and there, a cobweb or layer of dust decorating the odd bit of furniture, and a lot of empty space where you could see the electrical wiring of the house.

What was I looking for exactly? I had no idea really, I just figured that whatever it was would catch my eye somehow. I slowly took the attic in. Nothing really out of the ordinary here. That's another trick I've learned as a teacher. You learn how to sense things out of place. I looked around for a bit but found nothing. After what seemed like an eternity, I turned out the light and slowly climbed down the steps again, being as quiet as I possibly could. I felt a mix of relief and disappointment wash over me, which was an odd feeling. Shouldn't I have been happy to have discovered nothing was amiss? Yes, I should be, but I wasn't.

Telling myself that I tried, I climbed back into bed. Kyle didn't move an inch when I did. That was also a relief. I half expected him to confront me about lurking around in the attic or something. After a few minutes, I felt myself drift off to sleep.

Since the next day was Saturday, it meant Kyle was off to his golf game. He and his friends played golf at the local club every Saturday, and then they had brunch. Of course, there was always the possibility they might do something else after as well. Like watching a football game or something. Not to mention it was also a great way to network and meet clients. A country club is the place to see and be seen. But no matter what, Kyle always enjoyed it. Since it seemed to help him relax, I always supported it.

He left at 10 am sharp and wasn't set to come home until late in the afternoon. I had just finished up with some chores and was relaxing with some television while I was going through the mail. Mostly a couple bills, the usual suspects of car, electric, and gas. I was just about to put them away when I saw a statement from our health insurance provider. Skimming it, something caught my eye.

They documented that they had covered an office visit on September 15 with a Dr. Neil McFarland. From the looks of it, it was a pretty expensive visit, which meant it wasn't just some random checkup. September 15 was a Friday, and I remember Kyle had to leave work early. He said it was a meeting with a client downtown.

I was instantly suspicious. None of us had any such visit to a Dr. McFarland, at least not that I knew of. I tried calling our health insurance provider, but since it was Saturday, they were closed. What really had me uneasy was that there was also a prescription that had been covered. I had no idea what the drug was, so I looked it up. It was a sedative, a really powerful one.

I sat there, dumbfounded. I stared at the document for what seemed like an eternity. The crisp white paper crinkled as I gripped it tighter in my hands. Shock slowly gave way to panic, which began to claw at me. Slowly at first, then it came in great rushes, like a dam that had cracked wide open. Taking a deep breath, I tried to steady my nerves. Even after all this time, whenever I think of sedatives, I can't help but think of Zane.

"Come on, get it together," I told myself. "You've been through stuff worse than this."

Just telling myself that helped enormously. It was also quite true.

About 7 years ago, I had a student in my class named Zane. When I taught him, he was one of my top students. He also happened to be one of the nicest kids you'd ever want to meet. Zane never talked back or did anything wrong. His parents were by all appearances normal people, and it was a pleasure to have him in my class.

One of the most extraordinary parts of being a teacher is seeing your former students grow up. You see them grow into maturity; but no matter what happens, you can't help but always see them as the children you taught. Sort of how a parent sees their child.

Most of the students who have passed through my class have grown into sensible, well-adjusted young adults. Zane, well, he was one of the others.

I don't know what happened exactly, but for some reason he changed. It was right as he was about to go into the Junior High levels. In a small private school like White Pine Valley, word travels fast. All of my colleagues began to whisper about Zane's sudden behavior change. I tried to never pay attention to it, thinking the gossip was petty and beneath them. But deep down, I knew they had a point.

This previously hardworking and happy young man became quiet and withdrawn. He became something of a loner, which, while not uncommon for kids at that age, it still broke my heart to see. There was just something about it that made you do a double take. Whenever I saw Zane in the halls, I would say hello, and he would quietly respond, and that was the end of it. Eventually, Zane graduated and moved on to High School. I never forgot about him and checked on him as often as I could, but sadly he was out of my reach. All I could do was hope for the best.

I will never forget that day. November 17, 2011. I had just come home from work when I got a phone call. It was my boss Sheila Farnsworth, the principal of White Pine Valley.

"Vanessa, it's Sheila, I have some bad news." I felt my heart sink as she spoke. Sheila sounded so strained. I had never seen her like that before, nor has she sounded like that since.

"What is it?" I took a deep breath as I braced myself.

"It's Zane, he was arrested this morning." I almost dropped the phone in shock. No, this couldn't be happening.

"How?" I managed to mumble out.

"There was a bomb threat at the High School this morning. The police traced the call to Zane. Well, I guess one thing led to another, and they searched his house. They found posts on his computer where he talked about committing a mass shooting." Thank God I was already sitting, because if I hadn't been, my legs probably would have given out from under me.

"I can't believe it."

"I don't blame you Vanessa," Sheila agreed. "But there is more."

"Oh God."

"Oh God is right. Apparently Zane wasn't just talking. In his locker, they found a few hunting knives, along with a list of his fellow students. Beside each name there was a phrase explaining why they 'needed to be punished' in his words. Zane also got a little creative, in that he had plenty of drawings to go with his list. Pretty detailed, gruesome ones too. So as you can imagine, they took the kid into police custody. They called me for background on him."

"I feel like I failed him." I shouted more at myself than at Sheila before I let loose with a stream of swear words. I had never felt so useless as a teacher.

"Hey, don't you go blaming yourself," she gently corrected me when I was done. "You are the best teacher in my school. You bent over backwards for the kid and tried to help him." In my head I knew she was right. But in my heart, it still ripped at me to know what happened to one of my students. If I had done something, anything, would it have made a difference?

"You're right," I mumbled.

Sheila said a couple more things, but for the life of me I couldn't tell you what they were. I felt numb to everything. As I laid in bed that night, my thoughts were all over the place. I kept replaying everything I knew about Zane in my head, obsessively micro analyzing every interaction I had with him. Looking back, it was an impressive act of self-flagellation.

The next few days passed in a similar fashion. I would drag myself through the days at school, but come nighttime, I would lie awake and fester over what happened. This kid, a student in my own class, had seriously thought about going on a rampage at school. Would he have done that to me? Disbelief turned to fear, as I suddenly began imagining myself being in the position of Zane's High School peers.

Believe me, as a teacher these days, I am well-schooled in procedure for a lockdown. But somehow this was different. Perhaps because it was so close to home, someone I had actually known and taught. He could have easily turned on me as well.

One day when I was instructing my students, I began to imagine Zane sitting there. It was only for a moment, but it was still terrifying. I still wasn't sleeping at night, but during the day I was a mass of energy. I guess I thought that if I was the perfect teacher, I wouldn't have another student like that pass through my class.

After a particularly brutal night of not sleeping, I decided to do something about it. I went to the school counselor and asked for a recommendation for someone to talk to. Since she knew all too well of the Zane situation, she recommended me to a psychiatrist who specialized in traumatic incidents. After a few sessions, he put me on medication to see if it would help me relax and sleep. At first it seemed to do the job, but then on the fourth day, it came with an unexpected side effect.

That night, I dreamt I was running through a maze of lockers. My feed thudded on the black-and-white checkered floor as I sprinted down the halls. I was terrified, my heart was pounding so hard I thought it would burst through my chest. It seemed like no matter how hard I tried or how fast I ran, something or someone was always faster. I heard myself scream out to whatever was chasing me, saying I hadn't done anything. All I heard in response was a cold, emotionless laugh.

Then, I suddenly found myself facing a wall. With my back to it, I turned to face what was following me.

It was Zane. Just standing there staring at me.

"Why are you doing this," I screamed at him. "I was good to you!"

A sick smile twisted its way onto his face in response.

"So you think," he hissed in a voice that was nothing like Zane's. I was then staring down both barrels of a shotgun. A deafening blast emerged from it, and I woke up in my bed with a jolt.

I was panting like I had just ran a mile. I frantically looked around my room to make sure it was all real. Everything was as it should be, but I was still pretty rattled from that nightmare. I didn't immediately go off the medication in the hopes that the dream would be a one-time thing. Sadly enough, it wasn't. The dreams got even worse after that.

Once I even had a dream where I arrived in my classroom to see *Welcome Class* written on the blackboard in blood and the desks were dotted with bullet holes. Believe me, it only took a few days for me to drop the medicine.

I took up meditation and found it quite helpful. Slowly, things began to go back to normal. But I won't lie, there is an occasional moment where I am reminded of Zane. Once, I could have sworn I saw him at the mall. When that happened, I almost screamed. But I immediately realized that it wasn't him. Zane and his family had moved out of the area after the incident long ago. But that still doesn't quite totally stop the adrenaline you get when something like that happens.

I put the statement away after a pause. Time to focus on the matter at hand. This was all a simple process of elimination. Kyle hadn't slipped me the sedative, because I would have known it. Not to mention it would have been obvious to others as well. He hadn't given it to Hunter, because I was able to observe his behavior. Jayne hadn't been acting unusual either. No, the only possibilities were that he was taking it himself or was using it on someone outside the family.

I'd have to keep an eye on Kyle when he slept. Maybe that was the connection. Hunter always said that his dad went to fight the bad guys at night. Taking a deep breath, I knew what I had to do.

Moving quickly so I would be done before Kyle got home from his golf game, I looked up pictures of the drug in question. Tiny little orange capsules. Then I went to the upstairs bathroom. Combing through the medicine cabinet, I looked through everything, especially all the pill bottles. Nothing. I slammed the cabinet shut in irritation, and I realized something.

Inside Kyle's desk was a container of Tic Tacs. They were filled with what I assumed were the orange flavored ones, so I didn't think anything of it before.

Sprinting down to his office, I flung open the desk drawer and there they were. I opened the container and smelled it. That refreshing citrus smell was nowhere. There was no way these were orange Tic Tacs. I felt my stomach turn itself into a knot. Why does he have these? Even better, why was he hiding them like this?

Right at that moment, I heard the garage door opening. I hastily tossed the container back into the desk and closed it. Running upstairs, I threw myself back on the couch and turned on the TV just as Kyle was unlocking the door.

"Hey honey, how was your day?" I called out nonchalantly. "Good time on the green?"

"You know it, I had a good day. I put Charlie Fielding in his place. Today he couldn't hit the side of the Empire State Building."

"That's great, so he had to buy you brunch?"

The grin on his face said it all. "It was the greatest brunch ever." Kyle practically beamed as he remembered it. "I don't think Eggs Benedict and Hash Browns have ever tasted so good."

"Wonderful," I changed the channel as he was reminiscing.

"I'm gonna go take a shower. Any thoughts on dinner?"

"No, but I am curious about this," I said while handing him the health insurance statement.

He glanced at it for a minute, then looked at me. I could feel him briefly considering what to say before he sighed deeply.

"I should've just told you up front," he began. "You know I've been stressed about work lately?"

"Yeah? What about it?"

"It isn't my work per se. It's what came with it. Someone was threatening me."

"Threatening you?"

He nodded and seemed to age 10 years before my eyes. "Yeah. Not overtly. At least most of the time. One of the exceptions being the incident with the dead deer."

"The dead deer?"

"Yeah. One night I got up to go to the bathroom and there, right on top of my car, was a deer. Dead from a gunshot wound. Such a mess. I discreetly called Bill to help me get rid of it, and we did it before the sun came up. And I was hoping that would be the end of it. But it wasn't. Because not long after, I found a bloody skeleton in my car. Not outside, actually in my car. And there was an accompanying note saying next time it wouldn't be a fake."

"Wow. But why would someone threaten you?"

"Because I refused to represent someone on the grounds that they were unethical. And unethical is putting it lightly. They tried to bribe me with fancy jewels and cash, leaving it in our mailbox, but I always gave it back." He paused for a moment. "Do you remember Zane?"

I shuddered internally. "What about him?"

"The guy in question is his uncle."

That was a gut punch. "You're kidding me?"

He slowly shook his head back and forth. "I swear. That's the main reason I tried to keep you out of this. I know how that was horrible for you. And I know you had a bad experience with the kind of pills they wanted me to try."

I immediately walked up to Kyle and put my arms around him. "I don't blame you at all. I've been worried about you." Then I explained the whole thing about Hunter's story.

He listened to what I had to say and then immediately burst out laughing. "That's a good one. I told him a tiny bit and his imagination did the rest. But he was observant, so good for him."

"But what happened to Zane's uncle? What was he up to?"

"Drug trafficking. Amongst other things. Tried to get me and two others at the office to help him out. He refused. And we all started getting the same little messages."

"Why didn't you go to the police?"

"We were about to when he was found in a storage unit somewhere. Dead. So nothing to report and nothing's happened since."

"Wait a minute. Wasn't that on the news just the other day?"

Kyle nodded. "That was him."

My jaw dropped. "I thought he looked vaguely familiar."

"And now you know why."

I could see the relief in Kyle's face. It was all out in the open now. And I took a deep breath. "Well that explains it. But promise me something?"

"What's that?"

"Next time just tell me."

"Hopefully there won't be a next time."

I chuckled. "Fair point."

Seasonal Landscaping

I've always loved my job as a landscaper or lawn care specialist. I make my own hours, get to work outdoors, and best of all, I get to embrace my passion. I view lawn care as much more of an art form like architecture. Because no two trees, lawns, hedges, or ponds are the same. When you're a landscaper, you basically take the nature equivalent of raw material and craft it into something unique. That's why I view it more like an art form than just cutting the grass. And there is no telling what you may encounter while working. I thought I knew that until my last job.

By far the busiest times of year in this line of work are spring and fall. Spring, because after winter the grass and plants are finally starting to bloom and need tons of attention, especially because of the frequent rain, and fall, because it's the final bit of time to keep an eye on things before the months-long cold of winter makes my job irrelevant. I'm usually pretty busy in the summer depending on the weather, because I either have to work hard to make sure grass on lawns doesn't dry out in the heat, or there is no shortage of lawns to mow if it's a rainy summer. But fall also means that in addition to the usual landscaping tasks, there are leaves to rake.

Which was just fine with me. I've always loved raking leaves, as I find it calming and the vivid colors on the trees give you plenty to look at while you're working. Most of my clients are long time ones, so much so that we can communicate in what is essentially shorthand. But of all my customers, my favorite land to work belongs to Mr. and Mrs. Allen.

They have a large stone house with double doors and blue shutters, and the property is set on 7 acres with a solid blend of all kinds of trees. Lots of pine trees and plenty of beautiful maple and other trees that shed their leaves come fall. And I was due there for a job on a lovely October afternoon. It was a short drive there, and on the way, I passed numerous storefronts with orange lights or cobwebs in the windows before I arrived at the Allen's neighborhood.

It's filled with people who are actually pretty cool and friendly. That's one reason the neighborhood is one of the most prized places to go Trick-or-treating around here. All the houses are spaced pretty close together, there's plenty of sidewalk, and the homeowners get really into the holiday spirit. All down the street were houses decorated in their own unique ways. One was covered with cobwebs and a giant spider, while others were filled with a cemetery, an open coffin, and a collection of monsters.

Mr. and Mrs. Allen kept it simple with plenty of orange lights, pumpkins, and some dried corn stalks arranged around the garage. Once I parked in the driveway, I got out of my truck, got everything ready, and got started on my job. First, I mowed the front lawn. There is nothing like the smell of freshly cut grass on a refreshing fall morning. And when that was done, it was time for me to take care of the leaves. It was early October, and the trees in the backyard were only beginning to shed their leaves. So raking them all out from under the trees where the mower couldn't get them only took about half an hour, and all of them could fit into a small pile.

The Allens always liked me to mulch their leaves, which works for me. So I got the mower ready and methodically went about turning the leaves in the backyard into tiny piles that wouldn't cover the grass. When I was done, the smell of leaves coated the air. Also on the schedule today was for me to plant some mums, which was always a big request for me once fall arrived. When that was all said and done, I went home and had a grilled cheese sandwich and some soup for lunch.

Several days later, I had an appointment with the Sullivan family, who lived next door to the Allens. So I went right on schedule and took care of their lawn. They generally had less trees in their backyard than the Allen house, but they were bigger, and their leaves proved to be falling at a faster rate.

There was a bit of fog that morning that hung thickly in the air, and when I arrived, I could see the grass and the leaves scattered on it were soaked with dew. The Sullivans liked me to use a leaf blower and bag up their leaves, so that task quickly took up two hours. As I worked, I could see the one tree that was technically on the Allen property but would occasionally drop leaves on the Sullivan property. Thankfully, it wasn't a big deal. The two families got along great and had been friendly for decades. I've met far too many families where a leaf falling on their property from a tree that wasn't theirs was a huge problem.

Farther down in the yard, Mr. Sullivan was reading a book by his fire ring, which had a fire lit in it and was crackling along in the gentle breeze. The smell from it casually billowed my way and made the fall air with the crisp breeze and earthy smell of leaves that much more invigorating. Definitely a pleasant atmosphere to finish my work in.

The next day was one of those rainy October days where you can feel that fall has arrived. It was grey and rainy all day, and everywhere I drove you could see evidence that the steady rain had caused numerous trees to shed leaves that had thus far managed to stay on the branches. Although I spent the day indoors watching scary movie marathons, I was mentally gearing up for the inevitable post rainstorm calls that would arrive as soon as things dried up.

Sure enough, the very next day the calls came in to repair one thing or another. And out I went to tidy things up. No matter how old I get, it never ceases to amaze me the difference just a few days can make for how fall can look and feel. The color creeping into the trees was much more noticeable, with a particularly vivid red making itself known on a tree in the Allen yard that I could spot when I drove past it.

Later that week, there was a nasty storm with intense rain and wind that caused numerous trees to fall. Which meant I was constantly being called out to help get rid of tree limbs that had been snapped off in the wind or help cut up trees that had broken in half or been uprooted. One of the many trees damaged from wind was one of the massive ones in the Sullivan's yard.

Once I arrived, I took out the necessary equipment and carefully went to work on the fallen tree limb. It was a massive branch, but steadily, the fallen limb became a pile of firewood as I worked under the bright blue sky. I worked until the sun started to dip behind the orange and red foliage. As I finished up, the sun was slowly descending, and the mellow autumn light was peeking out from the gaps in the trees. A sight I never get tired of.

I had just finished up with one section and was heading to the other side of the yard to get the last bit of tree that had fallen. The final bit of fallen tree was right in the middle of the yard, where the surface was flat. As I stepped on it, I could tell how soft and wet the ground still was. But as I took another step, I felt something snap, and before I knew what was happening, I was falling through the earth.

Moments later, pain shot through my body as I landed on rocky ground. I waited for a moment before getting up. Fortunately, I always keep a tool belt filled with tools on me whenever I work, so I quickly removed a flashlight and switched it on. Thankfully, it worked.

I checked my phone, which was fine, but there was no service down here. But I was able to shine my flashlight up and see the hole I had fallen through. Thanks to the rain, the soil had thinned out and revealed that right under that section of the Sullivan's yard was the entrance to a tunnel that someone had placed a board over. No doubt all the years of rain and other types of weather had worn it down, so that by the time of the recent heavy rain it had been ready to crack when I stepped right on it.

Oh well. Nothing I could do about it now. The Sullivans were out for the evening, which meant I had no reason to stick around and try to get their attention. Especially since there was no way for me to climb out the way I'd fallen in. So that meant I had to follow the small tunnel I found myself in.

It was big enough for me to stand in, and in reasonably good condition. No signs of a cave in. I could feel how the chill had soaked into the earth as I kept walking. There was no telling where I was going or what I would find. All I could do to get out was keep going forward.

Several minutes later, the tunnel opened into a cavern, and I realized I was in an abandoned mine. The tools and cart left behind were the giveaway. It wasn't exactly a surprise. I've lived in Pennsylvania my whole life, and there are old mines everywhere. And I've been in several of them before. So I wasn't exactly shocked or afraid as I followed it along. After the work on the Sullivan yard and the amount of walking I'd done to get this far, I could feel how my body was soaked with sweat under my jacket. But the air here wasn't as chilly as it was above ground, so that helped cool me down at least somewhat.

Eventually, the tunnel I was walking in narrowed a bit and the intense darkness of the mine began to fade. Then the tunnel got lighter and lighter, until I was facing a small ladder built into the cavern wall that went up, and beyond that, there was light coming from somewhere above.

I switched off my flashlight, and carefully climbed the old wooden steps, silently hoping they wouldn't give. They held just fine, and when I pulled myself up the last step, I found myself facing a small opening in the rock wall that I could just barely fit through. That was where the light had been coming from.

I took a deep breath and carefully stepped through it. As I did, I could smell the fresh air and relief flooded through my body. But that was immediately followed by confusion.

On the other side of the opening in the rock wall was a wide stretch of open space that was surrounded by trees. From the outside, the rock wall looked like a small remnant of a quarry built into the earth. But the open space wasn't exactly open because it was filled with RVs. Only they were not all of a similar type, like you would expect in a standard storage space. Far from it, as it seemed like every possible model or design was here. Giant RVs and tiny ones, ones that looked older than I was, ones that looked brand new, ones that you could see at any campground, and ones you never saw aside from in old vintage family home movies.

I slowly started walking through the rows of vehicles. They seemed to go on forever, and it wasn't long before I had the sensation that I was lost in some kind of endless labyrinth. It was nighttime by now, and my small flashlight was the only source of light. I was walking on cement, which meant that there were no footprints I could follow. But the upside was that I didn't have to worry about leaving them either. As I kept walking on the cement, I remembered that there used to be a factory somewhere around here, and it was demolished years ago. I guess the floor was all that was left.

Seeing all the RVs sitting there, silent and abandoned, was downright creepy. Because this wasn't some brightly lit warehouse. This was outside in the dark, and the faint light from my flashlight dancing over the various vehicles gathered here made it all the more unnerving. There was something seriously not right about all this.

For starters, it wasn't like this was an actual storage space for a business that sold them. I'd heard of graveyards for ships to say nothing of junkyards, but not RVs. And it wasn't like all these RVs were situated in a public space where anyone could come and look. No, these were hidden away in a place people didn't come looking, and I had no doubt it was for a reason.

For a fleeting moment, I thought that maybe this was part of some haunted attraction for the Halloween season. But I know all the haunted houses around, and there was nothing like this. Plus, there were no Halloween decorations around, and these giant luxury RVs were not the type to be used in a haunted house. So the only idea left was that something was up here, and it wasn't good.

Especially because as I took a closer look at all the RVs assembled here, it was clear that for all their differences, they had something in common; they had all sustained some kind of small damage. One vintage RV had a broken front window, while I saw a smashed-in side door on one of the giant expensive RVs, and the list went on and on. The sight of a windshield on a relatively new one that had been completely destroyed sent a particular chill up my spine.

If all these RVs had sustained damage, then the logical thing that should've happened was for them to be repaired and returned. None of the damage I could see made them uninhabitable. As someone who maintains people's property as his job, none of this seemed right.

I slowly walked on, trying to get my bearings. The space seemed endless, and I carefully wandered along looking at everything until I passed an average modern RV that I've seen plenty of my friends use on vacation. As I passed the door, I shined my flashlight, and the beam of light highlighted that something was on the door's window. I paused for a closer look, and saw that it looked like a handprint, and it was made by what looked just like blood.

The sight made my stomach sick with fear. Now there was no doubt I needed to get out of here, and fast. Almost if on cue, I heard a sound from far off in the distance. And from all the time spent in nature, I could tell it was a car driving on gravel. Ignoring the fear gripping my stomach, I looked at my surroundings. Some of these RVs, superficial dents aside, were beyond well built. So well built that someone stuck inside would not be able to get out easily if the door was blocked. And I had plenty of small landscaping tools still on my belt that I could easily jam a door handle. If I was able to trick whoever was out there inside the RV.

So I took a deep breath, switched off my flashlight, and put together a plan. I had several minutes, but not much more. Whoever was out there would most likely go up and down the rows of RVs, looking for anything out of place. Naturally, an open door would signal that something was amiss and should be checked. Once the person driving was well inside the RV, I could slam the door shut and jam it so there would be no getting out.

It was as good a plan as any, and I had to act fast. Thankfully, it wasn't hard to decide on an RV. One of the giant expensive luxury vehicles was the way to go. But even in the dim light, the vehicle's interior was beyond impressive when I briefly checked it. No doubt no expense had been spared from the interior's comfort to the basic strength of the vehicle, which included windows, all of which were in perfect condition without a single scratch on them. The RV also had the perfect main door with a metal handle similar to a refrigerator's. If I were to put my small trowel from my belt inside the handle's space when the door was closed, it would jam the door perfectly. And it was the only door in and out of the vehicle. No normal doors to the front or passenger seat.

I also was beyond thankful that this RV, like several on display, were built with plenty of space for me to crawl under and wait. So once I had carefully opened the door to lure in whoever was out here with me, I removed the small trowel from my belt and crawled under the middle of the RV as quietly as possible and waited. All those years crawling around bushes and hedges would definitely come in handy now as I ducked under the bumper and stared up at the RV.

I had barely gotten in place when I heard the tires on gravel stop. Then all was quiet while I was alone with my thoughts. The silence in the space was so thick it was unpleasant, and I felt like my heart was thudding painfully loud as I tried to listen. After what felt like an hour, I heard it. The sound of quiet footsteps coming my way.

I swallowed thickly as I listened and got ready to act as soon as it was time. The footsteps quietly shuffled around before they arrived at the RV I was hidden under. As the footsteps got closer, I could tell whoever they belonged to was carrying a flashlight as well, as the beam slowly bobbed along to remind me someone was getting closer until the beam was right beside me. I couldn't see who the footsteps belonged to or make out any details aside from some basic black leather boots. But as they moved one step closer, I could faintly see the figure's outline in the reflection from one of the RV's tire rims, and I could see they were wearing a belt with a large knife on it.

My throat clenched as I stared at them from no more than a few feet away. The stranger was painfully close as I laid there and silently willed whoever was out there to just take the few steps inside the RV. And moments later, the adrenaline in my body kicked up a notch as the boots walked the few steps forward into the open RV. I could feel the RV moving slightly under the weight of its new occupant as the stranger climbed aboard, stepped inside, and slowly began to look around.

Despite the fear churning in my stomach, I did feel better that the stranger didn't immediately summon a friend of his who had driven here with him when he saw the open RV door. That meant this was the only other person here. So once the figure slowly started walking towards the bathroom and master bedroom in the back of the RV, that was time for me to climb out and spring into action. With my heart pounding harder than ever before in my life,

I crept out from under the RV, took the trowel in hand, and gently grabbed the door handle while listening carefully.

Whoever was in there had no idea I was out there, as I could feel the weight of footsteps in the back bedroom. So I carefully closed the door, which closed with a quiet click, before I immediately jammed the trowel in the handle and made sure it was stuck. It was.

The stranger inside had no idea what happened, but it didn't take whoever was inside long to realize something had happened, because moments later footsteps were hastily walking towards the door before there was weight pushing on it from the other side.

It didn't give an inch, and some faint relief flooded through my body. I crept quietly away as whoever was trapped inside tried to apply more pressure to the door, and nothing changed. As I put more distance between the RV and myself, I thought I could hear a muffled yell from inside, but that was it.

I didn't stop walking and before long, I had reached the other side of the open space and found myself facing a wall of trees. There was still no sign that whoever was stuck in the RV had managed to make any progress at all.

With that hopeful thought, I took several more steps and finally reached the part of the woods that was well on the other side from where I had climbed out of the abandoned mine. When I finally walked through the trees and was lost in them moments later, I finally felt somewhat better. But I kept my flashlight off to avoid being detected, and I carefully crept along, listening carefully for any sound of movement or voices.

As I continued walking in the trees, I heard a second vehicle roaring up from the other side of the area. I immediately ducked behind a tree and turned to watch. Someone had driven into the area via a truck, and the driver wasted no time getting out and racing into the vast collection of RVs, their shoes echoing loudly on the hard floor. I had a pretty good idea what would happen next. And I was right, because although I couldn't see anything yet, I could hear the RV door being yanked open before it was slammed shut. Then when both people walked quickly back towards the truck, which still had its headlights on, I could see, and I got a good look at the person who unknowingly walked right past me. He was a tall guy, muscular, and if I had to guess, I'd say mid-30s. His associate fit the same description.

"What happened?" One of them asked the other.

"I don't know. I went inside to see what made the door open, and before I knew it, it was sealed shut and I couldn't get out. Just like I told you."

"Well, it was sealed shut with this," I could faintly see him holding up my trowel that was available at any store for a few bucks. "And there's no telling who's responsible for it and where they are. We'll just have to take it from here."

"Right."

Then I watched as they both got in the truck and roared out of there in the opposite direction from me. I let out a deep breath before I kept walking. I knew I would eventually reach a road, but every step was tinged with nerves, as I half expected someone lurking behind a tree to reach out and attack me.

But after about two hours, I managed to reach a road without incident, and when I saw it, I finally had reception to call for help. I immediately told the police what I'd seen, and they dispatched someone to find me while the dispatcher stayed on the line with me. And I'd never been more relieved in my life than when I saw the flashing lights of the police car coming towards me.

I described the general direction I had come from, but it didn't take long for the cops to find the place, because after I left, someone had set fire to all the RVs, and before long, everything there was burning intensely, and the smoke was visible for miles. They had to bring in a massive team of firefighters to calm the blaze down. And they were able to get the fire under control in time for the cops to find out that all the RVs that hadn't been totally burned were all listed as missing, along with their owners. The cases involved spanned many years and every region of the country.

After some time, the cops were able to use some of what was found at the RV collection to aid in solving some missing persons cases, but there was never any lead on who was responsible for it. Nor did they ever figure out what the specific motivation was.

As for me, I'll always be extra careful where I step while on a landscaping job from now on. The Sullivans felt horrible when they heard what happened and gave me a huge bonus for my work that day. They were even gracious enough to invite me over for when they gave out Halloween candy. Since they stuck to sitting out on the front porch with some hot apple cider, I happily accepted.

Nighttime Wanderings

MY DAD IS HAVING a hard time coping with his wife's murder.

As you can imagine, he isn't taking the whole thing well. My parents divorced when I was a lot younger, and she was his second wife. From all I know, they had a good relationship. In fact I always thought she was a good influence on him. Did I actually like her myself? I respected her and was polite to her, but I can't say I loved her. Don't get me wrong, what happened to her is horrific and I can't imagine she did anything remotely possible to deserve anything like it.

Not surprisingly, he seems like a totally different person since it happened. One night, she left home and was found dead in her car about two hours away. No one has any idea what happened. Not gonna lie, it creeps me out a bit. Especially knowing the person hasn't been caught.

About a week ago, I heard Dad talking. It was late at night, and I can't say I was surprised. The doctors had given him something to help him sleep, but I wasn't sure how effective it was. It made him groggy and susceptible to sleepwalking. He had also been indulging in a few drinks, which is not good for something like sleeping pills. Still, I couldn't really blame him. That's why I was staying at his place to keep an eye on him and all that.

I heard him get up and sort of fumble around in the dark. Believe me, I knew better than to try to wake a sleepwalker. So I tried to just lie there and let it pass. He might have gone to the bathroom or something, because I'm pretty sure I heard that door open. To my surprise, I heard him mumble something.

"Veronica is gone and here I am, stuck with the person who killed her. Almost every day, like clockwork, I have to look at that conniving scumbag. It's not bad enough you kill her, your face tortures me day after day. Well, one day you'll crack and you'll be locked away for good. If you're lucky. Because I hope to God I get to you before the cops do."

I didn't hear him say anything more before he shuffled back into his room. The door creaked shut again and everything was silent. My brain, on the other hand, was anything but. Part of me was wondering if I really heard that. I sat up gingerly, patting myself on the arm to make sure I wasn't dreaming. Yup, that really happened. So I just laid there dumbfounded. I didn't think it was possible, but I felt even worse for him than before. Not only was his wife taken from him, but it was because of someone he knew. Someone he was forced to deal with. I can't imagine anything more awful. It's bad enough when someone wrongs you, but being forced to behave as if nothing happened is downright unbearable.

The first thing I wondered was, why didn't he report it to the police? With a sinking feeling, I answered my own question. Maybe he did, and it didn't go anywhere. Or worse, maybe the police already knew and just couldn't prove it. It happens far more than people like to think. Feeling a chill run up my spine, I couldn't help but wonder who Dad knew that was capable of something like that. A quick mental check didn't yield any results. Someone who had a grudge against him was the most likely. Or someone who he had one against. While I admit I hadn't been in touch with him as much as I'd like, there still isn't anyone in his circle who I'd suspect of such a thing.

But that didn't make things any easier. If anything, it just made it worse. My own father thought his wife's murderer was someone he saw on a regular basis. Over the next few days, I tried to keep an eye on stuff. A handyman or cleaning lady, perhaps? But according to him the few people he did occasionally use for stuff like this were people he really liked. I didn't push the matter and tried to act as nonchalant as I could.

Inside though, I was on edge, mentally running through people he knew and asking, 'Could they have done it?' When I couldn't answer yes to any of them, I began to feel truly afraid. No matter who they were, they were around.

All I could do was wait for him to sleepwalk again to see if he said anything more. Every night when he went to bed, I felt my adrenaline shoot up. I would get out of bed, quietly walk to my door, and peer out the tiny crack I kept open at night. Every time I would silently scream 'Come on start talking again' to myself, but he wouldn't. I felt so weird peering at my dad sleepwalking. But hey, this was a bit of an unusual circumstance. While he did sleepwalk a little bit, he wouldn't talk. At least, not for a few days.

When he did it last night, I almost leapt out of my skin when I heard his voice. I was watching through the crack in the door and once he began talking, I felt my heart almost leap into my throat.

"You think you got away with it did you? Well, keep thinking that. Your day will come. I guarantee it. Sleep well," he said before murmuring a bunch of rather colorful swear words. He walked back into his room after that and shut the door.

I felt like my chest was going to explode. Seeing him in the bathroom talking like that had been creepy before, but now it was more disturbing than I could imagine. It had been bad when I thought all he was talking about was revenge, but now I realized something. He hadn't just been talking in the bathroom, he had been talking to something in the bathroom. His voice sounded exactly the same as last time when just now, I saw him lean in and address the medicine cabinet. The medicine cabinet complete with a large mirror.

Rattlesnake Roundup

THE GUY BUYING A Poinsettia had no clue I was watching him from my car. But that's no surprise. It doesn't matter if they are buying a Poinsettia in November, Halloween candy in October, or stuff for a 4th of July cookout in June. I'm invisible and well paid for it. A good private investigator is like a stiletto: discrete and unassuming, but lethal and relentless when the situation calls for it. And there's no telling which situations may call for it. It never fails that the worst cases always seem easy at first. That's just how it goes. Some cases are incredibly dull, while others haunt you for years. But there's no doubt that every case is unique.

Since Halloween had just ended here in San Sebastian, that meant the stores were already pushing Christmas. Which was why I was being paid to watch someone buy a poinsettia instead of Halloween decorations or something related to Day of the Dead. Although every day is Day of the Dead. November 1 just happens to be the day everyone acknowledges it. Because no matter what day it is, someone dies, be it from natural causes or not. And lately the ones not naturally related out here were getting a lot of attention. That was also why I was being paid to watch someone buy a Poinsettia from a small greenhouse by the road.

After a few minutes, the guy picked two Poinsettias in pots wrapped in gold foil, walked to the checkout, and paid. Then he walked to his car and started on his way home, with me behind him every step of the way. Once he pulled into his apartment building's garage, he was out of sight and my job was over for the night. Which meant it was now my turn to go home.

When I was safely in my apartment with the door deadbolted, I whipped up some pasta with pesto sauce and tossed some garlic bread in the oven. Then I carried the steaming plates into the sitting room, settled down in front of the TV, and ate with great gusto.

After dinner, I headed towards the smallest bedroom which served as my office. On a yellow legal pad, there were a list of names written down. Aside from the last one, they had all been crossed off with a blue pen. Now it was time to mark off the name of the guy buying poinsettias. When his name had a slash of ink through it like the others, I shuffled through some papers and began to reread the notes on my most recent case. One I had taken four days ago during my 5 pm appointment.

The sky was iron grey that day, which meant the impending darkness was more pronounced than usual. I had just turned on my desk lamp and pulled out some forms in anticipation of the appointment when she knocked on my open office door. She was right on time. She was also gorgeous. Long slender legs, soft olive skin, and long brown hair. Since she was dressed in a red t—shirt and faded black jeans, I could see that her left arm was covered in a tattoo sleeve: an explosion of colors, creatures, and designs that I couldn't begin to decipher. But the most striking feature by far were her eyes. They were emerald green and glimmered with intelligence. I could feel her assessing me as much as I was assessing her.

"Hello, I'm Patrick Wilder," I stood up and walked around my desk to shake her hand.

"Maddie Nielsen," her grip was warm and soft. "Thank you for seeing me on short notice."

"Sure thing. Please have a seat," I gestured towards the faux leather armchairs situated in front of my desk before I returned to my chair. "How can I help you, Miss Nielsen?" I asked, after taking out a notepad and a pen.

"It's my sister, she's gone missing."

"I'm sorry to hear that. What can you tell me about her?"

"Gretchen was always the life of the party. The wild one. I will admit she got into plenty of messes growing up. And a few long after that. But she's a good person. Caring."

"Where was Gretchen last seen?"

"She ate dinner at TGI Friday's on Tuesday of last week."

"With a friend?"

"Yes. Paula. An old friend from school who went to a movie with her mother immediately after. Gretchen left shortly after 8 and that was the last confirmed sighting of her."

"Was she a regular there?"

"Oh yes. My sister is a huge fan of the restaurant. She loved to go there and have margaritas with their appetizers. I personally could take it or leave it. Years back, when I was in college, I went through a phase where I would buy a lot of their frozen products at the store. The potato skins were my favorite."

"I know what you mean. When did you notice something happened to your sister?"

"The first sign there was any trouble was when she didn't show up to work. When no one could get ahold of her, we went to her apartment and while it was empty, there was no sign of foul play either. We filed a missing persons report, but there isn't much they can do since there is no evidence of violence or that anything is wrong. That's why I came to you."

"I understand. Believe me, it's how I get most of my clients."

"I'm sure. They were beyond useless. You would think since people have been going missing and turning up dead here in South

Texas lately, they might take it a little more seriously. But that would require critical thinking skills and common sense, which are practically extinct anymore."

I chuckled. "You are right on the money there. Alright Miss Nielsen, you know my retainer and fee. If you accept that, I'm at your service."

She clapped her hands together. "Thank you, Mr. Wilder."

"Feel free to call me Patrick."

"I will. Especially if you call me Maddie. There is one other thing," she stared down at the floor of my office for a moment. When she looked back up, there was a glimmer of fear in her eyes. "I think I'm being watched. Scratch that, I know I'm being watched."

"Ok."

"You don't need me to explain?"

"I'm a retired law enforcement professional and most of my work consists of being paid to watch people without them knowing it. The sensation is unique. If you feel you're being watched, you're being watched. And I'm guessing you know it's not the police."

"Absolutely. I didn't ask them to begin with, but they would let me know they came and went. This is different. I can feel someone getting near my house. Not inside, but close to the windows. It's like a drink you are so familiar with that you can instantly detect even the slightest bit of difference in it. Like if it's made in a different state or something."

"I understand. Is there any consistency to it? Like does it occur on a similar day or time?"

"No. Not that I've noticed."

"Is there a significant other in your life?"

"No, I'm single. Haven't had a boyfriend in a long time."

"Ok. My advice to you is simple. Be very careful. Keep your eyes open and stay mindful. And whatever you do, don't post anything on social media, especially if it has anything to do with your location or routine. No tweeting about your coffee run or checking into a restaurant with your friends."

"I understand. I've been staying away from that for a while now. Gretchen was always more into that than I ever was."

"I don't mean to scare you, but if something happened to her, that may have been how someone was able to abduct her."

"Believe me, I'm well aware of that."

"I have an important question for you. Feel free to take some time to think about it and get back to me if you need to. Can you think of anyone who may be responsible for Gretchen's disappearance?"

"No. No one comes to mind. I've thought about that a lot since she vanished, and I can't think of anyone."

"Alright," I made a note. "Did she have common sense? Or street smarts?"

"She was always more book smart while I inherited the street smarts, but she had a decent head on her shoulders. She wasn't an idiot."

"Ok. Is there anyone who seems really interested in the matter to you? Aside from people who should be interested. A neighbor or something like that?"

She sat there for a moment. "Not that I can think of. But I have to admit, I wonder if she's the latest victim of The Rattlesnake."

"I won't lie to you Maddie, you may be right."

"What are your thoughts on The Rattlesnake?"

"Someone with some brains, a basic working anatomical knowledge, and a career that gives them some kind of cover."

Maddie brushed a strand of hair away from her face. "I was just curious."

"As you should be."

"I read a lot of true crime books."

"Do you?"

"Yes. It's technically part of my work, but I enjoy it regardless."

"And what is your work?"

"Journalist. I used to work for the San Sebastian Gazette before it went belly up. Now I teach it at the local college. I've also written one book so far."

"Really? What was it about?"

"That couple who went around killing people in Louisiana about 5 years ago."

"That is interesting. I remember that. I'd love a signed copy if it's not too much trouble."

She smiled. "No problem. Gretchen was always saying how I was interested in morbid things, and it made me paranoid. Ironic right?"

"Yeah. People used to be told all the time that they had seen too many movies. There's a good reason people don't say that anymore."

I kept Maddie for a while longer while I made notes, and she eventually signed a contract. Her sister was now officially my next job. She thanked me again before leaving into the night.

As darkness settled in, I began to dig into the files on Gretchen Nielsen. Gretchen was also an attractive woman and shared some physical features with Maddie like brown hair, but she was different from her sister. She was pretty, but conventionally so, whereas Maddie crackled with energy and got your attention by sticking out. If I were a talent agent, I'd be tempted to say she had 'it'. It's no wonder Maddie was a journalist, as she was the kind of person you'd want to chat with. Even if it was about whether her sister was the latest victim of a serial killer stalking this part of Texas known as The Rattlesnake.

So far, the official body count for The Rattlesnake was 10. 7 women and 3 men. But that was just the official body count, as there was no telling how many more murders may have been committed by The Rattlesnake, especially if they took place out of state.

The Rattlesnake's first victim was Veronica Sinclair, who was killed one night after leaving her job at a bar. Her body was found in a garbage covered alley about 5 miles away from where she worked. Next was Lenore Torres, an accountant who was found dead in her duplex by her family. The next four victims were married couples: Charles and Beatrice Adams, and Lucille and Frank Stewart. Both couples were found dead in their homes by family members. The most recent victim was Tiffany Menendez, a college student who was found dead in an abandoned field. Tiffany, like all the other victims of The Rattlesnake, had been strangled to death before numerous post mortem stab wounds were inflicted on her body. The police currently had no leads and no suspects.

But one witness claimed they saw Veronica Sinclair with some guy wearing cowboy boots made from rattlesnake skin, a detail repeated by a neighbor of the Stewarts who claimed that while getting ready for work, they saw a figure wearing similar boots leaving the Stewart house at approximately 5 in the morning. Someone jumped on the detail and that's how The Rattlesnake was born. As serial killer nicknames go, it's a pretty good one. I'm not sure who first came up with the nickname, but it was picked up by the local media and it spread.

Whether or not they caught The Rattlesnake was up in the air. But there was no doubt that they would go on killing until they were either in jail, physically incapacitated, or dead. It boggles my mind to think of how many people behind bars have committed murders that no one knows about.

A rattlesnake was a common sight here in San Sebastian, as most people encounter a rattlesnake by the time they're in grade school. I remember my first encounter with one when I was 10 years old. I was with my best friend Bill and we were going outside to play after we finished watching *Batman*. On the way out, we heard a sound coming from the corner of the garage. When we saw it was a rattlesnake, we immediately ran screaming into the house. Because of the noise we were making, Bill's Dad sprinted downstairs like his hair was on fire and we ran over to him babbling incoherently while pointing to the garage. After he figured out what we were saying, he called a friend who came over and got the snake out. Bill and I watched the whole thing while we stood on the cement steps leading from the kitchen into the garage.

So here I was, facing a rattlesnake yet again. The fact that I was currently handling a case involving a woman who may or may not have fallen victim to a serial killer in November was ironic, as it's been pointed out that an uncanny number of killers and murderers have November birthdays, with Manson and Bundy being two of the more famous ones. My friend Bill happens to be one of those people with a November birthday. But this state probably knows better than any other how November can have an eerie connection with murderers, as one of the most famous murders of all time took place here on November 22, 1963.

I don't know if anyone else does this, but I tend to associate different time periods with different places. For example, I associate the 50's with Middle America suburbia, the 60's with California, and the 70's with big cities, New York in particular. In many ways, music of the latter half of the 20th Century progresses almost like human development. The 50's and early 60's were times of innocent fun. But the music of the 1960's, much like the decade itself, underwent drastic change. Pop standards capturing love and longing morphed into something raw and poetic that captured the tensions and strife of an era.

Once the 60's ended, the 70's were a time when people came down from the high of the previous decade and wrestled with what came next. But the 1970's also came with a rising interest in serial killers. Before then, the only serial killer people really knew about was Jack the Ripper. But by the 1980's, everyone knew the names of people like Ted Bundy and John Wayne Gacy. Not only were people disturbed by what they did, they were terrified by the fact that they seemed so normal on the surface.

Odds were good whoever was responsible for Gretchen's vanishing was a solid citizen as well. But there was no doubt that whoever was responsible for Gretchen's vanishing was someone known to her. It didn't have to be her best friend, just someone she was familiar with to some degree. Someone smart doesn't even consider going off with someone alone at night unless you know them, and Maddie confirmed Gretchen was pretty smart.

I spent the next few days going through a list Maddie had made of people in Gretchen's life who may have had something to do with her going missing. Once I crossed off the last name, that of the guy buying poinsettias, I went through the rest of the information I had.

There was always the possibility of an anonymous tip. It's happened before with some frequency, but no such luck so far. The reason why I'm not surprised by the number of anonymous tips I get is because people love to tell secrets, so long as the secrets belong to someone else. In many ways, someone spilling dirt to me is simply a different type of gossip. But unlike telling your neighbor, if people tell me something, they know it will stay with me. On top of that, most people would love to be able to give the one tip that catches a criminal or turns out to be right. Shows like *Unsolved Mysteries* and *America's Most Wanted* aren't just for entertainment, they're also made in the hopes that a viewer somewhere sees it and recognizes something.

I kept reading until it was late and then I went to bed. After breakfast the next morning, I went to the TGI Friday's Gretchen was last seen at. I wanted to get a feel for the area and what was around. Perhaps there were some choice spots where someone might hide and watch besides the abandoned strip mall. Aside from the fact the police had already searched the place, it was an obvious candidate for where a potential killer or kidnapper could hide and watch for any amount of time. City council has been talking about redevelopment and all the usual slogans for the old strip mall for years now, but nothing ever happens. So it just sits there, silently overlooking the area from the hill it's perched on.

I parked my car on the cracked blacktop that had once served as the strip mall parking lot. Years ago this spot was packed with cars. Now the painted lines that marked spaces had all faded away, the blacktop was full of potholes, and gnarled weeds were steadily popping up here and there. Facing me was window after window of blackout paper. These buildings used to be home to Cicis, Blockbuster, and a liquor store, amongst other things. Now they were home to wild animals, dust, and mold. I started at the end of the strip mall and carefully walked past each set of windows, keeping an eye out for anything that caught my attention.

It wasn't long before I reached the final storefront, a former tuxedo rental store. On the bottom right-hand side of the windows, a faint corner of the window covering was crooked and through the gap I could faintly see the arm of a mannequin that was lying on the floor. Its pale grey arm was barely visible in the filthy storefront window. The carpet had been rolled up long ago, so the mannequin laid on the stained cement floor. But as I tilted my head, something gleamed in the afternoon sunlight.

A bracelet.

Mannequins don't wear bracelets. And mannequins left in long abandoned stores definitely don't wear expensive charm bracelets. So I crouched down and got as close to the Plexiglas window as I could and squinted, trying hard to see anything. But all I could see were some black high heels and some hair. Dark brown, almost chocolate colored. The moment I realized that the hair was identical to Maddie's, my stomach lurched as I realized I had just located Gretchen.

After I called the police and told them what I found, I did what was by far the worst part of my job and called Maddie. She managed to get there before the police did and I spent the remaining time waiting, being used as a makeshift tissue by Maddie. I've been a shoulder to cry on for clients before, but Maddie's anguish was particularly painful to watch, as she wasn't just crying, she was bawling. Her entire body wracked with sobs and she was struggling to catch her breath. When the police arrived and needed to ask me some questions, I gently managed to extract myself from her and placed her in my car before I walked them through who I was and how I found the body. Then I sat down beside her in the driver's seat and waited.

It gave me time to make a few notes. Gretchen had been placed here after the police searched the place. Meaning whoever was responsible was expecting that and was merely waiting for the right time to stash the body here. Why here wasn't difficult to figure out. It was an abandoned location no one would think to look after it had already been searched. But that also meant they would've had to stash the body somewhere in the meantime. So that meant the killer had a place to keep Gretchen until they killed her or had a place to keep the body until they dumped it here. I was leaning towards the latter, as holding someone hostage for a few days is incredibly difficult.

By now Maddie had calmed down a bit and I could feel the fatigue beginning to hit her. She would probably doze off on the couch for a while tonight but would find sleep evasive if she tried to go to bed normally. We sat there for what seemed like ages before she broke the silence.

"Is it bad I've thought about writing about my sister?"

"Not at all. Aside from the fact it's literally your job, it's your story. No one deserves to tell it more than you."

"I suppose."

I waited a moment. "Do you have someone to be with tonight?"

"What do you mean?"

"I'm asking if there's some friend or whatever who can come over tonight."

"I was gonna go over to my parents. Is that ok?"

"That's great, I just didn't want you to have to be alone tonight. There are circumstances where I like to make sure a client isn't alone. This would be one of them."

She sniffled. "Thank you, that's greatly appreciated."

"And I'll be there at the service if you choose to have one."

"We will. Gretchen deserves it. She deserved a lot of things. Definitely far better than she got."

"I'll do everything I can to find out what happened."

"I know you will."

The coroner eventually placed Gretchen's body in the standard black bag and Maddie was escorted downtown to do what she needed to do. Three days later, she dropped by my office with a copy of the coroner's report. In addition to listing her cause of death and cataloging her effects, the report left no doubt she was a victim of the Rattlesnake, as the cause of death and postmortem stabbings were identical to the other Rattlesnake killings. When Maddie told me the time and date of the funeral, I gave her a hug and told her I'd be there. And I was.

Whenever a client experiences something like this, my presence is a non-negotiable, and not simply because there were good odds whoever was responsible might show up. When someone hires me, that means I'm there for them in their hour of need, whatever that may entail. They pay good money for the peace of mind my presence offers, and I make sure they get it when it's needed.

The funeral home Maddie and her family chose was nice. One of those modern funeral homes that's far more user friendly than what most people grew up with. If you didn't know any better, you might mistake it for a banquet hall.

As I anticipated, the media was lurking outside the entrance, trying to grab a quote from anyone connected to the family or the investigation. They were kept at bay by cops who were there to keep an eye on things. I knew they were paying just as much attention to the visitors as I was. And there were a lot of them. A huge line that stretched through the building and out the door. To accommodate the crowd, a few appropriately dressed women in sensible shoes walked by periodically with trays of bottled water.

Despite its length, the line moved quickly and silently, which was no surprise to me. This wasn't a funeral for some beloved grandparent who died peacefully at a ripe old age and the neighborhood came together to celebrate a long life that was well lived. But no one could deny it was fitting that Gretchen met such a grisly end in San Sebastian, a town named after a martyr. I've never liked the word martyr. It sounds too much like murder, which I suppose is the point.

It didn't take long for the empty strip mall to turn into a makeshift shrine with some candles and balloons all clustered in front of the storefront where Gretchen was found, and the sight had been replicated all over town since they found Gretchen's body. Too many people in this town have had their picture surrounded by cheap flowers and large candles in colorful holders with icons on them.

It was a pleasantly cool day, but the funeral home soon became uncomfortably hot, which meant the scent of flowers became overwhelming. By the time I made it through the line and offered my condolences to Maddie's parents and gave Maddie herself a hug, it was well past noon and I felt like I was going to suffocate on the smell of overpriced roses. The service was mercifully quick, and I left along with everyone else who was not part of the immediate family. Once I was free from the scent of flowers, I drove to a pizza place and ordered myself the lunch buffet. Since my favorite thing to get there is the breadsticks, I got plenty of them along with a few slices of supreme pizza. Then I went back for a few slices of the dessert pizza, another favorite menu item of mine.

But instead of leaving as soon as I was done eating, I sat and sipped my iced tea while I thought about the service I had just left. I didn't know for sure whether or not whoever did that to Gretchen was there today. But I did know they would have a plausible reason to be there and would almost certainly not overdo any emotion. That's the thing about most killers, especially serial killers. They know how to put on a good act. But just like a rattlesnake, most serial killers can send out vibes that make someone back away.

Taking down a serial killer is a major rite of passage for a detective. It's the equivalent of a musician playing Carnegie Hall. And just like getting to Carnegie Hall, you have to work, work, and work to take down a serial killer. Technically, I had already fulfilled part of my contract and found Gretchen, but there was no way I was stopping now.

I already knew The Rattlesnake had some knowledge of the strip mall and was someone Gretchen was familiar with. But aside from that, there was still a lot I didn't know. Since I was going to my friend Bill's birthday tonight, it was a perfect chance to let my mind rest and see what else I could come up with.

So I went home, caught an excellent nap on the couch, and woke up at 4:30. It left plenty of time for me to take a shower and head to the restaurant, an Italian place in the center of town. At quarter to 6, I grabbed Bill's gift, a gift card for the movies, and headed downtown.

I got there right on time, grabbed a spot in the middle of the parking lot, and headed inside, where I was greeted with a blast of air conditioning. The smiling hostess dressed in black wasted no time in escorting me to Bill's table. I greeted the birthday boy with a big hug, gave him my gift, and sat down at the end of the table near his parents.

Eventually the other guests drifted in, and a comfortable camaraderie began to settle over our table. The two waitresses assigned to our table began to take orders, and I went with the lasagna. While they moved onto my tablemates, I wasted no time in digging into bread that was served with olive oil and seasonings. It was perfect. Crusty on the outside, super soft on the inside, and warm still from the oven.

At some point in the evening, I turned and talked to Chris, a son of the guy who lived next door to Bill's parents. After some casual chit chat, we started talking about work. He told me he worked as a contractor, and I told him what I did.

"Were you that private investigator who found the body at the strip mall?" he asked after a sip of wine. Chris was tall, fair skinned, and had fine blond hair. The kind that shimmered in the restaurant's artificial light.

I nodded. "That was me."

"That had to be a shock. Mannequins don't wear expensive heels."

Adrenaline exploded through my chest at that remark. How in the hell did he know Gretchen was wearing high heels? It was never made public in any fashion. There were only a few people who knew what Gretchen was wearing when she was found: myself, the officials at the scene, Maddie, and The Rattlesnake.

"No they sure don't." I smiled and nodded along, careful not to give a hint about what I was thinking.

I spent the rest of the evening paying attention to Chris. While eating my lasagna, which was delicious, I learned that he had once done contracting work at the strip mall. I nodded along nonchalantly, but inside I was on pins and needles. When the meal was over, we all paid our bill and spilled out into the darkened parking lot. Chris was parked at the opposite end of the lot, so all I had to do was wait for him to pull out and stick behind him. He drove a bright blue Mazda Miata that glimmered in the beams of the various headlights.

Once he eased out of the parking lot, I wasn't far behind, and we both cruised along at a leisurely pace. Chris got onto the highway and drove until he reached the east side of town. The roads out here were mostly dirt, gravel, and a touch of sand.

As I took care to stay a good distance behind Chris, some dust occasionally kicked up behind my car and the illumination from my tail lights cast an ominous red glow to it. People can try to develop this land as much as they like, it's still barely removed from the days of the Wild West. In fact, it's still the Wild West, except instead of outlaws riding horses and carrying Winchester rifles, they've upgraded to all-terrain trucks or SUVs and carry an AK-47 or an Uzi. I'm no stranger to this upgrade either, as my grandpa and great grandpa shot at outlaws with a revolver, while I typically use a Glock.

You hear people talking all the time about how they don't recognize something or someone anymore. But recognizing something isn't the problem. It's when you find that deep down, it's not what you thought it was that's really disorienting, if not downright terrifying. It's like a nightmare: something looks familiar, sounds familiar, smells familiar, feels familiar, but it's not what you thought it was. It's like when someone goes through your stuff behind your back and tries to put it back the way it was, but you can sense that something small is off.

Speaking of knowing something is off, Chris was now going down a long road towards a single residence, which meant I had to stop here, or risk being seen. So when I spotted a lone cul-de-sac of split-level houses, I pulled down the road and parked while he drove up the rocky driveway and parked in front of a ranch house which I could now see occupied a massive stretch of land that was otherwise untouched.

I took a few photos of Chris exiting his car and going inside the house, as well as of the house itself and the surrounding grounds. The land was wide open for almost a mile. It definitely made my job harder, as aside from some cover of darkness, I would be completely exposed if I approached the house. But since Chris' was the only one in the driveway, that meant I could go in for a closer look if he left. Since the house was dark until Chris unlocked the door and turned on some lights, that meant the house was, by all appearances, empty. Or he wanted it to look like it was empty.

I sat there watching for about 20 minutes when all the lights inside were suddenly extinguished and Chris came back out, hopped in the car, and bounced back down the dusty driveway. Once he was past the road I was parked on, I grabbed the revolver I always keep in my car, quietly stepped outside, locked my car from the inside, and began the approach towards the ranch house. With each step, I took care to observe my surroundings and make sure no one was sneaking up on me. As I got closer, I could see the house dated back to the 80's and was painted beige, but the color had faded in the sunlight over time.

No matter how quiet I was, my footsteps sounded painfully loud. Eventually I was within feet of the house and managed to circle it to get my bearings. The windows were all small and the only thing visible in the darkness were the various blurs and shapes of furniture. The easiest room to see based on the moonlight was a TV room with a recliner facing away from the window. The back porch was outfitted with a deck that led to a sliding glass door, but that was covered with a curtain from the inside. I climbed the deck and tried to peer inside, but there was nothing I could see from out here.

I was about to head back to the car when I smelled it. Something rancid and so overpowering it almost knocked me down and made my eyes water. Doing my best to breathe through my mouth, I looked left and right to try to figure out where the smell came from. But there was nothing around.

As one of the wooden deck planks creaked, I looked down and a chill ran up my spine. Operating on instinct now, I took out my phone and turned on the flashlight app to peer between the cracks of the sun-bleached deck. When I didn't see anything from the top, I went down the deck's steps and crouched down to peer through the latticework covering an opening.

The beam from my phone illuminated two pallid human shapes laid underneath the middle of the deck, the limbs all splayed out at haphazard angles. The image was an eerie reminder of Gretchen, and my stomach gave an angry lurch as I looked at the source of the smell. From what I could tell, they were both female and one had auburn hair, while the other was platinum blond. Both bodies were laying on their back and were dressed in jeans.

But before I could look any further, I heard a car coming back up the road. Ignoring the rising panic flooding my body, I quickly switched off my phone's flashlight, dashed to the other side of the deck for cover, and crouched down. When I heard the car door open and shoes crunching on the ground, I didn't dare make a sound. And when I heard the creak of the front door open, I took a silent breath and waited. And waited. After what seemed like the longest minute ever, the door closed. From this side of the house, a light flipped on before the shifting colors and patterns of a TV filled the window.

By now my legs began to ache, so I carefully walked away from where I was crouching and went back towards where I saw the bodies without taking my eyes off the back porch, which was still dark. Once I was on the opposite side of the house, I checked my surroundings again, and carefully began the walk back to my car. My shirt was soaked with sweat, but I ignored it as I carefully took each step as silently as I could as I ducked under windows and listened for every hint of sound.

It seemed like an eternity, but eventually I made it to the driveway. Using the car as a form of cover, I ducked behind it and waited. The minute I was sure the coast was clear, I carefully walked sideways back to my car. That way I never had my back to the front door and no one peering out the front would see me. As the ranch house receded into the background, I felt a small sense of relief.

When there was plenty of distance between me and the house, I felt safe enough to walk forward on the sun cracked earth. I was also thankful that the driveway was so long that by this point you couldn't make out the features of anyone walking on it. But it felt like miles before I was finally back to my car.

The minute I was back inside it, I inhaled like I hadn't experienced fresh air in months and took huge gasps of air. I was covered in sweat and a bit of dust, but I ignored it as I dialed the police and told them who I was and what I found. The cops wasted no time getting here, and Chris could not have been more surprised when he answered the door and found San Sebastian's finest waiting for him. It also didn't take them long to find what he had stashed under the deck and while a forensic team came onsite to extract the bodies and investigate the scene, Chris was escorted downtown. One detail that came out later was that when ordered to step outside, he put on the closest pair of shoes there was. Which happened to be a pair of rattlesnake cowboy boots.

The forensic team did a first-rate job and the evidence against Chris was massive. A respectable defense lawyer did the best job that could be done, but no one was surprised when he was found guilty of all the murders committed by The Rattlesnake and the sentence handed down meant he would never set foot outside a cell again.

I wasn't surprised when Maddie attended every day of the trial or when her reporting got attention nationwide. She earned it. On the day the verdict was read, she sat next to me during a lull in proceedings.

"Do you like *James Bond* films?" She asked.

"I do."

"I won't ask you about your favorite *Bond* film, or your favorite *Bond* actor. Too easy. But what about your favorite *Bond* villain?"

"Definitely far more interesting and more variety there. You first."

"Goldfinger."

"Good choice. Mine is Christopher Walken in *A View to a Kill*."

"Really?"

"Yup. It's Christopher Walken. It needs no explanation. Plus when he says 'More powah!' all I can think about is that More Cowbell sketch."

She smiled. "Can't argue with that. And thank you. For everything."

"My pleasure."

Then she reached into her purse, pulled out a package wrapped in brown paper, and handed it to me.

"This is for you. I promised it a while back."

I unwrapped it to find a brand-new copy of her book on the killer Louisiana couple. When I began to skim through it, I saw that she had signed it as well.

"I'm planning to write one on The Rattlesnake crimes. Offers are already pouring in."

"I'm sure they are. You earned it Maddie."

"It will be dedicated to you. And Gretchen."

"I'm flattered. Any idea on a title?"

"Oh yes. Rattlesnake Roundup."

"I like it. Very catchy."

"If you're free, I'd like to watch a *Bond* movie with you sometime."

"Which one?"

She laughed. "I'll let you pick."

FARM TO TABLE

MY COUSIN HOWARD RECENTLY bought a house with a lot of land, and he's spent a lot of time renovating the house and planting a huge vegetable garden. I knew how long he and his wife have worked towards this and wanted it, so I was very happy for them. As was everyone else who knew them. So once they were all settled in, I drove out of the city to see them.

Howard had taken plenty of pictures, but pictures hadn't done it justice. It was the coziest little farmhouse you could imagine, with a neatly mowed front lawn and a beautifully landscaped backyard with rows and rows of planted vegetables and other plants. Once I parked my car in the driveway, I got out and took a closer look at the backyard, which seemed to stretch on forever. From what I could tell, there was corn, carrots, lettuce, cabbage, peppers, tomatoes, green beans, asparagus, eggplants, blueberries, blackberries, apples, and a bunch of other things all growing in the neatly maintained field.

"Hey there, Eric!" Howard's wife Jody waved to me as she approached. "I see you've found our little garden."

"Little nothing, this is incredible."

Jody smiled. "Thank you so much."

"Seriously, this is amazing."

"We love it."

"It shows. Well done."

"Come on in, and we'll get down to having some of what we've planted to eat."

She didn't need to tell me twice. Once I followed Jody into the comfortably furnished farmhouse, I greeted Howard, and he gave me a glass of iced tea before we sat down in their little screen enclosed porch and chatted. It was a beautiful summer day, with a light breeze and a sky that was bright blue. Inside the porch there was a small glass table that we took our seats at before we started to eat.

First, we started with some spinach dip and stuffed mushrooms for an appetizer. Then, we moved onto stuffed cabbage, mashed potatoes, salad, and dinner rolls. It was all fantastic. We finished with dessert, which was apple crisp with ice cream.

"Did all the vegetables and fruits come from the garden?" I asked while we were all finishing off dessert.

"Everything but the potatoes. We haven't gotten around to that yet."

"It's all fantastic. Everything was delicious."

They both murmured their thanks before we grabbed some coffee and left the porch to sit outside around the fire pit. Then Howard built a fire, and we sat around it as night set in. Eventually, it got late enough for me to head home, so I said my goodbyes and left. But not before the two of them gave me plenty of leftovers to take home. Not that I needed much convincing, because I happily took everything they offered before I hit the road.

By the time I headed home it was late, and everything was dark. The roads were quiet, but not deserted. But just as I was about to reach the highway to go back into the city, I passed a large stretch of woods. As I was halfway down the road that ran alongside it, I looked over and for a moment, I thought I saw a person walking through the woods towards me.

The sight was shocking, so I immediately looked again. But the person was gone. I sighed with relief and told myself I was just tired after having a long week at work.

The rest of the drive went normally, and I got home safely. It was late by then, so I watched a little TV before I got ready for bed and went to sleep. I slept a little restlessly but woke up feeling fine. Then I went on with my usual Saturday of errands and other things I did on the weekend. I even went to the movies later and treated myself to some candy. When it was over, I heated up some of the leftovers from the night before, and they were just as tasty. Then I watched some TV until I inadvertently dozed off on the couch. The fact that I'd just ate meant that it wasn't surprising when I had a weird dream.

In it, I was standing on the side of a lake at night. It was a clear night, and you could see the moon reflected off the surface of the lake. It was a beautiful sight, but the feeling I got wasn't calm and peaceful. I felt uneasy, like I was waiting for something. Then, I looked beyond the lake and saw there was a cluster of trees sitting just beyond its surface. Thanks to the clear night and the moon, which seemed brighter than I'd ever seen before, I could see shadows moving in there. I could tell they were people, and they were walking steadily in rhythm. I had no idea what exactly they were doing, but I knew it wasn't good. Right at that moment, one of the figures turned towards the lake, saw me, and pointed at me. The others took notice, and that was when I woke up with a start.

It was creepy for sure, and I felt tense and on edge. But it was just a dream, so I went and got myself a glass of water. Then I took a deep breath and watched some more TV until I headed to bed. This time, I slept much better and woke up feeling refreshed.

The next few days were nothing out of the ordinary, and it wasn't long before Jody and Howard invited me back to their place for dinner the following weekend. I happily agreed, and by the end of the week, I was driving back out to their place and looking forward to their company and a delicious meal.

They didn't disappoint. This time, we began with asparagus soup and rolls before we had eggplant parmesan, cucumber salad, and blueberry cobbler. Today was much hotter than the last time I was here, so we ate inside in the dining room. But just like last time, we ended the evening around the fire outside after it was nighttime, and things had cooled down a bit. And just like last time, I got some leftover eggplant parmesan and blueberry cobbler to take home when it was time for me to head out.

I had been driving for fifteen minutes when I had to stop at an intersection. On my left was a house that looked like it had been long since abandoned. The lawn was overgrown and filled with numerous weeds, and Jody had mentioned over dinner last week that the place had been unowned and unoccupied for years according to their realtor. I was just about to look away when, from the corner of my eye, I saw motion from the right window on the first floor, and I could swear I saw someone peering out at me from between the boards in the window. But in an instant, it was gone.

I ignored the sudden cold chill that shot through my body and kept on driving while I told myself it could've been anyone. Some random person trespassing. Or it might have been nothing. So I focused on driving until I was back in my apartment. After I put my leftovers away, I made myself a cup of tea and relaxed with a book until it was bedtime.

By then, the beautiful night sky had filled with clouds, and a steady rain was pounding on my roof and the windows in a calming rhythm. It was still going on when I went to bed and drifted off. But unlike the rain, my dream was anything but relaxing. In it, I dreamed I was being chased through some incredibly dense woods I didn't recognize by someone I had never met before, or couldn't even see, but I knew they were there. It felt like I ran through the forest for hours. I hid behind trees, rocks, and listened to find out where the person after me was. I could feel the sting as I fell on the rocky ground or got smacked in the face with a tree branch. Just as I could see the end of the woods, I heard the snap of a tree branch and knew the person following me was right behind me, so I sprinted as fast as I could. Just as I heard a harsh voice whisper, "Got you now," I woke up, and it was morning.

I sat upright in my bed as I tried to calm down. I knew it was a dream, but it was one of the most vivid dreams I'd ever had. I could physically feel the woods, smell them, and the sensations had lingered as I woke up. After a moment, I got out of bed, walked to the kitchen, and started making myself some coffee. Once I had my first cup, and then another, I made myself some scrambled eggs and toast for breakfast. Then I went on with the first part of my day before returning home for lunch. I heated up the leftover eggplant parmesan and pie and ate it before I was due to meet some friends at the museum one of them worked at. They were having a fundraiser, and we'd all gotten tickets months ago.

Everyone got there right on time before we helped ourselves to some of the snacks provided while we wandered around and looked at the various exhibits on display. I'd always liked coming to the museum. It was full of interesting items, and the architecture and design alone was beyond impressive. Eventually, I found myself in one of my favorite parts in the whole museum. The dinosaur exhibit. No matter how old I got, I always loved this part. With my small plate of appetizers in hand, I walked over to the T-Rex skeleton on display behind the barrier that kept you from getting too close. As I stared up at it, the smell of mud and earth hit me full force in the face, like I had just fallen in mud. And for some reason, I could hear the sound of grass rustling.

But I shrugged it off and resumed walking around the rest of the museum. I had always had a very vivid imagination, especially when it came to history. So I forgot about it, caught up with my friends, and we stayed for a while longer. The event was a huge success, so we all left in a good mood.

Jody and Howard were busy with work, so I didn't hear from them for several weeks after that. But they invited me back over soon enough, and this time when I went over for dinner, they went all out. We had homemade potato chips and cheese dip, buffalo cauliflower, roasted chicken with carrots, asparagus, and potatoes, and strawberry pretzel salad for dessert.

But this time we didn't get a chance to sit outside, because the day had been intensely humid, and by the time I arrived, it had started pouring rain and thundering. And it hadn't slowed down, so it wasn't long before there were reports of flooding in the area. By then, it was obvious that there was enough flooding that I couldn't get back home immediately, but Jody and Howard immediately offered me the use of their spare bedroom for the night. I happily accepted, and we spent the rest of the evening relaxing with coffee while we listened to the rain and watched a movie together.

We eventually said goodnight to each other and went to bed. The bed itself was comfortable enough, but my mind wandered since I was in an unfamiliar bed, and I'd never slept well in unfamiliar places. So I tossed and turned for a while as the rain showed no sign of letting up. Eventually, I started to drift off. But as I did, I glanced out of the bedroom window, which looked down on a stretch of trees. All thoughts of sleep went away as I saw a lone figure staring up at the window. The figure was standing under a tree, so I couldn't really see who it was, but I could feel the figure watching the house. And watching me. Despite the sense of panic that immediately hit me, I just laid there in bed, staring out the window. The figure didn't move an inch, and it seemed like an eternity passed before the figure slowly walked away and disappeared.

I had dozed off at some point during this, so I immediately wrote it off as a dream. With how bad the storm was, there was no way someone would be just walking around outside. I managed to fall asleep eventually after this and woke up to light streaming through the bedroom window.

The smell of cinnamon rolls filled the air when I came downstairs. Jody and Howard were both casually sitting around the kitchen as the cinnamon rolls were baking in the oven.

"Coffee?" Howard offered with a smile.

"You know it," I accepted gratefully.

"How'd you sleep?" Jody asked as Howard poured a cup of coffee and handed it to me.

"Ok. Had a weird dream though. Someone was watching me outside. From the bedroom window."

They both went quiet at this. I could feel something in the air change.

"What?" I asked after a moment.

"I," Howard began. "I had a similar dream. Recently. A figure was lurking around the backyard. I couldn't see who, but I knew someone was there."

"We've had a lot of weird dreams since moving here. Creepy dreams," Jody said. "Stress of moving."

Now it was my turn to go quiet. When I did, they both looked at me, knowing something was up. So I explained the weird dreams I'd had and how I'd experienced other strange things recently. They both admitted they'd had similar experiences, but we couldn't figure out why. So we thought about it as we ate the cinnamon rolls, which were delicious.

"We never had anything like this happen before," Howard explained.

"Me either. I've had dreams before. Even bad ones. But these feel so different. Like they're feelings more than dreams."

"I know what you mean Eric," Jody nodded. "It's so creepy."

"I hate to mention this," I began. "But the only thing I can say is that I've only ever had these things happen after I've had food you guys made."

"Uh huh," Howard nodded.

"And you guys are both amazing cooks. I've had your cooking for years, and nothing like this has ever happened before. So what changed?"

"We moved here and started growing so much of our own food," Jody whispered.

It didn't take long for them to ask several other people they knew and find out they'd had similar creepy experiences. Nor did it take long for us to find out the cause. After checking with his friend he usually bought gardening material from, Howard found out that one of his suppliers had just found out that the location he usually got dirt from was actually an abandoned graveyard. Due to the passage of time, most of the headstones had broken down and were reduced to tiny rocks. So no one had any clue until someone inadvertently dug deep enough and found that the plot of land was a graveyard, and that all the dirt taken from the area was graveyard dirt.

The thought gave me the chills. But Jody and Howard had already used up most of their garden, and the storm had caused enough flooding that much of the soil had been washed away. So all that was left was for them to dig up the garden, get rid of the old soil, and start new next spring. Which they did. And while the delicious meals returned, the creepy dreams did not. A fact everyone appreciated.

The Great Cinema Event of Our Era

IT WAS A WARM night as I parked near the multiplex located inside the Forrest Valley Mall. The weather was perfect; not a cloud in the bright blue sky, which was slowly fading into a deep purple with splashes of red. Up ahead, the mall's gleaming white façade loomed over the horizon. Fireflies drifted through the air and dotted the parking lot with glowing yellow specks.

"Ready to go?" I asked Erica.

"Sure thing Casey."

She smiled, and I tried to act like it didn't make my insides do backflips. Erica was one of the most beautiful women I had ever seen. Long brown hair, piercing blue eyes, a beautiful smile, and perfect golden skin. She was dressed casually, but nicely in a red blouse and classy jeans. I nodded and we both got out of my car, a beige 1981 Chevy Malibu, and headed towards the massive glass double doors facing the parking lot, which was packed.

When we stepped inside, I was immediately hit with that flawless temperature that is just cool enough, the innately soothing background music, and the oddly calming smell of suburban retail.

We strode past the massive fountain splashing in the atrium, the escalator leading the way to the second floor, the food court with the vendors' names spelled out in neon lights, and walked towards the theatre, which was located by Sears, one of the anchor stores. When we passed the fountain, the pennies lying on the bottom gleamed in the fading daylight.

As our shoes clicked quietly on the white tile floor, you could feel that it was a Friday night. The air crackled with that unique mix of adrenaline and excitement that only a Friday night in summer creates. Toys "R" Us was jam-packed with overexcited kids and their frazzled parents, while the older kids were busy down at Sam Goody's or greedily gulping down drinks from Orange Julius. School had just let out, and no matter what your age was, it's a reason to celebrate. Since Memorial Day had come and gone again, summer was here.

It wasn't long before we arrived at the theater. The line stretching out front meant that we weren't the only ones who wanted to see *Return of the Jedi*, which was spelled out on the marquee in tall black letters. Erica and I got in line, which hummed with a pleasant buzz of chit chat, the usual inconsequential stuff you talk about in lines anywhere.

I had been looking forward to seeing this movie since 1980 and now that it was here, I could hardly believe it. I could also hardly believe what had happened in the world since 1980 either. Or since the first *Star Wars* film came out in 1977 for that matter. But I guess that's the entire point. No matter what happens, *Star Wars* is always there for you, waiting to be picked up and experienced. Just like no matter how cold and dark a winter is, summer always comes.

Standing there amidst the sea of blue and purple neon lights of the mall, I was on top of the world. There's something inherently nostalgic about summer. Perhaps it's because the season itself is so memorable. Summer sears itself into memory with electric blue skies, brilliant white sand, and grass so green it doesn't look real.

With long heady days and balmy nights, summer literally sears your flesh if you don't slather on enough sunscreen. Or maybe it's because summer is irretrievably connected to memories we all have about summer vacations when we were young. The vacations we took and the fun we had. Going to the movies to see the latest summer blockbuster. There's a reason a summer romance is something special. I've never heard anyone talk with longing about a spring romance or a winter romance. There's no denying summer is a magical time of year.

The last summer before you went off to high school or college is a lot like the last Halloween you went trick-or-treating. There were good times before it and good times after it, but there's no denying that things were different after.

Summer is also the most euphoric of seasons. That roar of energy you feel when school lets out; the giant shimmering promise of tomorrow being all your own. The only assignment for summer is to get out, enjoy every day, and make it count. It's practically in our blood as Americans to cherish summer, as the declaration of our independence was created during the hot, sticky summer of 1776.

Although this summer, my assignment was getting to know Erica Ashton. I had met her last week at a Memorial Day cookout at my friend Drew's house and I knew the instant I saw her that I had to go talk to her. Approaching her, I can't remember the last time I was that nervous about anything. Even though she was sitting outside by the pool while eating a hamburger and some potato salad, she may as well have been on another planet from me. But when she started talking, Erica was so friendly and warm that it put even a nervous wreck like me at ease. I was shocked at how much we had in common. And when I mentioned I wanted to see this movie, she mentioned she did as well and despite the nagging voice in my head saying that she would never come with me, I went through and asked. To my eternal surprise, Erica said yes. Quite frankly, that's more surreal to me than any science fiction movie.

The line steadily moved up until it was our turn and we got two tickets for the 9 pm showing.

"Let's grab seats first and once that's over, I'll head to the snack bar."

She nodded. "Good idea."

We walked past the ticket booths, the snack bar, and the restrooms before we entered our theater, which was theater number 3. We managed to find two seats in the middle of the left section. Row 12 still had two free aisle seats, which I was happy about.

"Which one do you prefer?" I gestured towards the chairs.

"Doesn't matter to me."

"Then I'll take the aisle seat."

I stood back and let her slide in before I sat down beside her and checked my watch. It was 8:45, fifteen minutes to showtime. The buzz of excitement was starting to fill the theatre, which was slowly filling up. From the way it looked so far, I suspected we'd have a full house, which made me happy. This was the kind of movie you needed to see with a packed theatre. Just like sports fans, movie fans speak a second language and feed off of each other's excitement.

"Want some snacks?" I turned to Erica. "I'm planning on getting a medium popcorn. Don't worry, I'll share."

She laughed. "I promise I won't sneak it all when you aren't looking. I'll take a Coke."

"Coming right up. Try not to let anyone steal our seats."

"No, I'm totally gonna be a pushover and let them just kick us out of our seats."

"Funny. Be right back."

I walked back into the lobby and headed towards the purple concession stand, the line for which was small, but still humming with activity. The area was filled with the buttery smell of fresh popcorn and the sounds of people talking, the popcorn popping, and the cash register clanging away.

"Two Cokes and a medium popcorn," I ordered when it was my turn at the register.

"5 bucks," the teenage guy manning the front said. Like the other employees, he was dressed in a red vest with a silver name tag clipped to it. After making change, he filled two paper cups with soda and placed them on the counter before turning to fill a paper bag with popcorn. He eventually placed the bag on the counter with the drinks.

"Would you like a drink holder for these?"

"Please." I nodded, and he quickly put both drinks in a cardboard container before I grabbed it and the popcorn and headed back to my seat.

"Thanks," Erica said as I handed her a Coke and sat back down. The chair creaked slightly as I sat.

"No problem."

As soon as I sat back down in my seat, I started munching on popcorn. It doesn't matter if the movie is on or not, popcorn needs to be eaten fresh, otherwise it gets stale. For the last few minutes, the anticipation in the room built up and the minute the lights on the deep red walls went out, the crowd started to cheer. I didn't blame them one bit. No matter how many times you see it, there is nothing like it when a screen goes from blank to a full-fledged picture in the blink of an eye. Everyone is instantly a kid again.

For the next few hours, Erica and I experienced the finale of the great cinema event of our era. Once the ending credits came on, the entire theatre, which included the two of us, burst into applause and gave the movie a standing ovation. As I clapped along with everyone else, I smiled with both a sense of happiness and a touch of sadness. I thought of who I'd been when the first *Star Wars* came out and who I'd gone with; my best friend Jimmy and his siblings. Jimmy and his family had moved away, and while I still had his address, we'd lost touch, but I thought of him often. I silently hoped he was somewhere having as much fun watching this movie as I was.

"I need to use the bathroom before we leave." I told Erica as we made our way to the exit.

"Me too. I'll wait for you near the snack bar."

"Sounds good."

When I was done, I found Erica where she said she'd be. By now the theater had quieted down and the mood was much mellower than when we'd arrived. Two uniformed ushers were sweeping the floors while patrons were steadily trickling out of the mall. We made our way out in relative quiet until we reached the front doors we came in through.

"Thanks for inviting me. I really enjoyed the movie." Erica said as we stepped outside and walked to the car. It was chillier now and a light breeze gently shook the few trees that were around.

"I enjoyed it too, and I'm really glad you came with me."

"I'm thrilled you invited me. Definitely one of the better summer memories I've had recently."

"Well I'm glad you had a good time. But I'm sorry to hear you've had a rough go of it recently."

"Oh no, don't worry about it, Casey," she paused while we both got in my car. "I was just thinking out loud."

"It happens." I slammed my door shut and started the car.

"I'm just really glad Donna made me come to the Memorial Day cookout."

"Me too." I laughed.

Without saying a word, she reached over and quickly gave my hand an affectionate squeeze, a gesture I returned.

"Did you not want to come? Believe me, I get Ray can be a bit over the top at times."

"He can, but that wasn't it at all. Last summer, something bad went down at a summer camp I was a counselor at."

"I'm sorry to hear that."

"Thank you. Believe me, there was no guy in a hockey mask or anything."

"Can you watch those movies after whatever happened?"

"Oh absolutely. Not a problem at all. For starters, I know it's not real. The only one that's even remotely realistic is the first *Friday the 13th*."

"Right."

"But aside from that, what happened at Camp Chestnut bore no resemblance to the movies at all. That didn't stop people from telling campfire stories about it, but it's not what happened."

"Of course not. Do you mind me asking what did happen?"

Right at that moment, I passed a streetlight, and the orange light briefly illuminated her face. She smiled, a wry, knowing, sad smile.

"Not at all. I wouldn't have brought it up if I didn't want to talk about it. One of the counselors went missing one night. It was towards the end of camp, right before Labor Day. Everyone went to bed one night and the next morning, we found out that Megan had just vanished. There was no sign of a struggle, no sign of an intruder, no nothing. They searched the lake and found nothing there either. Since there was nothing for the police to go on, the search was over fast. Megan's parents hired a private investigator and even he couldn't find anything."

"That's wild."

"It sure was. The camp hadn't done anything wrong, but that didn't stop it from being shut down immediately. Fortunately, camp was due to let out in a few days anyway, so it's not like the whole thing went down and ruined the kids' whole summer. But still. It shook the rest of us up pretty badly."

"I'm sure it did."

"Megan was the kind of girl who never met a stranger. In all the time I was there, I never heard her say a bad word about anyone. She was responsible, caring, and hilariously funny. That's one reason why it shook us up so bad. There are a few counselors there who it wouldn't have shocked me a bit if something happened to them. Megan was not one of them."

"I can imagine. That's awful. Where was Camp Chestnut at?"

"Way down on the south side of the state. Past Philadelphia and close to Maryland."

"Wild."

"Sure was." Erica added as I pulled up in front of her house, which was only a five-minute drive from the mall. "Thanks again for tonight, I had a really nice time."

"You're welcome. I'm really happy you came."

Without saying another word, she leaned in and kissed me on the lips. Her lips were beyond soft and gentle. But before I knew it, she pulled away with a knowing smile.

"And thank you for that as well."

"My pleasure."

She smiled again before we both got out of the car. I stood there with my hands in my pockets as she dug through her purse for what I assumed were her keys.

"Do you want to see what Megan looked like?" she asked without looking up.

"Sure."

She pulled out a polaroid and handed it to me. The photo showed a dozen people standing in front of a stunning lake on a beautiful summer day. I could practically feel the humidity in the photo. Everyone in the shot was wearing blue shorts and white shirts with blue lettering that spelled out Camp Chestnut.

"That's her," she pointed to the far-left side of the picture.

When I saw who she was pointing to, I felt like I had just been sucker punched. The person in the photo was a little older and a lot taller than when I last saw her, but I knew exactly who she was.

Megan Cartwright.

My old friend Jimmy's sister.

I stood there silently as I took the piece of information in. Jimmy's sister, who I'd spent time with at countless family cook-outs, holidays, and every other possible event, had just vanished one day. And no one had ever said a word to me about it.

Erica could tell something was up. So I swallowed hard and told her what was going on. She too stood there speechless when the realization washed over her.

"What are you going to do?" She asked after what seemed like a long time.

"I don't know. I guess I'll give Jimmy a call."

"That's a good idea." Erica nodded before we called it a night with a hug that seemed to last both an eternity and no time at all.

On the way home, the radio was nothing but indecipherable white noise as I was alone with my thoughts. The car seemed to be on autopilot as it wove up and down the streets and finally parked in my driveway. My house was dark, as my parents were already asleep for the night. It was only 10, so it wasn't too late yet. I knew from experience that Jimmy stayed up late like I did. We'd spent countless nights up late watching movies at the Twilight Drive-In.

Careful not to make too much noise as I came in and switched on a few lights, I crept over to the kitchen and grabbed the address book where we keep all contact information for family, friends, and everyone in between. Once Jimmy's info was in front of me, I dialed the number.

I stood there awkwardly as the phone rang. I had no idea what to say if anyone even picked up the phone. But on the fifth ring, someone answered.

"Hello?" A slightly out of breath male voice answered.

"Jimmy?" I heard myself ask.

"Yes?" He asked in a hesitant voice.

"It's Casey."

"Casey. Casey Flanigan?"

"That's right."

"Well this is a surprise." His voice was a lot warmer than it was a few seconds ago. "Been a long time."

"It sure has. How are you?"

"I'm good, and it's good to hear from you. But I'm more than a little curious as to why you're calling me."

"Of course. Well, I just got back from a date, and the girl I was with says she was a counselor at the same camp your sister went missing at. Camp Chestnut. I'm so sorry Jimmy."

He was silent for a few moments. "Mind if I ask you the girl's name?"

"Erica."

"Always liked her. Although I have to admit, I'm shocked she went out with you."

"You and me both. But I'm truly sorry to hear about your sister."

"Thanks. It was rough for a while, but we're doing better now. The worst part about it is not knowing what happened. No one has a clue."

"I'm sure."

"But we haven't given up looking. My family and a few others have been doing our own detective work, and we have a place to check out in the next few days. It's an island off the coast of the Carolinas. You're welcome to join us. I... I'd really like to see you again. For old time's sake. We're even gonna be taking my dad's boat. Remember it?"

"Do I ever. Remember the time he took us out fishing and we couldn't catch so much as a piece of seaweed, so we spent the rest of the trip home watching *Scooby Doo*?"

"Absolutely. So will I see you in a few days?"

"Yes. Looking forward to seeing you again."

"You too. And Casey? Thanks. For joining us. And thanks even more for calling."

"You're welcome."

"Here's where to meet us at." He added before he listed the address and time. It was a Maryland boat harbor. "See you then. Goodnight."

"Goodnight, Jimmy."

I hung up the phone and stared out the back porch. I was really going to go on a search party to find my old friend's missing sister.

Years ago, we would've invented some sort of game like this. Now it was all too real.

After a drink of water, I went to bed and slept soundly. I woke up the next morning to the smell of eggs and bacon, and while I ate with my parents, I told them about what I discovered and how I would be joining the search party in a few days. My parents were shocked at the news, but they were supportive of me joining the effort to help.

The day to search for Megan arrived sooner than I expected. Once I grabbed a flashlight and some other gear, I was heading down the road to the tail end of Maryland. The sun gleamed high in the sky as I eased through woods and weaved down highways.

It was stiflingly hot by the time I arrived at the location the boat was anchored at. It was late afternoon, and the salty sea air was sticky and humid. Seagulls squawked loudly overhead as they circled for food and the waves lapped against the various boats docked at the harbor.

Jimmy was there to greet me the minute I parked my car. Despite my sunglasses, I had to shield my eyes from the sun to see him. He looked good, he'd put on some muscle since I last saw him, and he was a bit taller than I remembered. But despite that, he still looked like my old friend.

He immediately ambled over for a hug that I swear made my shoulders pop.

"Take it easy son, we need Casey to be able to lift a flashlight." I heard his father say with his usual dry sense of humor.

"Mr. Cartwright." I turned to face him and held out my hand to shake. "Good to see you again."

"You too Casey. Always liked you. Thanks for coming to help us." Mr. Cartwright was a bit greyer and a bit bulkier than when I last saw him, but he still had the same mustache and beard he'd always had.

"Sure thing. Glad to help."

Then Mr. Cartwright took a moment to introduce me to the other 4 men joining the search party. Simon Bancroft, Jim O'Malley, Pete Jennings, and Mitch Portman were old family friends and had joined the Cartwrights on numerous outings like this to find Megan or whatever had happened to her.

"We're going to Green Cove. It's just off the coast of the Carolinas. We should be there in a few hours. There's plenty of food and entertainment aboard, so settle in and enjoy the ride, gentlemen." Mr. Cartwright clapped his hands and led us aboard his massive boat, which was unsurprisingly named Megan.

There was indeed plenty of food laid out in the sitting room, which was equipped with a TV and radio. Once we were all settled in, Mr. Cartwright went up to start the boat and steer us out to open water. The rest of us grabbed paper plates and loaded them up with potato chips, pretzels, several kinds of dips, and some cheesy potato casserole that we ate while we debated about what movie to watch. I was pleased when we decided on *Raiders of the Lost Ark*. Once we popped it in the VCR next to the TV, we all settled down on couches and relaxed as we cruised down south on the open water. Sipping soda and eating chips while watching one of my favorite movies made me forget what we were up to, which I suspected was the whole point. I had no doubt this was a way for them to decompress and relax despite everything.

We arrived off the coast of the Carolinas just as the movie was ending. Green Cove was stunning. The views of the water around it were spectacular, and the sand looked soft and comforting. I could easily see myself curled up there with a paperback for the afternoon. The beach was dotted with palm trees, and there was a pleasant breeze that made them all flutter in a calming rhythm.

But something was off about Green Cove.

From the looks of it, the island was deserted. Everything was unnaturally still. But that didn't make sense, since I could see plenty of small boats parked on the shore. So where did all the people go?

"Do you see the boats, Mr. Cartwright?"

"Sure do Casey." He said before he grabbed a pair of binoculars and peered through them. "There are people there. Or there were. The question is what happened?"

"What do we do Dad?" Jimmy asked.

He thought for a moment. "Son, you and Casey stay with the boat and keep watch with Pete and Mitch. Jim and Simon, you two come with me to look around."

The men all nodded and grabbed their gear before going to shore. Pete and Mitch stood on the top deck with Jimmy and me, and we watched as they set foot on the island. Jimmy's dad and the other two had walkie talkies with them, so we could contact them if need be. But it was too quiet. Every moment they were gone felt painfully drawn out. I couldn't help but think about how if there were people out there, they would've heard us approach in the boat and knew exactly where we were.

I did the best I could to push those thoughts out of my head as we waited. We had several pairs of binoculars that we took turns passing around, and we'd been keeping watch for about 15 minutes when static suddenly started coming from the walkie talkies and they crackled to life.

"Get the boat started and ready to go immediately. We're getting out of here," was all Mr. Cartwright said before the walkie talkie went silent again.

We all stood there, unsure of what to do. But within moments, Jimmy's dad and the others burst out of the greenery, sprinted towards the boat, and climbed aboard. Without pausing to take a breath, Mr. Cartwright started the boat, and we sped out of there. The water splashed behind us as we peeled away from the island and went out to sea.

But as we pulled away from shore, Pete and I looked behind us and saw the shape of someone watching us leave. From that distance, I couldn't make out much, but I could tell they were wearing a burlap sack with eye holes cut in it as a mask. The figure just stood there and watched us as well. There is absolutely no way to confirm this, but I felt the figure's eyes on me as the boat roared away.

I had no idea what was going on, but I knew something was deeply wrong. And I couldn't wait to be far away from here. I wasn't the only one either, because Jimmy's dad was going way faster than before, and the water splashed around us with a vengeance. I had to hold on to my seat to make sure I didn't fall out of it, but I wasn't complaining.

As he piloted the boat, Jimmy's dad was also radioing for help. I could only make out a few words, but I would find out later what happened, as everyone who had left the boat was just sitting there in complete shock. That frightened me more than anything, and I was dying to know what they had found or what had happened.

But nothing could prepare me for the story when it was finally told to me several hours later. When they came ashore, Jimmy's dad and the other two had found three bodies strung up in trees and several heads impaled on spikes, with no sign of any human life around. By the time the cops were able to arrive and search the island, there was no trace of anyone there, either. Nor was there any sign of Jimmy's sister.

Things eventually calmed down after that, and life went on. Erica and I went out on a few more dates, and things steadily got more serious. I had practically forgotten about that day on the boat when we went to see *Indiana Jones and the Temple of Doom* almost exactly one year later. Personally, I preferred *Raiders of the Lost Ark*, but Erica absolutely loved it. Jimmy, who had come along on a double date with his girlfriend Julianna, loved it as well, while Julianna agreed with me.

Once we left the movie, we went to a local pizza place for dinner before we grabbed some ice cream at the place next door. It was a wonderful evening that we ended at my house, where Jimmy was due to spend the night. If there was one positive thing to come out of the awful situation, it was that Jimmy and I had rekindled our friendship.

Jimmy fell asleep quicker than I did, and I had to get up to grab a drink of water in the middle of the night. Once I grabbed my drink, I stood in the kitchen while looking out over our backyard through the window.

I was just about to head back to bed when I saw it. A shadow looming out from the tree line where our property ended. At first, I wasn't sure I saw anything at all, but when I took a closer look, there was no mistaking it was there, and that it was a person. I couldn't make out any features, but there was no doubting it was there, and whoever was making the shadow was watching me.

So I looked right back. I couldn't tell you for how long, but I met the shadow's gaze with equal intensity. Because in life, sometimes the only thing you can do is look right back and dare the other person to blink first. And in what seemed like moments later, the shadow vanished.

I shook my head as if to clear my mind. The whole thing seemed like a dream. I eventually walked back to my bedroom and drifted off to a restless sleep hours later. After breakfast, I told Jimmy what I had seen. He didn't know what to make of it either. What could I do besides just wonder and speculate? Eventually, the conversation moved on to what movie we should see next.

"*Ghostbusters* or *Gremlins*?" he asked.

I had to stifle a laugh. "*Ghostbusters*."

Jimmy stared at me for a moment before he realized what he had just asked. "Oh. Oh yeah. Good point."

So *Ghostbusters* was our next movie outing. And it was a blast.

Smile for the Camera

In the mid 90's I used to be a photo technician. Those were the days when all you could do on phones was dial a number and if you wanted to take photos, you bought a camera containing actual rolls of film that you had to drop off at the store to be developed. Amazing how times change.

As far as jobs go, I couldn't complain. The pay and hours were solid, and I was pretty much my own boss, but there was one thing I never really got used to. Looking at the photos of complete strangers always felt slightly intrusive, even if they knew I was doing it. Spending hour after hour in an ominously lit dark room filled with chemicals so you could take a peek at the memories of people you had never even met is inherently voyeuristic. It's almost like going through someone's stuff. So that's why I always made sure to not get too interested in what photos I was developing. Some days I liked to pretend I was in a government lab developing film for some kind of top secret project, but the reality was nowhere near that. Usually the most exciting pictures I dealt with were holiday pictures of parents wearing ugly Christmas sweaters before they were a joke.

One day, I was developing some photos from a drop off order. I had done the initial process before checking my work to make sure it had come out ok. Everything looked fine. The colors were all normal, and the images were just as they should be. Since this was back when someone could have red eyes in pictures, they weren't exactly the model of clarity and detail we have now, but they were acceptable.

I was just about to put them away and start on my next order when, for some reason, one of the photos caught my attention. Most of these pictures were shots of the outdoors that someone took near a park or something. There were some beautiful shots of a lake filled in on every side by dense pine trees. It was gorgeous to look at, but there was something a little off. One of the last pictures showed a family of 5 gathered together in front of a cluster of blue spruce trees near a pond in the afternoon.

In the left corner near the edge of the shot, there was the shape of a person. There wasn't much you could tell, but it was definitely a person standing there, wearing what looked like a black shirt and blue jeans. It's clear from the picture that the photographer was either ignoring the person, or more likely, had no idea the person was even there. There was nothing obviously alarming about it, but it reminded me of those blurry bigfoot pictures that were on the front page of some of the tabloids located out in front. It was something about the lone person lurking out in the woods that looked slightly creepy. But a random person making it into the shot happened in a ton of pictures, especially back then. So I finished the order, went on with the next batch, and forgot about the picture.

About three weeks later, I was going through a totally different order when I found another strange picture. Except this one was different. Instead of the great outdoors, this picture was from a birthday party of some sort. In the picture I was looking at, everyone was inside a massive dining room and clustered around the big dining room table while the birthday girl, a blond girl who looked to be about twenty, was blowing out the candles on her extravagant white birthday cake. But what caught my attention was the large bay window that everyone was facing away from. There was a man standing outside, closely watching everyone inside. He was average looking from what I could tell, but what stood out was his expression. He wasn't standing out there with a woeful expression that said he felt left out. No, this guy was intently watching them, like he was carefully studying them for something. I wasn't 100 percent sure, but I thought that he may have been looking at whoever was taking the photo.

Either way, I had no idea what to think. Was this a relative about to pull a prank on the birthday girl or something? I've seen plenty of awkward and downright weird family photos, but this one seemed different. I'd seen enough awkward family pictures to know that you can recognize them almost immediately. They have a unique charm to them that gives you a good laugh, but in a heartwarming 'oh my family is just like that,' way.

Since there wasn't much of anything I could do about a weird picture, I checked the rest of the pictures, packaged it up, and kept on with my work. But this time I couldn't shake the image.

Over a month later, there was another weird picture. The setting this time was at some kind of pool party. From the looks of the flag themed décor, it was some kind of Fourth of July get together. It looked like a fun time; plenty of people waving sparklers and eating grilled hamburgers and hot dogs in between taking a dip in an in-ground swimming pool. As the day turned into nighttime, the pictures now showed people gathered around a large campfire where they roasted marshmallows.

My stomach dropped when I saw someone in a picture who looked just like the guy from the birthday party. What gave him away was the same expression I had seen before; unflinching, unsmiling, and out of place amidst all the holiday festivities. This time he was in the next-to-last photo. The picture was of a huge gathering at some public park. With all the people spread out on blankets and folding chairs, I figured everyone was there to see some fireworks.

I didn't recognize the location or the other people in the shot, but there was no mistaking the man I saw peering at the group from far off in the background. Was this some stalker or something? Because there was no way this was all a coincidence, especially because the orders were all placed under different names. The weird part was that the people in these pictures were completely different from the ones I had seen before. The only similarity I could tell, aside from the strange man, was that in both instances he had only appeared when there was a photo of a large group of people.

The old saying "a picture says a thousand words," is very true at times, but sometimes you wished they would say a thousand more. I had no idea what the context was for the stranger in the picture. Not that there was anything I could really do. All I had was the name the respective orders were placed under, and that was it. Ignoring the chill that had just washed over me, I finished the order and went on to the next. I managed to forget about what I'd seen until one night about two months later.

I was manning the customer service counter for the night and was just getting ready to go on break when I heard the tell-tale bell clinging that meant we had a customer. Putting my stuff down, I strode out to the front to take care of things.

"How can I help you?" I asked the customer, whose back was turned to me.

"Hi, I have an order to pick up. I believe my wife placed it under the name Crawford."

He turned to face me, and my stomach dropped to somewhere around my knees. It was the strange man from the pictures. Same closely cropped hair and unreadable expression.

"Of course," I managed to say while checking the cartons of packages ready for pickup. Crawford was mercifully near the top. I wasted no time in grabbing it and returning to face the guy.

"Here you are. It'll be $7.95."

"Here you are," he gave me a 10, and I quickly made change.

"Is there anything else I can do for you?" I asked over the deafening sound of my own heart rate.

"Oh no thank you, this is plenty. Between the two of us, I'm just happy to finally get some time off work. I'm in law enforcement so my schedule is a mess," he added while showing me the legit badge and ID on the inside of his wallet.

"No kidding?"

"Yup. I've been doing undercover work for the last few months and it's finally over. That's why I'm thrilled to be doing something as ordinary as running errands. You should be able to read all about it in the paper tomorrow, but there was this serial killer operating around here. His victims were all people he knew personally. He would go to their houses for holidays and stuff and they never suspected a thing. I'll give him this, he was clever. Since he never wanted to have his picture taken there, he would instead volunteer to be the one to take the big family photos of everyone. I even watched him do it a few times myself. Scary stuff huh?"

"Very," I agreed as relief began flooding through my body. "It's easy to forget that a photo shows everything except the person taking it."

Cat People

IT BEGAN WITH A call from my brother Owen. That was all the heads up I needed to brace myself for whatever was coming. I love my brother, but that doesn't mean I like him or what he does at times. Owen's not a bad person by any stretch of the imagination, but he gets himself into the worst messes and always needs someone to bail him out. By default, that usually means he comes to me. And boy, does it get old. He's my half-brother and before our Dad passed, he asked me to look after Owen, who's been the black sheep of the family from the beginning.

"I know you'll always be ok, but I'm worried about your brother. He's not strong like you. Try to help him if you can, but you have your own life to live. If he wants to go under, he will, and there's nothing any of us can do to stop it," is what he specifically said.

I certainly don't mind helping family out when they truly need a hand, but when all you hear from people is when they need something, it's beyond insulting. So when I answered the call from Owen, it's why the first thing I asked was, "What did you do now?"

A pause on the other end. Never a good sign.

"Well?" I asked, the irritation plain in my voice. "Spit it out."

"I'm stuck somewhere," Owen said sheepishly.

"You're stuck somewhere?"

"Yeah, my car stalled and now it won't start."

"So why call me? Why not a tow truck or something?"

Another pause.

"I kinda just finished something."

"Finished what?"

"A job."

"Owen, just tell me what's going on. Quit beating around the bush." I already hated where this conversation was going.

"Ok, I needed some money, and I needed it fast, so I took a job that required me and a bunch of guys to go overseas and work on a dig. Some kind of archeology thing that needed contractors or something. So I said yes. The pay was too good to turn down. 25,000 bucks, plus all meals and living arrangements covered for the week I was overseas."

"25,000 dollars?" I couldn't keep the shock out of my voice. "For what?"

"Not much, just some digging and hauling of stuff. A lot of grunt work. They gave me the cash when we landed back here about two hours ago, and I was trying to start my car when it stalled."

"What stuff did you haul?"

"Mostly rocks, but there was also some ancient Egyptian stuff found within the tomb we were supposed to excavate. Some of it came back with us on the ship we went over on. The last part of the job was for us to haul it onto trucks, which are going to museums."

"And they paid you 25 thousand for that?"

"I know, unbelievable right?"

"Exactly. Something smells fishy to me. Especially since they gave you the cash up front. You sure it wasn't all a front to smuggle in drugs or something?"

"They swore it was all legit. Told me I could let the local authorities know, but it was all in the open and the port authority knew exactly what was being shipped. They even gave me a business card with their contact info. The reason I'm calling you instead of a tow truck is I don't exactly want to be out here alone with a stranger when I have 25 grand in cash."

"That actually is good thinking," I said, shocked at how he had thought that out. "I'll be right there."

"Thanks. There's no one around, but there's a bunch of fog not too far off, so visibility is a bit difficult."

He gave me directions to his location, which I could find easily enough. But as I left and drove towards him, something was off. Legit business or not, you don't pay someone 25 thousand dollars just to dig overseas and move antiques for no reason. Owen had been in messes like this before, usually when he'd been drinking.

When I arrived where Owen had directed me, I saw he wasn't kidding about the fog. It was so thick it almost looked like something out of a machine you get for Halloween. The streetlights lining the road cast an ominous orange glow onto it. I saw Owen's car and gave a quick honk of the horn to let him know I was here. In no time at all, he bounded over, hopped into the passenger seat, and we were off, my car's high beams casting shadows off the fog's surface.

"Thanks Ethan," he said as his car faded away behind us.

"Sure."

"I was actually getting kinda spooked back there, all alone in the fog. Once I actually thought someone was there and it gave me a good scare."

"I'm sure it did."

"Thanks again for coming to get me bro, I don't know what I'd do without you at times."

"Don't mention it."

"No I have to, I know I haven't been the best sibling, but I'm really gonna try to do better."

It was a nice sentiment. Or at least it was the first time he'd said it. Not so much on the 20th time or so. But maybe this time he'd pleasantly surprise me. We got to Owen's apartment without incident, and he got out of the car, muttering a "Thanks again," as he did before I headed home. When I parked in my spot in the garage, I spotted what looked like a handprint made in the condensation on the passenger's side window. I didn't think Owen had touched the window, but he's always a bunch of flailing limbs and fidgety hands. If the idea had existed at the time, Owen would've probably been diagnosed with ADHD when we were kids. So I ignored it and once I was back inside my condo, I resumed watching episodes of *Stranger Things* on Netflix while my cat Sebastian snuggled up on the couch next to me and dozed off. I eventually dozed off as well.

I woke up the next morning and made myself some oatmeal with blueberries for breakfast. On the way to the kitchen, I saw a text from Owen.

"Thanks again for helping me out." I noted the late hour it was sent. 4:57 AM.

"Nightmare?" I texted back.

"Yup. I haven't had one like this in a while. Have a good day at work!"

I went through my usual day at work, and I assumed Owen did whatever he did during the day. Since it was Friday, I splurged on a pizza for dinner and watched *House of Cards* while I ate. I had a great night's sleep and woke up late that Saturday. I noticed another late-night text from Owen.

"Hey, I can't sleep. A terrible nightmare woke me up and now I don't feel like going back to bed." This one had been sent at 3:22 AM.

"That again, huh?" I texted back.

"Yeah, but it was worse than before. One of the worst I've ever had. I dreamt something was chasing me. I haven't had a dream that bad since I was using."

"It happens," was all I responded before I went about my day.

Later that night, I dozed off in front of the TV. Sometime later, I woke up in a haze, not knowing what time it was or what had woken me up. It took me a minute to realize I was hearing my phone going off on the table in front of the couch. It was Owen.

"Hello?" I mumbled out.

"Hey Bro," I heard him gasp out. "Are you ok?"

"I'm fine," I said, knowing something was up. "But it sounds like I should be asking you that."

"I'm... fine." It came out more like a question.

"Come on Owen. You don't sound fine, and you don't call someone at this hour just to ask if they're ok unless you have a good reason."

"Alright, I had another nightmare. Not only was something chasing me, but this time it got close. I couldn't see what it was, I couldn't even look behind me because I was focused on running. But it was there. And it was terrifying. And I woke up just before it caught me."

"Look, I'm not one to knock nightmares. They can be scary like nobody's business. But it was just a nightmare, wasn't it?"

"Yeah, I guess. It just felt so real. I had a drink or two earlier to calm myself down and then I took a sleeping pill to help sleep better."

"There's your problem. Don't mix those two. Ever. I don't even take sleeping pills solo. Those things don't help you sleep. They drug you and knock you unconscious and you wake up feeling like a zombie. That's not a restful sleep."

"You're right. You've always been right. Thanks for being there for me."

"Sure."

The next few days passed without incident and Owen was fine until about a week later. Instead of a late-night call, I got one early in the morning as I was sitting in traffic on my way to work.

"That thing in my dream finally caught me," Owen informed me. "The first time it slashed at me and I woke up with scratches on my back and chest. But the second time it caught me, grabbed me by the arm, and started to choke me. When I woke up, I was struggling to breathe and panting. Then I went to the bathroom and took a look in the mirror. This is what I saw."

My phone dinged as he sent me a picture. Sure enough, there was a massive bruise on Owen's left arm. But what caught my attention even more than that was his expression. Complete and utter terror.

"I'm so scared Ethan," he whispered. "I think I'm going crazy. But I know I'm not. I only had a drink or two to help get to sleep."

I'd heard this Owen before. There were countless versions of my brother I'd seen over the years, but this was the version that was using again. The bruise was the dead giveaway. I felt exhaustion hit me. Here we go again, this same old song and dance.

"No you're not," I said, using the calm, soothing voice I always used for this Owen. "Just get some rest. It'll be ok. It always is."

"No," he whispered. "This time it won't be. I can feel it."

And there it was. My other favorite personality trait of this Owen. Paranoia.

"Why? What do you think is going to happen?"

"I'm going to die."

"Yes, well, there's something we can agree on, especially if you keep this up. Honestly Owen, I'm amazed you've lasted this long. All of us are. All those times Dad had to rush you to the ER because you overdosed on one thing or another. I would think after all this time, death wouldn't be scary to you at all because you've gotten close to it enough times you should be on a first name basis with it. So I don't know what you expect me to do. Please, tell me, what the hell do you want me to do? Do you want me to come over there with a baseball bat and guard you while you sleep or something?"

"Well, no," he said feebly.

"Remember that time you swore there were animals in the walls, and they were scratching and trying to get you?"

"Yes," he mumbled.

"But we looked and there was nothing there."

"I just don't want anything bad to happen. I feel like something might. I really, really do."

"Welcome to how the rest of us have felt about you for years, Owen."

"I know how you feel, Ethan. You and everyone else. That I was what drove Dad to an early grave."

"I didn't say that."

"No. You don't have to. I can see it when anyone looks at me. And I can't blame anyone for it either. If I were you, I'd probably think the same thing."

We sat in silence for a few moments. This is the worst part of dealing with someone like Owen. The sitting and watching part, knowing they're dancing on the edge of the knife. No matter how many times they pull the maneuver off, all it takes is one miss, and it's all over. There was absolutely nothing I, or anyone else for that matter, could do. Owen was Owen, and either he'd vacate the land of the living or pull himself up yet again.

"Would it be ok," he eventually began. "If I spent the night at your place and slept on the couch. Just to see if it helps."

"I guess. So long as you don't make any problems."

"I promise I won't. I'll be over later this evening when you're done with work."

When I answered my door later that night, I was shocked. Owen looked as awful as I'd ever seen him. He was gaunt, his eyes hollow. It looked like he'd lost some weight since I'd last seen him. Owen was always tall and slender, but now he was so skinny he looked emaciated.

"I guess I really do look as bad as I feel," he said, noticing my demeanor.

"Well here's to hoping you sleep better tonight," was all I said as I shut the door behind him. "Do you need to eat something?"

"No I'm fine," he took off his shoes and made himself comfortable on the couch, taking care to spread a blanket over himself. "But thank you. I really appreciate this Ethan."

"Sure."

"No, really, I mean it. You're much better to me than I deserve. You and your Mom. She always treated me like I was her own, God knows I didn't deserve it. And I lorded the fact that my own mother died when I was two over Dad until the very end, whether I knew it or not. So I'm just gonna lay quietly here and try to sleep."

"Ok. Good night." I walked back to my bedroom and closed the door. Once I switched on the TV, I found myself listening intermittently for the sound of Owen talking in his sleep or any other telltale signs of whatever was happening to him. But there was nothing. Not a sound. I eventually dozed off myself and woke up late the next morning, the sun streaming in through the cracks in the blinds.

I shuffled out of bed and walked towards the kitchen, stepping over Sebastian on the way. Last night he had decided to crash in the living room as opposed to her bed in my room. Silly cat. I turned to check on Owen, who was still out like a light on the couch, his quiet snoring barely audible.

By the time I had finished making Nutella pancakes for breakfast and was beginning to eat, Owen had finally woken up. He yawned while lumbering towards me.

"I forgot where I was at first," he rubbed his eyes as I dug into my breakfast.

"How'd you sleep?"

"Amazingly. I feel so much better. The best night's sleep I've had in a long time."

"Good deal. You want some?" I pointed a fork towards the Nutella pancakes.

"No thanks, you've done more than enough for me. I'm gonna get going."

He stood there quietly for a second, like there was something else he wanted to say.

"Could I give you a hug?" he eventually asked.

I froze. Never in my life can I remember Owen asking me for a hug or giving one.

"Who are you and what have you done with my brother?" I heard myself say.

"I know right? But I'm really gonna try to be a better brother from now on. I know I've said it a million times, but this time I mean it. So how about a hug Ethan?"

"I guess," I put my fork down and stood up from the kitchen island I usually ate at. Owen walked quickly into the kitchen and embraced me in a deep hug I was not expecting. I stood there awkwardly for a second before I carefully raised my arms and wrapped them gingerly around him. I let it last for a moment or two until I pulled away.

"Thanks," he smiled. "I'll see you later Ethan. Have a great day."

That was the last interaction I ever had with my brother. According to the coroner, Owen died approximately 24 hours later. At some point he had gotten incredibly drunk and took too many sleeping pills. I like to think he slipped away quietly and without any pain. I got the call a few days later. The call I had expected for years but would never be truly ready for.

Despite the conflicting emotions I was feeling, planning the funeral was easy. I had him cremated and had the box buried on top of my father's plot, which was next to his mother's ashes. At the funeral home where the memorial service was, a striking blond walked up to me after the short service where a small group of family and friends came to pay their respects to me, his closest surviving relative.

"Are you Ethan?" she asked when the last person had offered their condolences.

"Yes, can I help you?"

"I'm Sabrina Townsend, I'm so sorry for your loss." She was very pretty, but there was something in her expression that was all too familiar. An unsettled look. Tired. Like she was ground down from worrying about something.

"Thank you," we shook hands. "You're a friend of Owen's."

"How did you know that?"

"You look haunted too."

"I'm sure I do. Can I meet you for coffee or something tomorrow?"

"Sure, does the local Starbucks at about this time work ok?"

"That's great, thank you so much Ethan." She hugged me quickly before giving me her business card and making her way out the door. According to her card, Sabrina Townsend was an archeologist of some sort. I checked her out, and she was a lecturer at a local college.

The following day, I left my place right on time and found Sabrina already there waiting for me. I waved to her, and she rushed up to greet me. I could feel the anxiety radiating off her like sweat.

"Thanks so much for coming," the relief plain on her face. "Would you like to order now?" She gestured towards the short line.

"Sure," I let her go in front of me as we waited for the two people ahead of us.

"I insist that whatever you get is on me," she said when it was our turn.

"Thanks. I'll have a regular Java Chip Frappuccino with a Pumpkin Scone," I told the girl at the cashier's register.

"Chestnut Praline Latte with a Vanilla Bean Scone," Sabrina added while she dug out her credit card and paid our bill. Once we had our coffees and pastries in hand, we headed towards a table at the back. By now the sky had clouded over and a light rain had begun to fall. I felt a chill just looking at it.

"Thanks again for meeting me Ethan," she took a sip once we sat down.

"Sure, so what's this about? Besides Owen, of course."

"Before he died, was he having any problems?"

"Owen was always having problems. Could you be more specific?"

"Anything out of the ordinary?"

"He was having nightmares. The worst kind he'd had since he was using or was a kid. Something was chasing him. But he slept at my place the night before he died and had no problems at all. He said it was the best night's sleep he'd had in a long time. Are you having sleeping problems too?" I took a bite of scone and watched Sabrina. She was nervously clutching her coffee cup.

"Of a different sort. No nightmares, but I feel like I'm being watched. Not all the time, but often. I can feel it. And sometimes at night I look out my window and see something in the shadows. I can't see anything, but I know something's there. I'm having a horrible time sleeping."

"I'm sorry"

"The reason I asked to speak to you is this," she pulled a large glossy photo out of her bag and pushed it towards me. It depicted a large group of people standing in a quarry filled with digging equipment. "It's the entire team who worked on the Finnister dig. Our job was to excavate a tomb located on the outskirts of Cairo that was found a few months ago. The entire expedition consisted of 47 members. 23 of them have died within three months."

"That's insane." I peered at the photo and Owen stared back at me from the second row, a light smile on his face.

"I know. The causes of death range from accidents of various nature, sudden medical mishaps, and murder. Much has been made of the curse."

"The what?"

"At the sight we found an inscription that loosely translated means 'Death shall be an unwanted guest of anyone who disturbs this tomb.' There has already been a growing interest on both the internet and within the media regarding the unnatural number of deaths associated with the dig."

"I'm sure there is," I said nonchalantly. "Is this why Owen was paid good money for basically digging in the sand?"

"Yes, the tomb's reputation amongst locals made it hard to hire local workers, so we headhunted here in the states and offered good salaries for the trouble."

"Gotcha."

"Do you believe your brother was cursed?"

"Are you kidding me?" The tone of my voice made her flinch. "My brother just died. The hell is the matter with you?"

"I apologize, I didn't mean to upset you. I just thought you might like to know what may have been bothering Owen before he died."

"I know damn well what was bothering him before he died. My brother was a train wreck from day one. You don't need a fucking PhD to see that. You want to know if I think he was cursed? Everyone is cursed, it's just a matter of how. Some are cursed with a bad heart, a bad kidney, a bad lung, or a bad liver. Others are cursed with bipolar disease, depression, OCD, schizophrenia, alcoholism, or drug abuse. People are cursed with abusive parents, abusive spouses, or abusive siblings. No one gets out of here unscathed or alive, it's the curse of being human. We're all cursed to shuffle off the Earth in some fashion, it's just a question of how and when. Some people are blessed to die quietly of old age in a warm bed, while others aren't. My brother, like many, was not given that luxury. He was cursed alright, cursed to be the black sheep of the family. Do I think his death was unusual and a bit uncanny? Absolutely. But that's what death is, the last great mystery. Try as you might and people certainly do try today to make death as straightforward and clear cut as they can, there are some things they just can't unravel. And I don't expect that to change anytime soon. So if you plan to get your 15 minutes of fame by saying my brother and a bunch of others are the victim of a mummy's curse or something, you can get the fuck out now."

She sat there silently for a minute.

"I'm sorry," she eventually whispered. "Please forgive me. It's just, I'm scared. I'm so scared. I don't know what to do. I've gone to New Age shops, burned sage in my apartment, hired a medium, the whole nine yards. Nothing worked. I'm just trying to live in peace. I don't want to exploit anything, I just want this to go away."

"And how do you propose to do that?"

"I don't know. That's what scares me so much," she sniffed. "I looked into the deaths of everyone associated with the expedition and they all seem to match up to some fact in their life. No one died any crazy deaths out of left field. In short, the only reason the deaths are noteworthy is because they all occurred in a close time frame. I've also read up on other alleged curses and strange happenings. Like the ones on movie sets and stuff like that. Nothing as bizarre as that has happened yet."

"So in other words, if there is something going on, it's not blatant and that's why it scares you."

"Correct. And it doesn't just scare me, it terrifies me. I once had an abusive boyfriend who stalked me. I feel the same way now as I did then. That's how I think whatever is going on works. It doesn't invent something, it just amplifies something you are already dealing with in your life."

"Question. Why do you call it the Finnister dig?"

"Because that's the name of the man in charge. Charles Finnister."

"Is he still alive?"

"Very much so. He just posted a picture of his cat on Twitter."

"Well, I'm sorry Sabrina, I don't know what to tell you. Wait a minute," I stared at her for a moment. "Didn't the Egyptians think cats were special?"

"Very much so. They were the original cat people."

"What if that's the solution to your problem?"

"Getting a cat?"

"Yes. Owen claimed he felt better after sleeping at my house and my cat was sitting nearby."

"That's bizarre."

"No shit," I snapped. "Bizarre is what you got. And if you got any better ideas, you go for it honey. This isn't my problem, so if you don't like my ideas, feel free to hit the road and have it your way."

"Look, I'm sorry Ethan. It's an idea." A look suddenly came over her face and she frantically tugged out her phone and scrolled through it for a few minutes until she froze.

"On the night this photo was taken, everyone in it was discussing their cats. All 12 of them. Every single person in this picture is alive and healthy."

"So I guess you're adopting a cat," I took a sip of coffee.

She looked up and suddenly seemed ten years younger.

"Would you believe I've always wanted one? I just never took the step and thought I never had the time. Guess this is the universe telling me to just do it. Would you like to come with me? I'm definitely getting a rescue."

"Absolutely."

We left Starbucks and made our way to the local shelter and, as I expected, I automatically wanted to take at least three cats home with me. Sabrina walked through the cages until she found a cat that caught her eye. A little black and white tuxedo one.

"That's Giselle," the woman volunteering told her. "She likes you, but just a heads up, she has a brother and it's best they're not separated."

"Where is he?" she stood up and faced the volunteer at eye level.

"Harvey is right over there," she pointed in the next cage, where a slightly bigger tuxedo cat was rolling over on its back and looking amusedly at Sabrina before he stood up, stretched, and swatted at her through the cage. I recognized the look on Sabrina's face all too well.

"Then I guess that settles it," she said. "I'll take them."

While the staff got the cats ready for travel, it was time for Sabrina to fill out some paperwork.

"Congrats on your adoption day!" The perky brunette whose name tag said 'Bernadette,' cheerfully told Sabrina.

"Thank you."

"And thank you for getting a rescue."

"No, thank you for taking care of these cats. I'm the one who needs to be rescued here."

"Awe, I hear that so much," Bernadette said cheerfully. "I could tell you were going through a hard time before you got here, but your energy just seems so much better now. Would you like one of these bumper stickers?" She pointed to some that had "Who rescued who?" written on it alongside a trail of paw prints.

"Who rescued who indeed," Sabrina looked back at her. "I'll take one alright."

I helped Sabrina take one of the carriers to her car and bid her farewell. Several hours later, she sent me a picture confirming both cats had already taken over her bed.

"Get used to it. Now you're gonna learn why the Egyptians found cats regal and otherworldly," I added with a smiley face.

"I named them Ramses and Nefertiti," she texted back

"Good for you."

"Thank you for everything. I feel so much better. The mood here is normal again. But I'm now a cliche, the crazy cat lady."

"Isn't that preferable to the archeologist dead from a mummy's curse cliche?"

"Well played."

Campfire Memories

I've always loved campfires. It doesn't matter what is going on or what the setting is. The feeling of sitting around a campfire, in the middle of nature, with your friends gathered around you as you make s'mores or tell stories, is like no other. So when I went camping with my friends one weekend last year, there was no doubt we'd be having a campfire and roasting some marshmallows.

So I packed up my gear and waited for the date of our departure to arrive, which it did. Right on schedule, my friend Jake picked me up at my apartment building. Once my bags were in his car, we headed to our destination, which was a new area he had picked out after checking with his dad. Our friend Bo has a camper that we always used to camp, and we all loved it.

We got there, and it was beautiful. Tall, majestic pine trees everywhere you looked, a cozy pond filled with algae located within a mile of our campsite, and an atmosphere that just made you feel refreshed and alive. Our friends Zack, Aiden, and Bo were already there, and Bo's camper was all set up for us. So once Jake and I got settled, I sipped a bottle of water and enjoyed the view while I took a brief hike around.

We were the only people in the area, so we had the place to ourselves. While I was walking around, I was also making notes about what to use for our campfire. I'd already brought my usual stuff for starting a fire, so that wasn't a problem. I never know what might be available, so I always bring some stuff from my local camping store to start the fire and get it going. But I can't really bring that much firewood with me, so I usually have to find some local place that sells it or something.

Once I got back to the campsite, it was agreed that Bo, Aiden, and I would go into town to get the pizza for us to eat. Then we hopped in Zack's Jeep and headed for the nearest town. It was a cozy, but reasonable sized place with all the usual features. A hardware store, gas station, grocery store, and the usual variety of restaurants.

While Bo and Aiden were at the pizza place, I headed across the street to the hardware store in search of some firewood. It was quiet. I was the only customer there, and the counter was staffed by a guy about my age, who was dressed in a t-shirt and jeans.

"Hello, how may I help you?" He greeted me with a smile.

"Hi, I was wondering about some firewood for camping?"

"Ah, I got you. I'm sorry to say we're fresh out, but I know where you can get some. My neighbor just had to clear a bunch of trees off his property, and he's got more firewood left over than he knows what to do with. Just go on over, give him a ring, and tell him Toby sent you."

Then he wrote down the address and gave it to me. It was right on the way back to our campsite, so that was even better.

"Thank you so much," I said as I pocketed the address.

"No problem. He can't wait to get rid of it, so you'd be doing him a favor. Like to camp, huh?"

"Love it. Gotta have a fire too."

"Of course," he nodded with a smile. "Well you enjoy yourself and come back if you need anything else."

"Will do, thank you so much!"

With that, I left the hardware store, walked back to Zack's Jeep, and told them what I'd found out. They happily agreed to stop by on the way back to camp.

We arrived at Toby's neighbor's house ten minutes later. It was a beautiful little cabin in the woods with a comfortable front porch and a great view of the road. And, as advertised, there was a massive amount of firewood lying around in thick rows.

I got out of the Jeep, walked to the front door, and gently knocked. An older gentleman with bright blue eyes answered it.

"Hi, I'm here for some firewood. Toby said to let you know he told me to come by.

"Ah yes," he clapped his hands together and smiled at me. "He just told me he sent someone my way. Right this way, my friend."

He quickly led me to the firewood that seemed to take up half the yard.

"We had a nasty storm a few months ago that uprooted a bunch of trees. It was a miracle none of them crashed right on the house. It took forever to make it manageable, but here's what's left. Help yourself to them. Do you need a hand?"

"No thank you, I think we have it under control." I nodded to my friends in the Jeep.

"Alright. Well, you all help yourself to as much as you want. Truth be told, I'm sorry that all those trees got uprooted or broken in the storm. I've never seen anything like them before. They look just like any other tree, but they burn just a little bit different. I can't really explain it. Probably because I grew up with them or something."

"I understand."

"Well, you all have a good time. Come back if you run out and need more."

"We will, thank you so much."

I shook his hand before the three of us loaded a ton of firewood into the back of the Jeep. Once it was full, we drove back to camp, had the pizza, which was delicious, and relaxed for a bit. Then it was campfire time.

The others sat back and let me set it up, as they knew I loved it. Once it was done, we all relaxed and let the soothing warmth and flickering light settle into the area. Before too long, the fire was steadily consuming the firewood I had brought with us, and it was time to use what I'd gotten from Toby's neighbor.

It took some time, but I eventually began to see what he meant. It seemed like any old firewood, but it burned just a bit differently. There was a bit more heat and brightness to the fire, but that could be because it had aged or any number of other reasons.

Either way, with the fire in full swing and dinner behind us, it was s'more time. That was another thing I'd always brought supplies for on camping trips. Once I passed out the metal skewers to put the marshmallows on and the chocolate bars and graham crackers had been opened, we took turns roasting the marshmallows over the fire, which crackled happily in front of us. It was beyond calming. Once we all had our fill of s'mores, all that was left was to relax, talk, and enjoy each other's company around the fire. It was one of my favorite parts of the whole camping experience. The atmosphere was calm, mellow, and invigorating. We talked about nothing in particular, but we quickly passed the time. Before long, darkness had completely fallen, and the moon peered out at us from behind a dense cluster of pine trees.

It wasn't long before, one by one, my friends said goodnight and went inside the camper to grab a place to sleep. As usual, I was the last one awake and quietly sat by the fire. By now, the fire quietly burned away, not quite as big as before, but still going strong. I'm not sure how late it was, but it was getting late.

I was just about to start heading to bed when I turned my head and the fire popped. Not loud, but enough that it caught my attention. Then I turned my head slightly and noticed something. I thought I could see something in the fire. At first, I thought it was just my eyes, or something had fallen in the fire, but no, it was something else. There were shapes moving within the flames. Making images, like a movie on a screen, except it was in the fire. I sat there, unsure of what to think or do, so I sat there, quietly observing in my chair.

At first, I had no idea what I was looking at. The shapes were just blurs at first, vague outlines. But then they became clearer, and I realized it was the five of us. We were riding in the Jeep, going steadily along one of the roads we'd come down on the way to the campsite. Then, Zack turned down a road I'd never seen before and came to an intersection. As he did, you could see there was a nasty accident that occurred here, and we had to be detoured around it. Then the images stopped dancing in the flames, and the fire returned to normal, burning low over the coals.

I sat there stunned, unsure of what to think. Had I fallen asleep while sitting here? Or was it just my imagination? I chalked it up to fatigue, tossed one last piece of firewood on the fire, and went inside the camper to grab some sleep. Once I rolled my sleeping bag out on the floor and got comfortable, I managed to sleep ok and woke up to sunlight streaming through the camper's windows.

The others were stretching as they woke up, and they gradually made their way to the remnants of the fire, which had burned down enough so that only faint puffs of smoke drifted overhead. When they saw I was up, Jake and Zack took out the stuff to make breakfast, and before too long, we were eating biscuits and scrambled eggs in front of what was left of the fire.

Once I had finished eating, I tossed some logs on top of the smoldering remnants of the campfire in the hopes that given enough time, it would ignite again. Once that was done, we all got ready to head to the nearby park for a hike and headed out soon after. As usual, Zack drove.

We were halfway there when Zack said something, turned the Jeep, and headed down a road that seemed vaguely familiar. Then a moment later, the Jeep stopped at an intersection, and we could all just make out that there had been an accident, and they were detouring traffic down a side road.

My stomach clenched at the sight. How was this possible? It couldn't be a coincidence, or my imagination. I briefly wondered if there had been something inside the firewood that caused hallucinations, but that didn't explain this.

I did my best to shrug it off as Zack kept driving and we arrived at our hiking destination. The sight made it easy, as it was beautiful. Lots of tall boulders and canyons overlooking a quarry filled with water. We all started walking and took in the area. It was an amazing hike, and we returned to the camper, had plenty of water, and relaxed in front of the fire, which had returned to life and was crackling away. After that hike, our appetites returned with a vengeance, so Bo and I went into town to get some sandwiches from the local deli. We returned with them and some potato chips and pasta salad, and everyone ate heartily. Then we went inside the camper and watched a few movies until it was time for dinner.

Dinner consisted of spaghetti with tomato sauce and garlic bread followed by s'mores. We had our fill until we all sat contently around the fire, which burned with a calm brightness that was beyond pleasant to sit around. And just like last night, one by one, my friends went to the camper to sleep until only I was left awake.

I sat there, feeling more than a little uneasy as I stared at the fire, wondering what it would do or if it would do anything. It felt like I was daring it to do something, as it was just the two of us alone in the middle of nature.

After what felt like an eternity, the fire sizzled, and I saw shadows forming in the depths of the flames. I sat there, stunned by what I was witnessing. Because after a moment, the shadows became clear, and just like last time, I was watching a scene unfold like a movie projected from within the fire.

Several dark figures were watching a camper in the middle of the woods. They were dressed all in black and had on ski masks and leather gloves. I realized with a sickening lurch in my stomach they were watching our camper. Then, I watched as they got closer to the camper, and waited outside, just beyond the front door. For what they were waiting for or what exactly they were up to, I had no idea, but I knew it wasn't good.

I watched as the people lurking outside the camper held up a phone to do something, and Bo peeked his head out, clearly unsure of what was happening. Right when this happened, the people waiting outside rushed him and forced their way into the camper. That was when the shapes were reduced to shadows before they faded away, and the fire returned to normal.

I was stunned by what I'd seen. Despite the heat from the fire, chills had run up my spine, and I felt beyond isolated out here in the woods. Were there really people out there, watching us?

It didn't take me long to go to bed quickly after that, as I felt beyond uneasy outside now. So I went inside and laid down in my spot like last time. But this time, sleep was out of the question. I laid there, listening to the others contently sleeping, and I felt so alone and unsure of what to think. I was tense and uneasy, listening to every sound or even the hint of something.

After what seemed like an eternity, I heard the faint sounds of grass rustling outside before I heard what sounded like a dog barking.

Fear shot through my body like nothing I'd experienced before. I knew deep down that was no dog. After a moment, I heard it again. That was when Bo woke up and sat upright on the couch he'd been sleeping on.

"What?" He mumbled, still partially asleep. "What's going on?"

"Shhh," I whispered. "I think someone is outside."

That woke him up. Bo quietly crept over to me and leaned over so we could talk.

"I thought I heard the sound of someone outside, and that isn't a dog."

"Right," he nodded. "There's no way I'm opening that door."

Then he quietly went over to the kitchen, grabbed a knife, and held it close to him. Then he called the local authorities and made sure to whisper so no one knew what was going on. We sat like that for what seemed like hours until finally, it became lighter, and sunlight faintly started to peer through the windows. By then, we heard the sounds of police cruisers and from the window in the kitchen, we could see it was the cops.

I'd never felt so relieved in my life as we saw them arrive. Bo and I stepped out to talk to the two officers and explained what happened. They listened, agreed to check the area out, and praised us for our quick thinking. As we told our story, morning dawned, bright and vivid. Then they took down our contact information and told us to go inside and get some sleep.

We happily agreed. As Bo and I went back inside, the other three were slowly waking up, and we had to explain to them what happened. They agreed it had been suspicious and said they'd keep watch on the place while Bo and I tried to get some sleep. We managed to get some, and when the cops returned, they told us they hadn't found anything aside from some footprints by the camper. But they promised to be on the lookout for any other suspicious activity in the area.

After we thanked them, we got ready to leave because it was a weekend camping trip, and we all had to get back to our lives. Once Bo loaded up the camper and got it ready to go, I got back in Jake's car, and we headed home.

I never did tell them what I saw in the fire. We went on plenty more camping trips or just hung out outside around a fire after that, and I'd used the firewood we'd gotten, but I never once saw images in the fire again.

SCARY MOVIE SEASON

EVERYONE HAS THAT ONE job. The one job that all other jobs are measured by. The job that makes all other jobs look stupid, trivial, and downright awful. That job for me was working at Blockbuster.

But it wasn't just working at Blockbuster, it was working at Blockbuster in the 90s. Those were the days when video stores and VHS tapes were *it*. I imagine that working at Blockbuster, or any other video store in the 90s, was like being a New York adman in the 60s or working at Studio 54 in the 70s. If you wanted to soak up the culture and atmosphere of the 1990s, working at a video store was how to do it.

Don't get me wrong, I like Netflix and the other streaming services, but it's a completely different experience. Video stores were the 90s equivalent to what malt shops were to people in the 1950s because going to your local video store was an event, especially if you went with your friends on a Friday or Saturday night. That's because a movie being released on video was a huge deal in those days because you had to wait about 6 months for a movie to go from theatres to being available to buy or rent.

That sense of fun is what made working at a video store the best job I've ever had. Unlike virtually every other service job, there was very little customers could get upset or angry about. All you did was come in, pick a movie to rent, maybe pick out some candy, and leave. The worst thing a customer usually did was forget to drop a movie off or lose it. My coworkers there felt the same way, and we all knew the job was one of the easiest and best jobs you could ever have. Which meant everyone was almost guaranteed to be in a good mood every day.

One of my favorite parts of working at a video store was seeing what movies were popular with customers. Like being a bartender, you learned about the regulars and what their typical orders were.

This one customer was well built, rode a motorcycle, and had the most impressive mustache I've ever seen. He would always come in and rent romantic comedies and other movies like *Steel Magnolias, Waiting to Exhale,* and *The First Wives Club.* Another customer was a guy in his 20s who always wore a t-shirt dedicated to heavy metal bands. He turned out to be a huge fan of classic movie musicals. After he became a regular, he told me that his favorite movie was *The Sound of Music.* Good choice.

A favorite of everyone was Dorothy Malone, who we all called "Ma." An older lady in her late 60's who probably weighed about 115 pounds, she would come in and always get action movies. Her selections usually included the classic Clint Eastwood westerns and his Dirty Harry films, plus newer movies starring Schwarzenegger like *Commando* and *Predator.*

As we got to know her, we found out Ma had served in the army and worked for the state of Virginia in some civil service job before she moved north to take care of her mother, who was ill. Ma often came in later at night, but we didn't care because she had some of the best stories I've ever heard. And if some customer got a little snarky with her, she could silence them with a glance.

But of all the regular customers, Courtney was my favorite. She was one of the most beautiful women I've ever seen in my life, either in pictures or in person. Gorgeous black hair. Immaculate skin. Deep green eyes. And an appetite for edgy films. She won me over the minute she came in one chilly evening before Christmas and rented *Die Hard.*

Courtney was also a fan of scary movies, as one of her favorite movies was *Fright Night*, which she would often rent alongside other movies like *My Bloody Valentine, Poltergeist,* and *The Texas Chainsaw Massacre.* She was also a big fan of *Abbott and Costello Meet Frankenstein* and *Abbott and Costello Meet the Mummy.*

Whenever Courtney came in, it always made my day. She was my age, so I wanted to ask her out for the longest time. But of course, I had the chorus of "She's out of your league and you're not good enough," going through my head every time I saw her.

Angst aside, it was a wonderful time in my life. I wish everyone had the same opportunity to have an experience like that. Coworkers who are truly like your second family are a priceless experience and a low-pressure job where people come to have fun is something I wouldn't trade for anything.

So in October 1997 there was a crisp bite in the air, the leaves were turning shades of red and yellow, and it was officially scary movie season. I say officially because for a lot of people scary movie season is all year round, but September to November is when it's official. Or at least now it is. Back then, people didn't dare push holidays so early, so it wasn't until well into September when people even dared to mention Halloween.

The sense of fun that comes with Halloween was in the air as families, couples, and single people of all ages and backgrounds came in to check out scary movies or more family friendly Halloween videos. In keeping with holiday spirit, the store was decked out with cobwebs hung from the walls and decorative skeletons and pumpkins were posted on the windows.

The last Saturday before the 31st we were beyond busy, with people returning Halloween movies and us putting them back on shelves as fast as we could. But towards the middle of the shift, Courtney came in. As usual, my stomach gave a lurch that wasn't entirely unpleasant while I tried to be as professional and nonchalant as possible.

After browsing for a few minutes, she came to the register and checked out *Scream*. By now there was a lull in the customers, so I managed to chat with her for a bit.

Just before she grabbed her movie and left, she turned and said, "Hey Jared, want to come over tomorrow for a Halloween movie marathon?"

My chest felt like it was about to explode.

"A movie marathon?"

"Yeah, at my house. My parents are going to be out for a Halloween party, so I'll be home by myself."

I couldn't believe this was really happening. I somehow managed to have the following day off, so I was free to go.

"Sure, ok. When should I swing by?"

"Does 8 work?"

"It does."

"Great!" She grabbed a piece of paper and a pen off the counter. "Here's the address," she scribbled as I watched. "And my number, just in case."

"Thank you. See you tomorrow, Courtney."

As she walked out the door, I stood there motionless. It now felt uncomfortably hot in the store, despite the temperature being pleasantly cool as always.

I spent the rest of my shift in a daze. Once I punched out for the evening, I went home, heated up some macaroni and cheese in the microwave, and ate it without much thought. I felt simultaneously giddy and nervous and spent the rest of the night in a sort of limbo.

But once tomorrow arrived, chilly and grey, the nerves came back with a vengeance. But I tried not to focus on that while I did my best to look good for the evening without trying too hard. Time seemed to move both too slow and too fast, and by the time I was walking to Courtney's door, my legs felt like they were filled with cement. The rain, which had come down in thick cold waves, had mercifully stopped by now. All that was left was a sliver of fog and a slight breeze that made the soaked leaves rattle faintly on the sidewalk.

After I rang the doorbell, I stood there in the chilly night air for what felt like an eternity before she answered the door. As always, Courtney seemed to look effortlessly gorgeous in a white cashmere sweater and black jeans.

"Hi there, come on in," she greeted me with a smile. "Make yourself at home."

Her house was spectacular. Everywhere you looked there were high ceilings, plush rugs, hardwood floors, and marble counter-tops. After I gave her my jacket, which she put away in a huge closet located just inside the front hallway, she led me to a massive TV room that held a huge TV and several reclining armchairs and two sofas in similar shades of tan leather. The dark red walls contained several vintage movie posters from the 1950s and 60s in heavy glass frames. I was duly impressed.

"Popcorn or pizza?" She asked while I took the room in.

"Either's fine with me."

"Ok. How about we start with popcorn while we wait for the pizza?"

"Sure."

Courtney ordered us a large pepperoni, then I followed her into the expansive kitchen and watched as she tossed a bag of popcorn into the microwave. After pouring the steaming bag into a large glass bowl, she carried it into the living room.

At some point I looked at the movies sitting on the table near one of the sofas. They were movies she had rented before her most recent visit to the store. *Halloween* and *Night of the Living Dead*. Both classics.

"Do you have a preference on what to watch?" I heard her switch the TV on.

"No. I've watched them both a million times and could easily watch them a million more."

"Me too. Let's go with *Halloween*."

She picked up the box, pulled out the cassette tape, and popped it into the VCR before taking the spot next to me on the couch. The gesture made my chest feel pleasantly warm, and I leaned back in my seat to enjoy the movie.

But within a few minutes, it became clear something was wrong. Very wrong.

Instead of the movie's normal opening credits, what came on the screen was not *Halloween*. At first, I had no idea what I was looking at. The image on the screen was like something you saw in home movies; grainy, static filled, and shaky.

After the camera jerked up suddenly, I finally saw what was being focused on. A log cabin out in the middle of nowhere by a lake. As it came into focus, I realized that it was nighttime out and aside from a security light at the far end of the driveway near some tall pine trees, the area was pitch dark.

Another quick jerk made the camera pan to the people standing around it.

There was about 7 people wearing ski masks and the sight was unsettling. Unless they personally knew the cabin's owner, there was no reason they should be there. And there was no good reason they should be wearing ski masks and dressed in black at night. But the worst part was the quiet. Aside from the crackle of the camera and the occasional outdoor noise, the group was silent. There was no drunken laughter or stupid jokes. Just eerie silence.

The camera shifted slightly as the person holding it moved, and the rest of the group slowly began to walk towards the cabin, with the person holding the camera walking slightly behind the others. It was obvious this wasn't a group of drunk idiots deciding to pull a stupid prank. This was a group on a mission. They all walked with an athletic gait and a no-nonsense demeanor. Despite the patchy audio, I could hear grass crunching under their shoes as they walked.

My stomach sank as I watched someone quickly unlock the front door and the group stealthily entered the house. The cabin interior was nice; quaint but modern. But suddenly the sound of a woman screaming reverberated through the stereo, and I flinched as the camera abruptly cut off and all that was left on the television was static.

I quickly grabbed the remote and turned it off. Then the two of us sat there in stunned silence.

"Was that real?" Courtney asked, her voice slightly higher than usual.

"I... I don't know. It looked real, but anyone with a camera could stage that."

"Well, if they wanted to creep people out, it worked."

I had to agree. It was beyond creepy. Especially that scream. That was no surprised scream over finding a rat in your kitchen; it was a raw shriek of primal fear.

Courtney stood up. "My cousin is a cop, I'll call him and see what he has to say."

"Good idea."

She dashed to the phone and made the call while I watched. He told us to sit tight, and he'd be over soon with some colleagues to check things out. About 5 minutes later, the shrill ring of the doorbell made both of us jump out of our seats. I slowly crept to the window, with Courtney close behind me, only to see it was the pizza delivery guy.

She paid for it and the two of us quietly ate until Courtney's cousin arrived. It didn't take them long to fill us in on what they knew. Some local criminals were playing a sick game by making disturbing home movies and sending them to people disguised as normal movies. The footage being sent around was of all too real crimes and the authorities were in the process of matching up the footage they had gotten so far with files from unsolved cases.

With the tape in their possession, they left Courtney and I alone to digest what had just happened.

"Well," Courtney eventually began, "I invited you over for a scary movie night, and we both certainly got that. So you can't say I didn't deliver."

Despite everything, I felt a faint smile appear on my face.

"You got that right."

"And if you're not totally creeped out from spending time with me, I'd like to try again sometime."

"I'd like that too, but next time we can watch a movie at my house, and it'll be a movie I actually own."

A Lone Car in the Desert

IT STARTED OUT AS just a routine night on the job as a park ranger. Or more specifically, in my case, just a routine night on the job as a park ranger in Arizona. It was a job I loved, as I'd been on the team for years, and I had no reason to want to change that. I adored the scenery; the desert canyons, the saguaro cactus that dotted the horizon, and everything that came with it. I even loved the job at night.

In fact, I especially loved working at night. That's my favorite time to patrol the park. There had just been a recent series of dust storms in the area, so the park had been closed for several days, and tomorrow was the first full day back. Our job today had been to prepare for the reopening, and we had been tasked with double checking the park to make sure nothing was amiss or out of place. And, lucky for me, I had gotten the chance to patrol the area as night was settling in.

I had just rounded a corner and was straightening my Jeep out on the road when I noticed something looked slightly out of place. I'd been on this stretch of road literally a thousand times by now, but thanks to the huge dust storm, the nearby canyon wall had been swept cleart, and now you could see that a section of rock wall had been removed and replaced with something else. So I immediately pulled over, turned on my flashlight, and hopped out of the Jeep to investigate.

It didn't take long to see that this wasn't some random gap in the canyon wall, but a man-made opening that had been boarded up many years ago. The wood was badly damaged and weathered by the elements, and it had only been the years of sand and debris that kept it hidden this long. I felt a ripple of excitement as I held my flashlight up to it. From all the years I've been on the job and lived out here, I was pretty sure this was the opening to a mine. Not only had I seen plenty in my time out west, but part of the land that was now the park had belonged to a mining company. There had been rumors there was a mine under the land, but nothing had ever been found or confirmed. Until now. And I made it official by using my Jeep radio to let my colleagues know my location and what I'd found.

The ranger base radioed back they had received my message and were sending some of my colleagues to help investigate with me and I should wait until they arrived. I confirmed I understood my instructions, and then I returned to my Jeep and waited.

My fellow rangers arrived relatively quickly, and once they had their flashlights in hand, we all carefully approached the badly boarded up entrance. There were now four of us; Holly, Christian, Fletcher, and myself. The wooden beams were barely held in place by rusty nails and were pulled off easily. Once they were all lying cast aside on the rocky ground, we shined our flashlights into the now exposed entrance.

Now there was no doubt it was the opening to a mine. The wooden beams lining the walls and the rusty track lining the floor confirmed this had been used in mining. Since I had been the one to find this place, my fellow rangers let me do the honors, and I led the way into the dusty and arid tunnel.

The tunnel went on for about a mile until it passed by an open section of rock wall on our left. It was jagged and rough, but we could just see that it led straight to a mine shaft many stories below us. But when we looked straight down at the mine shaft with our flashlights in hand, I almost recoiled in shock.

The mine shaft floor was almost completely covered with snakes. Only the slightest bit of mine floor was visible for us to see, and even from this distance, it was obvious they were Diamondback Rattlesnakes. We'd all seen many of them while working here, but seeing so many of them in one place didn't feel real. I could practically feel their movements even though I was far above them. The fact that so many of them got here in one place was mind-boggling. It all looked like something out of a documentary, and if you stared at it long enough, there was the brief illusion that the floor was moving.

"Wow," Holly muttered as she looked at the snakes just below us.

"Wow is right." Christian agreed. "Definitely something to document."

We did just that before we carried on. Once we left the snakes behind, the four of us walked in relative silence for about 5 minutes until we came to a turn in the tunnel, and we could feel it descending further into the earth. The air was even cooler here, and we kept at a steady pace until we arrived at a fork in the tunnel.

"Alright, what do we do now?" Fletcher asked.

"Shall we split up?" Christian suggested.

"Works for me," I said. "I'll take the left."

"I'll go with you," Fletcher volunteered.

"Cool, then we'll head this way," Holly nodded.

Once we radioed the base what we were doing and got confirmation they understood, we proceeded. When Fletcher and I headed down the left tunnel, Holly and Christian disappeared behind the dense rock wall separating the tunnels, and that was that.

Fletcher and I walked at the same pace as the left tunnel veered far off from the path we'd been going down. After twisting sharply to the left, it evened out until we found ourselves in a narrow cavern that led to a dead end.

With my flashlight in hand, I took a closer look at where we were. The ceiling was dotted with stalactites, and the ground was covered in sand and a few rocks. Fletcher was right behind me as we quietly checked everything out. I was just about to say we should go back when I saw right in the corner, there was a section of wall that was a bit smoother than the rest. When I took a closer look, it appeared like a bit of the floor was boarded up.

"Come over here," I called to Fletcher.

He immediately walked over to where I was looking, and saw I'd found something. After we both took a moment to look at it, we were able to see it was a trapdoor, and there was a rusted handle in the middle of the wooden frame.

"Shall we give it a try?" Fletcher asked.

I nodded, and we both took hold and tugged. It was heavy and took a ton of strength, but after a moment, it jolted open with a loud crack. Once we eased it open, we shined our flashlights down into the opening. It was a simple climb down a bit of cavern steps, and it opened to another path. But why had it been closed off? People had probably fallen back when this was an operating mine.

After we briefly reported what we'd found back to base, we slowly descended the steps. Once we were both back on flat terrain, we took the space in. You couldn't see it from above, but this part of the mine connected to a winding path that led further down into what I assumed was the pit. This time, Fletcher went first, and I followed him. We had walked for almost a mile down the winding path when Fletcher moved a stationary mine cart out of the way, and it inadvertently crashed into the rock wall beside us with a loud bang that seemed to echo in the space.

"Sorry," he said to me.

"No worries."

In the beam from my flashlight, I could see the mine cart hitting the rock wall had disturbed the earth around it, and an opening had appeared in the ground. And moments later, I could see shapes coming out of it. I immediately recognized them as Arizona Bark Scorpions, and they were crawling out of the wall at a fast pace and, before too long, they had completely covered the space separating Fletcher and myself. Especially because we had both been in the job long enough to know you didn't want to get stung by one, much less the dozens crawling out, so we immediately backed up and away from each other.

"I guess I'll go this way, and you keep going that way," I said as I pointed to the other way the tunnel went.

"Sounds good. I'll catch up with you."

And with that, I was back on my own. I followed the path in the other direction, and before too long, I came to another end, but this time, it was marked by a huge pile of rocks. When I got close, I could feel the breeze coming from somewhere, so I knew this led outside.

So I slowly started removing rocks, and before too long, there was a narrow path for me to climb through to reach the other side. Once I put my flashlight back on my belt, I started to climb through the rocks and feel my way through.

Moments later, I was in the pleasant nighttime air again. The breeze felt amazing after being in the dusty mine for so long, and I took a moment to get oriented. I was far away from the park now, and I was in the middle of a rocky canyon overlooking the desert terrain a level below.

It was an incredible sight. All those saguaro cacti dotting the night landscape, while other brush lined the desert floor. But then, far on the horizon, I saw something coming this way. Something kicking up a lot of dusk. It was a car, and its headlights were blazing bright against the darkness that had settled over everything.

The sight filled me with dread, so I immediately ducked behind a rock wall and watched. A lone car driving out in the desert at night is never a good sign, especially when the road doesn't exactly lead this way.

It didn't happen often, but occasionally, rangers have found things out here over the years. Unnerving things. Things that suggested something bad happened without coming right out and saying it. It's no surprise because there's nowhere to run in the desert. There aren't many trees to climb up in, no forest you can camouflage yourself with, and no abandoned cabin you can run into. Unless you get lucky and there's an abandoned mine around, you are well and truly at the mercy of whatever is out there. And most of the time, that means you're at the mercy of nature, or even worse, people who didn't know the meaning of the word merciful.

Out of instinct, I checked my belt, and my stomach lurched when I realized my walkie talkie was gone. Probably got stuck in the rocks I climbed through. But I still had my heavy flashlight. That was more important, because it could come in handy if push came to shove. Then I quickly tried to crawl my way back to the mine to get help. Cold fear hit me as I realized there had been a cave in or something, as heavier rocks had replaced the much lighter ones I had moved. I quietly struggled for a moment until it was obvious they weren't budging. I had no choice but to return to my hiding spot and think of what else to do.

So I took a deep breath and watched the vehicle, which was a truck, bounce over countless dips in the ground. There were no paved streets out here, so the truck was constantly kicking up dust and swerving roughly. I had no idea what was going on, but I had a feeling, and it gave me a chill. Naivety is a luxury most people can't afford anymore. The truck's headlights were almost unnaturally bright, gleaming harshly against the desert sand. If anyone else accidentally stumbled onto the scene, I doubt they'd wonder about what was happening out here at night either. As I could tell, there were two most likely options. Money changing hands or something worse. It was just a question of which one it would be. In fact, it was entirely possible it could be both.

As the truck got closer, I could see it was grey. And although the windows weren't tinted, I couldn't see who was inside. Moments later, the truck slammed to a halt in an open patch of land that was just close enough for me to see what was happening. All was eerily quiet for a moment until all four doors opened at the same time and one man got out of each door. The truck's front was facing me, so I had a direct view as the two guys on the driver's side pulled a fifth guy out of the backseat and dragged him roughly along with them.

Not a good sign. Especially because even at this distance, I could see they were armed in addition to carrying flashlights to see where they were walking. And you could tell the guy was scared. No surprise there. Since they had no concern about him seeing their faces, that meant they weren't worried about what came after this little rendezvous. But even if they'd done that, he probably knew who they were. While I could practically smell the fear coming off him, he didn't look surprised or shocked.

In fact, I felt a shock of recognition when I realized the guy looked familiar. He was a local businessman who disappeared about a week ago. The story was some people had shown up unannounced at his house and without saying a word, kicked the door in, dragged him out, and stuffed him in the back of a car in the middle of the night. And rumor was the people responsible were a local gang famous for violence intended to shock and horrify. But since this guy was well known and had some power in town, rumor was they decided to make an example of him in another way by making him disappear.

By now they had dragged the guy, who I remembered was Mason Winters, towards a spot in the middle of the area. He was dressed in a suit that was clearly expensive, but had also seen better days. But then I realized that three of the four guys were dragging Winters, while the fourth was retrieving something from the back of the truck. I briefly wondered how many times they'd done this. From their demeanor, they seemed beyond nonchalant about it all.

Like it was the most routine thing in the world to them. Which very well could be the case.

Then the guy found what he wanted from the trunk. It was a shovel, which he tossed at the ground by where his associates had shoved Mason Winters and left him.

"Dig," I could hear him faintly say from where I was hiding.

There was no further explanation needed, as Winters picked up the shovel, stood up, and slowly started digging. I could see the first few shovelfuls were hard, but it started to come easier. He shoveled back and forth in what seemed like a never-ending motion. I could practically feel their gaze on him as each shovelful brought him one step closer to the end, and the air was thick with adrenaline and tension.

I was sweating despite the cool night air, and I didn't want to look, but I had no choice. It wasn't long before Winters began to feel the ache in his arms, because he definitely slowed down the longer he dug. The four men didn't say a word the entire time, as they merely leaned against the truck and one of them lit up a cigarette. When he did, the brief flash of a lighter stood out in the darkness for a moment.

The hole was slowly getting bigger and bigger, as was the pile of dirt beside it. Before too long, it'd be the proper dimensions and then it would all be over. Or it would be unless I did something, which is what I had planned. I had some rocks ready, and when the moment came, I would hurl some as far as I could in the other direction and cause some paranoia and distraction. Maybe give Winters the chance to get the upper hand. He didn't strike me as the type to back down from a fight easily. He may have been terrified, and his arms were probably aching with every movement, but he was dignified. Not once did he beg or plead for his life.

I also noticed it felt unnaturally quiet. No sign of any animals or any other forms of desert life. I'm not sure if that made the situation better or worse.

"Alright, that's good enough." One of the four armed men suddenly commanded. As Winters stopped digging, I gripped one of the rocks tightly in my hand. It was time. I was aiming to throw it where it would make plenty of noise.

Fear shivered down my spine as I got ready to act. But just as I was about to throw, there was a sound from somewhere out there in the desert. Something between a snap and a crack, and the suddenness of it after the deafening silence was disconcerting.

"What was that?" The one who told Winters to stop asked. He was about medium height, and he had an athletic build.

"No idea, come with me and look." The driver nodded at him. "You two, watch him," he said to the other two gunmen while pointing at Winters.

The two of them headed in the direction the sound had come from while Winters stood in front of the hole with two pairs of eyes on him. From where they were headed, it looked like the sound had come from behind a small canyon covered in sand.

"What the hell?" I heard the driver ask after about three minutes.

"Is that?" was all the other guy managed to get out before I heard a deafening roar that was immediately followed by the sound of gunfire and a blood-curdling scream.

The other two gunmen watching Winters immediately jumped and ran to check out what was going on. Winters grabbed the shovel again and watched from behind the mound of dirt as the two men ran to where their associates had been, only to be stopped dead in their tracks as the driver sprinted towards them, his clothes and face splattered with blood.

"Run for the truck!" he screamed at them.

But before he could lead them in that direction, something grabbed him from behind and dragged him out of sight while he thrashed and screamed. The flashlight in his hand lay there motionless on the ground, casting a beam onto the sand. The two remaining gunmen also dropped their flashlights as they tried to honor their instructions and sprinted towards the truck. Any thoughts of Winters long since forgotten. They were halfway there when something stepped in their path.

I watched in shock as a shape on four legs that seemed to loom out of the darkness launched itself at them with a ferocity I had never seen before. Like anyone, I had heard stories of what creatures may lurk in the desert. I hadn't given it much thought as an adult because there were many more pressing monsters to be afraid of. Who has time to worry about a monster that may or may not exist when you are surrounded by monsters you know exist?

Winters audibly gasped at the same time both gunmen yelled out. One tried to aim and fire his gun, but the creature stood on its hind legs and slashed his arm with claws that looked lethally long before he could fire a single shot. He let out a wail of pain as he fell to the ground.

The other one tried to keep running to the truck. I could hear his heavy breathing as he panted, but he was no match for the creature. It pounced on him and sunk its teeth into his neck, silencing him instantly. Meanwhile, his associate was still crawling on the ground, trying to get to cover in the truck. In the blink of an eye, whatever that thing was landed on top of him, and after the gunman briefly cried out, he went quiet.

Now it was silent again, and the only source of light out on the desert floor was the discarded flashlights. But that thing was still out there because you could occasionally hear movement coming from the darkness. Winters heard it too because he stayed hidden behind the massive dirt pile and kept quiet. Good move.

An eternity passed before I heard what sounded like footfalls going in the opposite direction. Then it was gone. Winters noticed the same thing, because he peeked out from behind the dirt mound and saw there was no sign of that thing. No doubt he was feeling painfully exposed out there in the middle of the desert more than ever.

Then, somehow, the feeling in the air returned to normal, and the desert felt more like the desert once again. I couldn't tell you how or why it happened, but something shifted in the air, and now this felt more like the desert I'd spent an incalculable amount of time in.

So after I cleared my throat and tried to shake off the shock of the situation, I stood up and called out, "Hey Winters, over here!"

He turned to look at me so fast it was impressive. I had no doubt the poor guy was on edge, but I thought that was better than sneaking up on him.

"Who are you, and how do you know who I am?" He yelled back to me.

"I'm a park ranger, and I've seen you all over the news."

"How did you get out here?"

"Found a hidden mine shaft and followed it here."

He paused while he took this in. "How long were you up there?"

"Not long, I got here right before you arrived."

"Did," he began. "Did something come out of nowhere and attack my unwanted associates?"

"Indeed."

"I thought so, but I wanted to check and make sure I wasn't hallucinating or something. Saying I'm lucky that thing showed up doesn't even come close to describing it."

"I was gonna cause a little diversion if it didn't. My walkie talkie got lost in the mine, otherwise I would've called for help."

"I appreciate that."

"On that note, do you mind lending me a ride?" I pointed to the truck that sat there silently.

"No problem. Come on down and we'll get the hell out of there."

He didn't need to say anything more. Now I felt better about turning my flashlight back on as I walked down from where I was to the truck. I still felt the adrenaline running through my body, but it was more muted. Plus, it was nothing compared to how Winters must be feeling. So I just put one foot in front of the other and walked towards the truck. While I was far less wary now, I did keep my eye on the truck and paid attention to my peripheral vision as I approached Winters while I walked through the cactus lined sand.

Eventually, Winters was in front of me. He studied my appearance, obviously checking my uniform. After a moment, he held his hand out in front of him, and we shook hands. I could feel how raw they were from digging, but he didn't flinch for a moment.

"Nice to meet you," I said sincerely.

"Likewise. Shall we get this show on the road?"

"Absolutely." But then I paused. "Is it alright if I drive?"

Winters didn't say anything, but I could feel him thinking over my request. After what seemed like a long time but was probably less than a minute, he chuckled. "Sure thing. And smart man. I would've asked the same thing. You may have an idea of who those men are and why they took me, but you don't know the specifics, and have no reason to trust me or where I might take you. By all means drive. I'm just happy to get the hell out of here at all."

With that, I hopped in the driver's seat while Winters climbed in beside me. I wasn't surprised that the keys were still in the ignition. They had no reason to even consider removing them. As I briefly checked the truck, I could see bits of stuffing coming out of the upholstery in the backseat. But the truck started without any difficulty, and I slowly pulled out of there.

As the area faded away in the red glow from the taillights, I watched the dust being kicked up in the truck's rear-view mirror. What was left of the four men who came out with Winters laid sprawled out on the ground, completely motionless.

After a few minutes, the sight had nearly vanished in the rearview mirror, and we were well on our way towards the road back to town.

"You want to know exactly what happened?" Winters asked after being quiet since we got in the truck.

"Of course."

"The reason for my disappearance and the little ride out here was that I wouldn't pay money to some people who claimed I should for my own good. Do you know why?"

"I have an idea."

He chuckled. "You seem perceptive, so I'm sure you do. It's all very simple. As a businessman, it's all a question of value. Paying money is absolutely useless if they keep raising the price or there's absolutely no guarantee of safety in it. When there are a thousand other people just waiting to take over turf or already in the area also demanding payment, it's a complete waste of money. Especially since I have no family in the area, so it wasn't like these people could use that as leverage against me. I'd learn to live with death a long time ago. It's like an old friend you've been expecting to show up to a party you're having. Sometimes he's early, sometimes he's late, sometimes he's right on schedule when you expect him, but he always makes a call. But like any party guest, most of the time you can't help but be nervous when he's about to come knocking."

There was a lot of sense in that, so the two of us sat in comfortable silence until the vast terrain of the desert was behind us and we were almost back to town. Right before I reached the road, he turned to me.

"What exactly did you plan to do if that thing hadn't shown up?"

"Throw some rocks to cause a distraction and some chaos."

"Interesting. What did you think that would do?"

"At the very least, give you an opportunity to get the upper hand and do something."

"Did it not cross your mind that might make the situation worse?"

I briefly glanced at him. "No."

"Why?" He sounded genuinely intrigued.

"I watched you the whole time. You were afraid, but you were defiant. You didn't beg for your life, offer to give them whatever they wanted, or anything remotely like that. You were ready to put up a fight."

Winters seemed genuinely surprised by this. Then I saw him smile for the first time.

"You are observant. And you were right. Had you started throwing rocks, I would've immediately swung into action. At the very least, it would've given me a chance. You know what I was thinking of while I was digging?"

"What?"

"How the four of them were small time and would always be small time, no matter what happened to me. They were all expendable. Know what's going to happen now? I'll turn up and it'll be a huge news story. I'll go back to my life, and people will look at me in stunned disbelief. It'll be the story to end all stories. Meanwhile, the four of them won't even be a name somewhere. They'll eventually be dumped in a hole in the ground just like that one, and they will be replaced like they weren't even there. By the time someone figures out all isn't well and finds the remains of their associates, they'll see how badly things went. Odds are very good they won't even get near the place because the cops will get there first, but everyone will know something attacked them without so much as breaking a sweat. And it's still out there. That'll be the story."

I had no doubt that was true. All of it. So I drove to the police station and escorted Winters in where we told them the story of how I got there and what happened. They brought us some coffee and contacted the ranger station to let them know everything was alright, but I'd be a while. It wasn't the worst way to spend an evening, as Winters and I got to share a pizza and some other food from a restaurant down the street. Everything Winters said came true, and his miraculous return was the big story in town.

In the meantime, I went back to work, and the mine was fully explored and documented before it was properly closed off for safety reasons. The thing that was out there that night was never seen again by me or anyone in the park. If anyone else saw it, I never heard about it. But that didn't mean it wasn't out there. The desert has always been a place of mystery, especially at night. I don't expect that to change because that's exactly what makes it the desert. And it's something I've always loved about it.

THE GRIZZLY

Eʟʟɪᴏᴛᴛ ᴀɴᴅ I ʜᴀᴅ just finished a job for our boss. It was a simple errand; make a drop off and collect payment for a rare treasure that a collector had an eye on. It was something we had taken care of many times as employees in the antiques and rare collectibles industry. Once the rare item was safely in the proper hands, we headed to a local diner for some food. The two of us had just finished eating burgers, fries, and some pie when Elliott looked at his phone.

"It's the boss Spencer. He wants us as soon as possible."

"Cool. Let's go."

The sunset was just starting by the time we left the diner, and it made for a spectacular sight. The two of us eventually arrived at a private airstrip where there was a jet waiting for us. I saw our boss's black sedan parked a safe distance away, and I pulled up alongside it and turned the car off. By now the desert air was much cooler than before as we stood face to face with our boss, Carlton. A slight man with impressive eyebrows in his early 40s, he greeted us with a smile while his driver Nash, a well built guy in his 30s, politely nodded at us. Carlton was the head of one of the most respected firms in the country that dealt with rare treasures, antiques, and items that had been lost and were in need of locating.

"Well done on the job today boys."

"No problem. So what are we doing here?" Elliott asked.

"Our friends up north were finally able to give us the location of The Grizzly's treasure."

A ripple of excitement went through the air. David "The Grizzly" Green was a prominent crime boss who died in an impressive shootout with law enforcement about 25 years ago. Before he went out in a hail of gunfire, it was widely rumored that he stashed a fortune in gold somewhere. Much of the fortune had been improperly taken from its rightful owners, and there was a longstanding legal claim on it.

"Really? After all this time?" Elliott whispered.

"Indeed," Carlton nodded. "Some old associate of his just died and when going through his estate they found a map to it." He held up a thick piece of paper to show us. "And according to this, the land it's on no one technically owns. And we've been contracted to recover it by the people it belongs to."

"No kidding?" I asked.

"Yessir. And I don't need to tell you the recovery fee is massive. That's where we're going on the plane. We'll go over the location in detail when we get there."

"Nice," I said.

We boarded the plane, strapped ourselves into the comfortable leather seats, and took the short flight. When it landed, we disembarked and saw that the arid desert of Arizona had been replaced with the crisp greenery of Montana in early October. There was still a small but fading amount of daylight that made the mountains and pine tree peaks visible. Different from the desert, but just as impressive.

"Alright," Carlton said as we all got into a waiting truck that had been arranged for us. "The word is the treasure is hidden under a log cabin where there is a labyrinth of caves. I have the directions to where there is an underground passage, and that should take us to what we're here for."

"But going in at night? Shouldn't we have special equipment?" I asked.

"Correct. Always thinking Spencer. That's why I like you. We already took care of it. Jackets, flashlights, knives, and bottled water in backpacks. Now it's only a short drive from here, and once we find it, then we'll gear up and head in."

The drive was proven to be short; a quick trek down a dark, quiet, pine tree-lined road that wound around until it stopped at a seemingly abandoned log cabin. Elliott and I strapped on backpacks while Carlton and Nash did the same. Once we were all fitted with gear and had flashlights in hand, we slowly approached the cabin.

"According to this, there should be a secret tunnel located in the back sunroom under the floorboards. The path should eventually lead to where the treasure is hidden," Carlton explained.

Without further ado, Nash slowly opened the door to the cabin. Its hinges were rusty, and it opened with a loud squeal. Not that there was anyone around to hear it. The cabin was in the middle of nowhere, with nothing but the mountain far off in the distance to see us.

We entered one at a time, our high-powered flashlights illuminating the ruined cabin. It might have had rustic charm once upon a time, but now everything was old and faded.

"The only thing missing is the guy with a hockey mask and a machete," I said as I slowly walked around the cluttered and broken remains of the living room.

"Come on Spencer, where's your sense of adventure?" Nash chuckled.

"My sense of adventure is just fine. I just prefer to leave the scary movie tropes for my time off."

Everyone laughed as we carefully walked through what had once been the kitchen and dining room to the screened-in porch. Despite everything, it did give us a superb view of the moon, which was a perfect crescent in the crisp night sky.

"Ok," Elliott began. "The passage has to be somewhere here in the floor."

We all murmured our agreement and began prodding and stepping on the floor to find something out of place. After a minute, Nash stepped on a section that gave off a loud creak. That was our cue to immediately start tearing out sections of the thick rug covering the floor. When I yanked a particularly thick section that brought up a cloud of dust and the thick smell of mold, a trapdoor in the floor was visible.

Elliott immediately grabbed the metal rung attached to the trapdoor and tugged. It easily opened, and a blast of cold air hit us as we found ourselves staring into a deep tunnel.

"Alright," Carlton clapped his hands together excitedly. "Let's go."

Our flashlights revealed we were walking into a long passage built off the structure of an interconnected series of caves. No doubt used by smugglers for a generation. Once I stepped down the wooden steps that led from the cabin into the earth, I tugged my jacket tighter around myself and we continued on our journey.

We'd been walking for about a half hour when I smelled it, the pungent odor of rot. And it wasn't long before we were face to face with the source, a man lying face down on the passage floor. Despite the smell, the body was still very much intact, and he was wearing what could only be described as hardcore hiking gear. There was no doubt the guy had been here very recently. But from what I could see, his gear and the exposed flesh was covered in what looked like a thousand rips. Almost certainly the result of an animal attack or an animal finding the remains. Maybe both.

"Come on." Carlton whispered. "We're almost there."

"What happened to him?" Nash asked.

Carlton shook his head. "I don't know."

Each of us stepped over the body in turn and continued walking down the tunnel. Then the ground began to incline, and we started to climb as the path twisted and turned through thick rock walls that were gnarled and twisted.

But then, our path began to even out and we found ourselves looking at a small opening in the rock wall. When we walked through it, we were in open air again. The cave had opened up onto a ledge overlooking an open field that was located between a cluster of pine trees. In the middle of the field was a cluster of sharp boulders that took up most of the space.

"Ok. According to this, the suitcase with the goods should be hidden under a giant flat slab of rock in the middle of the field," Carlton said.

The four of us slowly approached, and we did indeed see the giant flat rock. The natural light was actually pretty good here, so with the addition of our flashlights, we could see a lot. From the angle we were at, I could make out the faint outline of a battered old suitcase sitting right underneath the rock. The problem was that we could also see the rock wasn't empty, as there were three giant sleeping grizzly bears on top of it.

The sight caused each of us to go silent for a moment. The idea of going in there with grizzly bears, any one of which could devour me without a second thought, made me sweat.

"What do we do boss?" Elliott muttered while watching the sleeping bears.

"No problem," Carlton said as he shrugged off his backpack and took out several large pistols. The sight didn't phase us, as we all knew that sometimes you couldn't be too careful in this business. We'd all narrowly escaped more than a few sticky situations in this line of work.

Carlton handed one gun to Nash and gave me the other before turning to Elliott. "You go in and grab the suitcase. These two will make a diversion if need be, but that shouldn't be necessary. I can tell these bears are hibernating, so you should have nothing to worry about. But only if you're game for it. If not, no one would blame you."

Elliott had been through far worse than this, so I wasn't surprised when he nodded. After taking a deep breath, he slowly climbed into the open space, taking care with each step while the three of us watched. Despite the chilly air whipping through the clearing, I was sweating. Each step had me half expecting one of the bears to wake up and roar with a vengeance before charging at Elliott. As I held the gun ready, the handle quickly became slick thanks to my sweaty palm. All we could do was watch Elliott get closer with every step, which took a painfully long time.

When he finally reached the giant flat rock, he slowly ducked down for a moment while he fished for the suitcase. Two of the bears had their backs to him, but one was sleeping with its head facing Elliot, and I had no doubt that with it being only a few feet above him, Elliott could probably feel it breathing. When he finally tugged out the suitcase and stood up, I held my breath. Fortunately, the bears did not move a muscle, and he began to walk back to us. I was careful to never let the bears out of my sight, but they were definitely hibernating. They hadn't even made a sound.

Moments later, Elliott returned to us with the suitcase in hand. When he finally climbed back up the ledge and there was a barrier between him and the grizzly bears, he sat down, panting and sweating.

"Well done, Elliott," Carlton nodded approvingly while handing him a water bottle that he downed in a few quick gulps. "You'll definitely get a bonus for this."

"Thanks boss."

"We'll take a brief rest before we leave. Since you have already done more than your share of hard work today, Nash will carry the suitcase the rest of the way. All you have to do is stay ahead of us with a flashlight. But first let's look at the spoils."

He bent down and gently zipped open the suitcase. It unfolded easily, and the gleam of what was inside was stunning in the intense glare from our flashlights. Gold bars, jewelry, and coins were stacked thickly on top of each other.

"Not too shabby," Carlton nodded. "Not too shabby at all. We'll give it another minute or two and then get out of here."

After Elliott rested, Carlton collected the guns back before Nash carefully picked up the suitcase and Elliott and I led the way back to the cabin. In what seemed like no time at all, we were climbing back up the stairs to the cabin's trapdoor. Once we were back out in the fresh air and the suitcase was loaded into the back of the truck, Carlton shut it with a satisfied click.

"Now all that's left is to take it to the appraisers and lawyers when we get back home. When we return, you two can call it a night. Well done again, both of you."

"Thanks boss," Elliott said. "That was fun. Let's never do it again."

Carlton laughed. "No doubt. I've never cared for bears either. I've always been more partial to wolves myself."

With that thought, we all hopped in the truck and headed out of there. Everything was quiet until we got to the area where the plane was supposed to be waiting for us. We were about three miles away when Nash began to drive over a ridge overlooking a stretch of grass. Nash was about to say something when there was a loud crash, and in the blink of an eye, I felt the truck being hurled onto its side and all four of us were scrambling around while yelling profanities incoherently.

"Everyone alright?" Carlton asked once we had all extracted ourselves from the truck, which was badly dented and lying on its right side, which was a little too close to the edge of the ridge for comfort.

We all muttered we were. I was a little dizzy, but nothing too bad.

"What happened?" I asked Nash.

He shrugged. "I don't know. From the corner of my eye, I saw some shadow come out of the woods back there and moments later, I felt the impact like it hit us."

"That's insane," Elliott muttered.

"Agreed," Nash said.

"Well we won't be able to use the truck to get us the rest of the way. So we go on foot. Spencer, grab the suitcase. And since I don't like the looks of these woods, both of you take one of these," Carlton instructed Elliott and myself as he produced the two pistols again.

He didn't need to explain himself because I didn't like the vibe in the air either. What had just happened didn't seem normal. So I grabbed the suitcase and had a weapon at the ready just in case. For what exactly I didn't know, but it sure beat not having a weapon.

The four of us walked in complete silence, with the wind occasionally howling at our back. As unnerving as being alone in the chilly night air for miles was, it beat having to worry about random people finding us with a fortune in gold. So the quiet had its upside. We kept close watch on the dense pines surrounding us on all sides and we steadily followed the road to the private air strip. With my watch, I was able to steadily keep track of our progress as we walked one mile, and then two.

As more time passed, I was able to recognize the area we had first arrived in. But that sense of partial relief didn't last long, because just as I was starting to shake off the adrenaline from the truck being knocked off the road, I heard something. Voices in the distance.

We all immediately stopped and listened, our weapons at the ready and the suitcase clenched tightly in my free hand. The voices were not loud, or particularly close, but they were human sounding, and any human voice this far out in the middle of nowhere at night was something to pay attention to.

But the creepy part was that there had been no signs of footsteps or any other indicator of human activity. It was like a random sound in the woods that comes out of nowhere. The sweat began to dribble down my neck as we stood there. I had no idea what was going on, but I didn't like it one bit.

After we didn't hear anything for another minute, Carlton gestured for us to keep going, but to keep an eye on what was behind us as we did. Which was fine by me. So the walk continued on for what seemed like a painfully long time. At least once, I swore I could hear the sounds of someone, or something following me. But every time I turned around, I saw nothing.

When the sight of the plane on the private airstrip finally came into view, I had never been so happy to see a plane. And from the sighs of Elliott and Nash, I could tell they felt the same way. Our pilot opened the door to the plane's cabin to greet Carlton, and that was the exact same moment there was the sound of rustling in the woods less than a mile away, and I could just barely make out the sound of a laugh. It did not sound like any laugh I had ever heard before, as it sounded too high and almost inhuman.

"Get in the plane," Carlton hissed at us.

He didn't need to tell us twice, as all three of us immediately hustled up the steps behind him, slamming the door shut behind us as we climbed into the plane's cabin.

"And please get us out of here, NOW," he commanded the pilot.

He didn't need to be told twice either, because he hastily went back to the cockpit and, within moments, was easing us down the runway and out of there.

Nash, Elliott, and I quickly strapped ourselves into our seats and prepared for takeoff. Relief was starting to flood back through my system. But just as we reached the end of the runway and were beginning to take off, I looked through the window and saw that the space where our plane had been was now occupied by several humanoid type figures, who were just standing there watching our plane leave. Since darkness was rapidly consuming the area, all I could make out was their general shape, which looked vaguely human but not quite.

Once we were off the ground and out of there, I turned around and saw Elliott on the other side of the aisle. He was watching me, and from the look in his eyes, I could see he had observed the same thing. Nash and Carlton were sitting straight ahead, simply relieved to be out of there and enjoying the plane's steady ascent into the air back towards home. Good for them.

At some point I dozed off on the flight back home. Elliott woke me up when we landed, and we both happily went home and crashed. Carlton was able to return the treasure within the next few days, and we both received our cut of the finder's fee by the end of the week. It was nothing to sneer at. I never did figure out who or what was following us that night, but I'm happy we never have to go back there again.

Longstreet's Island

I AM A PRIVATE contractor who specializes in investigations. Meaning people hire me to investigate and deal with troublesome tasks they can't quite handle themselves, or don't want to get their hands dirty and want someone else to take care of things.

It has taken me to virtually all the world's major hotspots in addition to numerous other countries you wouldn't expect. Upon being given a new assignment, I met my superiors in a bland conference room where they filled me in. As usual, they were all dressed in overpriced business attire that looked good but did not justify the price tag while they sat around a mahogany table that was polished to a shine that was bright enough I could practically see my reflection in it.

"Your objective is this man, Dr. Longstreet." The guy at the head of the conference table said before he flipped to a picture of a man in his late 40's with a widow's peak and penetrating green eyes. "He is working on a project that is of great interest to many people."

"What kind of project?"

"Genetic engineering."

"Ok. And what's the problem?"

"The good doctor was contracted out to work on a research project, but for one reason or another, his employers lost contact with him. And his employers are people who never normally need help, and they want our help on this."

"You don't say?"

"I do. So that's where you come in. Your objective is to reach the island where Longstreet is holed up and report back what you see. Once that has been achieved, we'll have a better grasp of the situation and what to do about it."

"Understood."

"Your contact for this is Giselle. Rendezvous with her within a few days and she will help you the rest of the way. The dossier file on Longstreet and other background materials will be provided to you when you leave here. Good luck."

"Thank you."

Said background material was indeed provided, and I spent the journey to the island parsing through it. Dr. Longstreet was an interesting character to say the least. Born to a well-off family, Charles Longstreet had gone to the best boarding schools and graduated top of his class at Harvard and Harvard Medical School. After that came the usual litany of internships, residencies, and other assorted professional milestones, each more prestigious than the last. That was why when it came time to put a professional in charge of a big-time project, Dr. Longstreet was the top choice.

At first, he exceeded their wildest expectations, delivering encouraging results time and time again. But somewhere along the line, something went sour. The reports weren't quite sure what happened, but the why didn't matter so much as the what. At some point he'd abandoned his assigned tasks and had just invented his own. Then they stopped being able to reach him altogether. That made certain people nervous. And people who aren't used to being nervous don't like it. Which meant he was now officially a problem.

Flipping through the various reports, memos, and other notes in the files, it was clear that whatever was going on with Longstreet had truly disturbed them. It was a sight seeing the notes and communications go from mild irritation to full-blown concern. But the unwritten thing that screamed off the page was that it disturbed them because it should not have happened, as the Doctor was one of the best and the brightest. But that was no surprise to me, people can live with something going sour so long as it's something that makes sense. But when something bad happens that defies all logic, that rattles people.

That's why the whole mad scientist thing has been a staple of stories for so long. The entire reason I have this job, for which I am incredibly well compensated, is when illogical things happen, and it rattles people who never get rattled. And boy, were they rattled over whatever Longstreet was up to. Or more specifically, they were rattled that whatever he was up to was now out of their direct control.

More interesting to me personally was the fact that I wasn't the first person being sent to check on the Doctor. First, they sent in another doctor. But when he didn't check back in, they sent in someone else. Some in-house guy who handled security issues for them in the past. But when he went the way of their previous effort, that's when they decided someone else should handle it. And when I got there, my objective was to find my way to Longstreet's lab and report back my findings.

From what the dossier said, the Doctor was holed up on an island all alone with maybe one or two other people. That was bad news. Of all the things you could do to someone to slowly drive them insane without much effort, solitary confinement is number one on the list. What makes it so powerful is that you think it's easy. It's not an overt form of torture or punishment. In fact, some people think spending all your time alone would be heavenly. But it slowly gets to almost everyone, it's just a question of how long it takes.

I was eventually dropped off at my rendezvous point, an old freighter stationed off the coast of a chain of islands in the Pacific. There my contact Giselle was waiting for me at a spot near the water. With her soft brown hair and a knowing smile, she looked like any other content beachgoer on vacation. But it was her eyes that gave her away. Almost unnaturally blue, I could see them scanning everything and everyone around her. And not in an arrogant way either. She was simply observing and studying what was occurring in her vicinity. A trait I knew quite well myself.

"Carter?" She asked.

"Correct." I reached out to shake her hand. "Nice to meet you."

"Likewise. Thank you for coming."

"Of course. So what's the story? I heard he's working on some kind of genetic engineering project."

"That's one way to put it. I tend to put it another way. He's become the cliché mad scientist."

She took a large tablet in hand and swiped through it. After a few moments she handed it to me.

At first the footage was grainy, but then I could see and hear several people frantically running for their lives from a camera suspended from the ceiling above a giant tank of water so I could see the entire massive space. The water was deep blue, and I could see in its depths was a massive black shadow.

But then the camera zoomed in to something farther down the room, and I could see what looked like a giant glass greenhouse filled with trees and other plants. But unlike most greenhouses, the plants inside this one looked overgrown and wild. For one brief moment, I saw a giant shadow leap out from behind some tree and maul something lying on the ground with a guttural roar. Then the camera's feed went out.

I stood there in shock. I'd seen more than my fair share of disturbing things in this job, but this was unlike anything I had ever heard of before. In fact, watching that footage didn't even seem real. It was like watching a movie, and one with less production quality at that. But that's often how life goes, what isn't real can often look more plausible than the absurdity that can be reality.

I gave her the tablet back. "What exactly is he working on?"

"Charles was always fascinated with mythological beasts, but nothing held his interest like werewolves."

"Interesting. Why Werewolves?"

"Part of it was how the idea of a werewolf was so widespread across cultures and civilizations. But the majority of it came from the idea that it was treated like an actual disease that would manifest symptoms at certain times."

"I see where this is going."

"I'm sure. He kept remarking how the fact that the idea was so present in cultures made it hard not to think that there was more going on than just metaphors or scary stories. Like there was some underlying basis for it all."

"I see. So how do you know so much about Longstreet?"

"I used to be one of his many lab assistants, that's how I got the layout of the island and all the facilities."

"Interesting. So how do you feel about what I've been asked to do?"

"Fine," she shrugged. "The Longstreet I knew died long ago, I don't recognize the person he is now."

"What happened to him?"

She ran a hand through her hair and studied me. "I can't tell you how long I've thought about that question. Maybe longer than I've ever thought about any one question in my life. The best I can say is that I don't think it was a clear-cut thing. More of a slow evolution. But the short answer is this. I truly believe the line between sanity and insanity is far thinner than we care to believe, and sometimes the line gets moved closer without us even realizing it. Sometimes people even move the line by their own behavior. That was Charles. He got a taste of true power, the power of life and death, and it was not a good result."

"I see."

"And now you can see for yourself," she said while giving me a piece of paper." Here's a map of the island. Everything is on there. Good luck."

I thanked her for all her help before I got ready to head to the island. Once my gear was all set and the boat was properly equipped for the voyage, I studied the island map and steered out to sea. There was a light breeze that got more powerful as I cruised along. I occasionally passed a sailboat or yacht filled with happy ocean travelers, but apart from that it was quiet on the sea.

I arrived at my destination about an hour later. The humidity was so strong it hung in the air like a wall. It gave the atmosphere a surreal, almost dreamlike quality. Everything was like a mirage. For Dr. Longstreet, it seemed to be exactly that.

The island's appeal for the Doctor was obvious. This was no lush tropical paradise with white sand beaches like something out of a travel brochure. This place was a mass of jagged rocks sticking out in every direction. There looked like a few palm trees here and there, and who knows, maybe there was a beach in there somewhere, but it was not a welcoming sight. Which I'm sure was part of the plan. The island's layout showed that all the labs were underground and could be accessed on foot once you had gotten to the proper location via boat.

According to the map, the only way to get there was through a massive, rocky passageway. Getting through it took serious time and effort. Everywhere you looked there were jagged rocks and stalagmites descending from the ceiling, and it didn't take long before the passage was pitch dark and I needed to turn on the boat's lights just to see. As I slowly went along, I felt like the boat was being swallowed by a monster.

It wasn't hard to understand why Longstreet had changed out here in particular. Isolation is a bad influence on anyone, but when you add in power on top of it, that can be a uniquely awful combination. Out here Longstreet wasn't just a suit with an MD, he was the king of the castle. And suits with an MD have a lot of influence to begin with.

Since navigating the sea cave took so long, I had plenty of time to study the map of the island. I was currently in a series of interconnected caves that went from the ocean to the island's interior, where Longstreet's underground lab was. All I had to do was follow the cave until it ended, and I would eventually reach the labs.

Many minutes later, I arrived at a metal door that was set into the rock wall. After I carefully stopped the boat and dropped anchor, I got all my gear ready including my weapons to defend myself if need be, climbed over to the rock ledge containing the door, checked to see if it was unlocked, and when I found it was, I gingerly pushed it open.

I found myself facing the vast expanse of the lab I had seen on the video footage. Seeing it in person was an entirely new experience, as it seemed like every inch of space was taken up by some project that was sitting there incomplete. The room was one long corridor that allowed you to walk past and glance at everything going on. But all the various stations did was sit there. And that was the giveaway that the whole place was deserted.

I could feel it in the air, which was heavy and silent. This should be the heart of the whole island, brimming with activity. Instead, all the lab equipment felt abandoned here. There was no whirring or clicking of computers, no liquids simmering away. It all looked more like a film set that had been forgotten and had a sad, neglected air.

That meant something had happened, it wasn't pretty, and I was just now finding the aftermath with no idea what came before. That's something that applies for much of life in general. So many times we just stumble into the aftermath of something that's happened. We simply aren't aware of it. And we also aren't aware that we are cleaning up the pieces of a mess we don't even know exists. That's my job in a nutshell, with the difference I typically know what happened before. Or at least I have a clue about what happened before.

After I passed a bunch of brand-new computers that were sitting there with the screens off, it didn't take me long to find the wreckage of the greenhouse type structure. The glass had giant cracks in it, and when I got closer, I could see the glass also had giant claw marks embedded in it. That was my cue to take out my camera and get plenty of pictures and footage for those who had contracted my services.

Once that was done, I kept exploring while my findings were reviewed. It didn't take long for me to receive contact to check elsewhere and see if there was any sign for what may have happened and where the Doctor may have gone. So I stealthily crept through the maze of other lab buildings that also held living quarters and the seemingly endless expanse of vegetation that covered the island's interior.

After about two hours, I eventually came to a hidden dock, and what I saw made my jaw drop. It was a cavernous space completely filled with boats. They varied greatly from small boats to yachts that were probably worth the GDP of entire countries. Some were decaying and rusted, while others were in flawless condition, but they all sat there silently. The effect was more than a little spooky.

It seemed every inch of space was taken up by a boat, with one exception. A gap near the end of a row near the hidden opening in the rock wall that led to the sea. I had no doubt the missing boat was where Dr. Longstreet and his associates were.

So that was my hint to go back to my own boat and see what I could find. Steadily, I followed the same path I had taken and eventually, I was back on board and ready to go. But by now the sun had set, and the island was rapidly fading into darkness. I was pleased to be leaving, as it seemed either there was no outdoor illumination, or it was not being activated for one reason or another.

I quickly started the boat and steered my way back through the caves, mentally trying to decide where to search first once I was back in open water. As I finally found myself heading out to sea, I looked up at the sky and saw it was a cloudless night. That meant I got a crystal-clear view at the moon, which was full. I had to appreciate the irony. Maybe that was the essential truth about the werewolf story; the idea that the full moon does things to people. The terms lunacy and lunatic come from the word lunar, which means moon. The correlation between the moon and human behavior has been studied and debated, but when you're dealing with ideas and folklore that transcend cultures and go back centuries upon centuries, arguing there is no clear connection doesn't quite hit home.

Besides, just because people aren't sure how the full moon impacts humans doesn't give the full picture, because there are all those other creatures like wolves living on this planet as well. And sometimes we just don't know everything, because deep down, I don't think any person is meant to know everything. Just look at Dr. Longstreet. There's a huge difference between being knowledgeable and thinking you know everything. He clearly thought he knew something, and from what the shape of his lab says, turns out he didn't. The sea is like life; an endless mystery that although we are a bit closer to understanding, still remains unfathomable in many ways.

With the moon hovering above, I decided that Longstreet would take the boat to a location where he could presumably spend some time without anyone finding him. That meant another island or some kind of cove. According to the maps, the nearest thing to Longstreet's island was 15 miles away, and it was a lagoon. So that was my goal for now.

With that decided, I settled in for a comfortable ride. The water was calm and lacked waves, so I got to relax and sail along. I've spent a large piece of my life on boats. Going from one assignment to another means a lot of time traveling, and oftentimes it requires going to remote locations on water. So boats and I were very well acquainted. And while seeing the sun shimmer on the waves is stunning, nighttime was always my favorite time while out to sea. It's quiet and there's nothing but you, the sound of the ship, and the open sea. It helps you think and focus on the essentials.

Water is a witness to the entire scope of human history, and not just as a casual observer, either. The Nile River, the English Channel, and countless other names on the map have helped decide which civilizations rise and which ones fall. And unlike fire, water is eternal. The darker side of human existence is as steady and eternal as the sea; the appearance might change just like the ocean's rhythms and tides, but they're always there in some form.

And it's not just the sea itself that makes you think. Because people are creatures of habit and telling stories about things that may or may not have happened is one habit. People think tales of pirates are just some bit of ancient history or ghost stories designed to scare travelers, but they're not. The age of cannons and the Jolly Roger may have gone away, but piracy went exactly nowhere. If anything, the Jolly Roger got an upgrade, as now pirates have automatic weapons instead of flintlock pistols and instead of using a compass they have sonar. And they don't hide out at some charming tourist trap where hotel employees are paid to dress up as pirates and walk around with a peg leg and a parrot on their shoulder. In reality, they have far more in common with drug traffickers than something sold at a Halloween store.

Being out there on the open sea pursuing Longstreet reminded me that I was following in the footsteps of countless sailors going back centuries. I remember the first time I ever thought about the sea. I mean when I truly sat and contemplated its depths. It's astounding when you think about it. The Earth is far more water than land; about 70%. Not to mention what inhabits the sea. Just think of all the shipwrecks that have occurred over the centuries. The sea is the largest graveyard on this planet. The saltwater dissolves everything it touches. Just drinking sea water could kill a human. That is the cruelest irony of all, imagine being surrounded by water and dying of thirst.

The planet really belongs to the sea, and all its contents. It's easy to forget until it isn't. Nature has a pesky way of reasserting itself.

I was less than one mile from the lagoon when the ship came up on my sonar. The sound sent a shot of adrenaline through my body, and I quickly slowed down as I approached the ship's location. Eventually, the ship in question appeared on the water, and as I got closer, it seemed to grow larger with each passing moment. Despite the distance, I could tell the ship was either completely abandoned or had been mostly abandoned because something had happened.

I was still a careful distance away when I grabbed my binoculars to grab a closer look. And what a sight it was. Because before airplanes were a thing, ships were the way to travel across the sea, and for the rich, no expense was spared. These things were essentially luxury hotels that floated. The boat that sat there silently in front of me was like that. Its impeccably polished surface gleamed in the moonlight with a shine that seemed almost unnatural, and its wooden deck looked so well cared for that in any other situation you would be beyond excited to relax on it while looking out at the water.

But I wasn't in any other situation, and in the present one, the sight of the massive yacht all alone on the sea at night with no activity not only wasn't pleasant, it was a downright uncanny sight. It sat there silently, like a sleeping animal. What bothered me most of all was the fact that there were numerous ships that Longstreet and whoever else may be onboard could've taken. I had no doubt there were faster, and certainly far more subtle boats. Which means this one had specifically been chosen for a reason, whatever it may be.

Traveling like I do, I've spent a massive amount of time hanging out with people. Often in bars and restaurants close to the water. Many times listening to stories is part of my job, but sometimes it's just fascinating to do. It's easy to see why all throughout history, sailors and pirates have told stories in bars and in ship hulls about what may be encountered on the sea. And a favorite type of tale was of ghost ships that had vanished and perhaps miraculously reappeared. They made for a fun story, but I never took it seriously.

Seeing the giant yacht stationed out here in the middle of nowhere at night, seemingly abandoned and gleaming white in the glow of the full moon, was as close to a real ghost ship as I was likely to get. Especially because unlike the vast majority of ghost stories about abandoned ships, this one was real, and I could be pretty well confident something terrible had happened.

So once I got as close as I dared, I slipped on my diving suit, carefully swam over to the giant yacht, and climbed the boat using the shiny metal ladder that spanned the back of the ship. I took each step with as much caution as possible, and when I finally touched the luxurious wooden deck, I walked over to the door to the ship's interior and opened it.

That was when things got truly creepy because the impeccable exterior couldn't hide the chaos inside. Everywhere I stepped, something expensive had been smashed, shattered, broken, or ripped. Chandeliers and dinner plates that probably cost more than my apartment were lying on the floor, crystal beads were now scattered everywhere like marbles. Crystal glasses so nice you would be afraid to pick up were ground down into shards and beautiful red curtains were barely recognizable, as it looked like they'd been ripped to ribbons one uses to wrap Christmas presents with.

But the worst was the blood. It was scattered intermittently on walls and floors. By now it had dried, and it coated the expensive wallpapers and polished wooden floors in spots with thick black smudges. And it was coupled by numerous scratches in the floor and walls. Deep scratches. Ones far deeper than human fingernails could cause.

I took a deep breath and tried to focus. If there was this much blood that meant there had to be bodies somewhere nearby. I was just about to take a final look around when, without warning, I heard the sound of movements from below deck. The footsteps were slow. Careful. Stealthy. The kind belonging to someone taking their sweet time and looking for prey.

With my heart pounding in my chest so hard I thought it would explode, I quickly went back towards the way I had come in. If they found me, odds were good it would all be over. I was one man with one gun and there was no telling how many there were and what they were armed with.

Going as fast as I dared, I moved to the small wooden staircase I had climbed down on my descent from the top deck and moved up it until I was hidden from the floor I had just departed. And I managed this not a moment too soon, because soon there were shadows moving up from below deck somewhere.

From where I was, shadows were all I could see. I had no idea what was causing them, only that whatever the source was, it seemed huge. But somehow, that all became irrelevant when I heard an unearthly roar come from somewhere that made the hair on my neck stand up. I've heard numerous animals roar in many different circumstances, and I had never heard anything like that before.

And whatever it was, apparently it didn't mean anything good for the occupants of the yacht, because there was a brief commotion from some other people who had apparently been following the shadow, because several people started shouting before frantic yelling was quickly followed by gunfire.

That was my cue to exit, and fast. Fortunately, the gunfire continued and masked my footsteps as I climbed the stairs, moved past the wreckage, pushed open the door I'd come in, and found myself on the deck. Then I swam back to my boat.

The swim felt like it took an eternity, and when I finally flung myself back on the deck of my boat, I saw that a fire had somehow started in the yacht. It spread with an alarming quickness I had never seen before, and it wasn't long before I could smell and feel it, even from the distance I was at.

I'd been in and around numerous fires, but nothing like this. The fire burned with an intensity that wasn't natural. It sizzled and spat sparks in a way that telegraphed that it wasn't your cozy fireplace fire gently burning firewood. I had no idea what was now being consumed by flames, but good riddance to whatever was now burning up with a vengeance. All I could do was continue to quickly document and record what I was seeing for my associates. I watched helplessly as the expensive boat burned to a shell before it sank to the bottom of the ocean with a loud hiss as the flames were extinguished and all that was left was a thick cloud of smoke.

Then my job was officially over, because there was nothing left of Dr. Longstreet, his suspected associates, and his work. All that was left was for me to return home and meet with those who had dispatched me.

When I finally did return, I was met by uniformly stunned and demoralized faces. They had always thought that at least something could be retrieved from his work, but now there was nothing. Nothing but the money they would have to spend retrieving the yacht wreckage and whatever other expenses were awaiting them.

I couldn't really blame them for being so stunned. Truth was a hard thing to come by anymore, but a story like this, it just seemed too outrageous it had to be made up. But the footage didn't lie, and deep down, they knew it would end like this, no matter what they had hoped. But despite all the complications that were only beginning for them, whatever Longstreet was up to was over, and not only was I well compensated for my services, I got one hell of a story to share with people. And I couldn't ask for anything more than that.

So once the check from the job cleared, I wasted no time in going out to a local bar in a town nearby that I'd never been before, and chatted with whoever was hanging around. You never know when you'll find the perfect audience for your story, and you'll never know when you'll hear some undiscovered gem. Some charred wreckage at the bottom of the ocean was one of two things left of that yacht, while my story is the other. Personally, I much prefer the latter.

Nursing Duties

BEING A NURSE, YOU tend to see more than your fair share of sick things. What might come to mind for you is probably bodily functions.

Don't get me wrong, those can definitely make you a bit squeamish. But believe me, you can get used to that. But the body isn't the only part of a person that can become diseased. The ravings, screaming fits, and the general insanity, I don't know if you can ever completely get used to. The sad thing is, half the time the insanity comes just as much, if not more from the patient's family as from the patient themselves. But I won't lie, it's a remarkably satisfying feeling being able to help someone in their time of need. It comes with an emotional cost at times sure, but it is always worth it. Although sometimes you help in ways you never expect. Much like I did with old Pete McDonald.

From what I know, old man McDonald was a cantankerous SOB in life. But now all that remained was a gnarled, shriveled frame of someone who couldn't do much but lie in bed. Occasionally, he would speak a word or two. But most of his time was spent staring up at the ceiling.

It was just past 5 on my usual shift when I changed out the sodium thiopental solution in his I.V. and took care of the other usual tasks. He was the last stop on my round. I looked at Pete's vitals, heart rate and breathing, both normal. I checked his blood pressure; it was in the usual range, 160-90. A little on the higher side, but it was normal for him. I was just finishing up when he started talking.

"It's been so long," he began hesitantly. His voice had the weary tone of someone wanting to get something off their chest.

"Yeah it has Pete." It was quite common for people under medical care to talk at length to the staff. Believe me, sometimes a patient will tell a caregiver more personal information than their own family.

"I never thought I would want to talk about this. A man spends so much time with a secret buried, he never wants to talk about it. But since what's about to be buried next is me, what's the harm in talking about it."

"Go ahead Pete. I'm right here," I have no idea if he even knew my name, but he wanted to talk. Which meant I was here to listen.

"When I was younger, I was a real scumbag." His voice was completely hollow, lacking even the slightest bit of emotion. It wasn't a confession so much as a fact.

"Oh yeah?" This happened all the time with patients, especially elderly ones. All that time in a bed gave them endless opportunities for reflection. Since I don't think Pete had any visitors since he'd been admitted, that meant the guy was stuck with his own company.

"You have no idea. Back in my day, I was a first class hellraiser."

"Were you now?" I couldn't help but wonder. We always see seniors as they are now, in the twilight of their lives. Older, wiser, and wrinkled. We tend to forget that they didn't always look or act like that. They were the same as us once, young and vibrant. Our mistakes were once theirs.

"Let me put it this way. I probably shouldn't be alive right now. In fact, it's amazing I lived past the age of 50. Drinking, drugs, robbery, I even knocked a few men off in my time. Still haunts me to this day."

"Really?" I asked. He didn't respond to this but carried on as if I hadn't said a word.

"It was 1986, a very bad year for me and my family. Since I was infatuated with the bottle, I literally pissed away all of our money. I lashed out at everything and everyone around me. It didn't help that I messed around with the wrong people. It all came to a head on August 7, 1986."

"Go on," I whispered. Although I knew perfectly well he would continue whether I wanted him to or not.

"There was this guy who lived near my house. Went by the name of Snake Eyes Bennett. He was what you would call a big shot. All of us around town resented him. It wasn't just that he was rich. No, it was because Snake Eyes was shady and rich. Why do you think we called him Snake Eyes? It was an open secret that the guy had gotten his privileged status by rather unorthodox means."

"There's one in every town," I nodded in agreement.

"He was a hustler. But Snake Eyes didn't have the nerve to be a legit hustler. None of the hardcore stuff. No, he was a swindler. The suit and tie wearing kind. A real snake oil salesman. Ha, that's a good one!" A harsh laugh quickly filled the room for a moment before it turned into a racking cough that made his entire body convulse. But he had more to say after he caught his breath. "The rest of us would have had some respect if he actually went out there and got his hands dirty. But no, that wasn't for him. He was one of those Chamber of Commerce types who smiles at you when he's robbing you blind. So as you can imagine, that didn't sit too well with the rest of us. Not one bit."

"I'm sure."

"You gotta think, Oak Point was going through a pretty rough time back then. Unemployment was through the roof, most of us did an honest day's work for no money. Some of us had our vices, most of us in fact. But we made sure to toe the line as much as we could. Seeing Snake Eyes flaunt his wealth around town was just the straw that broke the camel's back."

"So what did you do?" I took the opportunity to sit down in a visitor's chair so I could face him as he continued.

"One night, a bunch of us were out on the town. When you are in a group, things sort of take on a life of their own. Especially when you are all hammered out of your mind. I don't remember who suggested it, but one of us knew Snake Eyes was holed up at some rat hole hotel about 15 miles away. His family was out of town for some reason. He was conducting one of his 'business transactions' as he called it. Naturally, we thought it was a great idea to go pay him a visit. He had ripped off everyone in town and it was high time to take back what was ours. It was only right."

I shuffled my feet and leaned back in the chair as Pete rambled on.

"It seemed like we were there in no time at all, crowded in front of that door. Room Number 12, the 2 was crooked and the grey paint was peeling. When Snake Eyes answered the door, all of us rushed him. He went to pieces quicker than a wet newspaper. Hell, I can still see it now. I mean, I knew he was a coward, but if you're gonna rip people off, you better toughen up, son."

"Right," I nodded in agreement. I wasn't surprised at what he was telling me. Part of me was hoping that what Pete had to say next would never come out of his mouth. But the rest of me just wanted him to spit it out.

"In no time at all, we had Snake Eyes all tied up. We made out good when we went through his stuff. $700 in cash, a gold watch, and some jewelry. It wasn't bad for a night's work. There were five of us all together; Luke, Brendon, Travis, Jamie, and yours truly. All seeking our own version of justice for how Snake Eyes ripped us off. Take Luke for example. He lost his farm that had been in the family for generations because the bank jacked up his mortgage rate, guess who sat on the board?"

"Snake Eyes."

"That's right my boy. The same goes for the rest of us. Well, since Snake Eyes stabbed us all in the back, we decided to do the same to him. But don't worry, we didn't neglect the front either."

There it was. I knew it was coming. But knowing something is coming and experiencing it in the moment are two completely different things. It was the way he said it that was so profound. So matter of factly, like Pete was talking about a routine trip to the mall or something.

"So what happened next?" I felt myself stiffen in the chair as I asked the question.

"We got rid of the body. Threw it in some old freezer with a padlock, tossed it in the backseat of what had been Snake Eyes' Cadillac, and drove it down to the swamp just off the old highway. We just cruised that thing right into the water. I can still hear the sounds of it sinking. As we walked away, Luke said something. 'Boys, I'm amazed we just did that. I was expecting the swamp to spit Snake Eyes right back out'. We all had a good chuckle at that."

"I bet. Did anyone ever find out?"

"No. It didn't hurt that no one in town was exactly sad to see him go. I gotta admit though, for years I was terrified his family or someone would come for revenge. But they never did. I guess they hated him as much as the rest of us." He looked out the window for a second as he seemed temporarily absorbed in thought. But after a moment, he turned back to face me. "Although one by one, we all lost touch. It wasn't long after that when I went to the slammer for a few years. Armed robbery, amongst other things. I was in and out for a few years, and my wife and kids were long gone during one of the in periods. I haven't seen any of them in years. Apart from me, everyone who was there that night has passed on."

"I'm sorry to hear that." I wasn't sorry for a moment, but what else do you say to something like that?

"Kind of you son. So anyways, that's my little story. Hope you enjoyed it." He spoke like he was reminiscing about a pleasant afternoon fishing or something. It was pretty messed up.

"It wasn't dull, that's for sure. Anything else you need, Pete?" I asked as I stood up from my seat.

He shook his head.

"Then it's my time to head out. I'll see you later." I walked out of his room as he turned on the TV.

I had never been so happy to leave work. The front doors to the hospital glided open smoothly as I walked out into the cool evening air. I felt like I was in some sort of trance as I unlocked my car, put the key in the ignition, and drove home. My body seemed numb, like it was on autopilot. Somehow, once I got on the highway, my mind suddenly switched back on. A million emotions flooded through my body at once. I spent the rest of the drive in silence, processing what had just happened.

I got back home about 20 minutes later. As I saw my front door, I relaxed a bit. When I walked into my condo, I switched the lights on. The dark blue walls and crisp white carpet never failed to make me feel at home. My mom was asleep on the couch, the TV blaring on in the background. She's been in town for the week and has been staying with me. When I switched on the lights, she bolted awake.

"What time's it?" she slurred out as she rubbed her eyes.

"I just got home from work, Mom," I told her as I got a bottle of water out of the refrigerator. She instantly sat upright at that.

"How was your day?" she asked. Mom was always curious to hear stories about my job.

"Well, a patient told me a little secret of his. I guess he killed some rich big shot decades ago out of spite. He finally spilled the beans after all these years. As soon as I'm done with my drink, I'll call the missing person's hotline. That reward money isn't gonna collect itself."

"Did it shock you?" Mom looked at me, her expression full of concern.

"Wish I could say it did. But nope. Not one bit." She nodded solemnly. "But then he mentioned how he was always afraid of Snake Eyes' family coming after him," I added.

"Oh yeah?" she looked faintly amused.

"Yup. Then he mentioned his own family as an afterthought. But nothing new there. Thank God his wife took their kids and ran."

"Indeed," Mom agreed. "Best decision I ever made. I cringe to imagine what would have happened if I didn't. You know the man I don't dare call your father was always way more interested in Snake Eyes' family than in us."

THE PURPLE CANDLE

YOU ENCOUNTER SOME PRETTY interesting people when you work at a store that specializes in things like tarot cards and other items connected to the occult. Although encountering interesting people is the norm when you work any retail job anymore, it's a unique experience in my case.

Personally, I think it's worth it to not have to deal with the usual nonsense like Black Friday, and the upside is that the store always smells amazing from the variety of incense you can buy. Most of the time customers are a little quirky, but respectful and polite. The store is in New Orleans, so it wasn't like I was working at an occult store that stuck out like a sore thumb or didn't fit in with the community. But most of all, the job was simple and straightforward, and the store itself was quiet, calm, and peaceful. And what more can you ask for from a job?

But there is one particular customer that stands out above all the rest. It was on a Tuesday afternoon when the shop was quiet. I was in the middle of adjusting some crystals we had on sale when I heard the telltale chime of the bell that announced we had a customer on the premises.

So I stood up and headed to the front of the store to see what was up.

"Hello, welcome to The Purple Candle, can I help you with anything?" I asked the figure with their back turned to me as they were looking at some books.

"I'm not sure. Let me look around and I'll let you know." The customer said as he turned around.

The guy was gorgeous. Deep green eyes and a jawline so sharp it could cut through bricks. But what got my attention most of all was his attitude. Many of the people who set foot in here often do it on a dare, or because they're getting a tongue in cheek gift for a friend, and it shows.

That wasn't this guy. As he browsed through the shop with a hint of seriousness, he methodically studied the various items on display. I could see his eyes sweeping over everything while I walked back to the checkout counter and busied myself. I could also tell he'd never set foot in a place like this, because he had the telltale uncertainty and awkwardness of someone who was out of their element. But that's usually how it goes; people who come in here either know exactly what they're looking for or don't have the slightest idea of what's going on.

"Do you like Ouija Boards?" He asked me out of nowhere after a few minutes.

"Not particularly."

"Why's that?"

"It's best to avoid asking questions you don't know the answer to. I don't care if it's your boss, your landlord, or a wooden board and a planchette."

"Fair point. What about some questions you do know the answer to?"

"Those can be just as risky."

"That they can." He nodded. "Do you do witchcraft?"

"No but ask my ex-boyfriend and he'll tell you something different."

He chuckled. "I'm sure. Well if he left you, I'd bet money the other woman is a witch and has him under a spell. It's the only possible explanation for leaving someone like you."

"Actually, it was a mutual decision. But nice try."

He smiled at me. "You know it."

"But if I'm being honest, I would've absolutely been accused of being a witch back in the day. Aside from working here, I have a black cat."

"Definitely grounds to be viewed with suspicion back then. Which means you would've been sent right to the gallows."

"Not burned at the stake?"

"Not here. They burned witches in Europe. Here in America it was hanging."

"That's correct. But at least I would've had good company. Me and virtually everyone else I know. Literally anything was grounds for being called a witch back then. Just like most things were fair game for being committed to a psychiatric hospital for centuries after that."

"Indeed."

"If I recall correctly, they even put a psychiatric hospital right where old Salem used to be. Fascinating, right?"

"Absolutely. Speaking of witchcraft, do you like working here?"

I shrugged. "I got no complaints. It's a job, like any other."

"What if a better offer came along?"

"I'll decide what to do if it comes along."

"I understand." He paused briefly and went to look at the display of tarot cards that occupied a table nearby. "Do you have a favorite deck?" He asked a few moments later.

"Not particularly. They all have their own unique style."

"Do you believe in them?"

I was quiet for a moment. "I tend to think of them as a form of meditation. If you're quiet and in thought, it's amazing what can come to you."

"I can respect that." He shuffled through a few decks and held one up to me. I noticed that the Devil card was displayed on the back of the box. "What would you do if I told you this was me?" He pointed at it.

I shrugged. "The same thing I'm doing right now."

"You don't seem surprised or shocked."

"Because I'm not. I get asked weird things all the time working here. Besides, everyone's got their own version of the Devil and everyone's the Devil to someone, it's just a question of how many people share that version. You know what the difference between an angel and a demon is?"

"What?"

"About thirty seconds."

He chuckled. "Well said. But what's your version of the Devil?"

"I haven't quite decided yet. Probably because there are countless versions. To some the Devil is that bottle of booze, while to others it's a bag of powder, the abusive spouse, the nasty boss, or the treacherous coworker. But they're all accurate. It's just a matter of picking your poison. My version, like most people's, all depends on what's happening."

"Very interesting observation. I like you."

"Thanks." I had no idea how I felt about this guy.

"One last question. What do you think of all this stuff in general?" He gestured around the store. It was a common question for me.

"Humanity has existed for thousands of years. Certain practices have come and gone over the years, but a lot of the tradition and folklore has endured. It's just a question of whether it's simply changed shape or gone underground. Many ancient ideas and practices are still out there, they're just hiding beneath the surface or practiced on the margins."

He nodded. "I see where you're coming from."

"Alright, I give," I said. "What are you here for?"

"Do you read cards?"

"No, even better, I read people. And you, my friend, are here for a specific reason. I'm just not sure what it is. Yet."

"Would it be ridiculous to say I was looking for some help?"

"Not at all. Most people are looking for help anymore. But as to what brings people in here, I find people are typically looking for assistance related to job, family, or romantic troubles. And since you don't carry that unique sense of misery that comes with job issues, I'm gonna guess family or dating."

"You're observant. It's family."

He paused for a moment while I stood there, quietly waiting.

"It's my sister. Kelly's her name. She's in trouble."

I remained silent while he stood there, trying to articulate his thoughts.

"She ran away a few months ago. We couldn't find her, so we hired a private investigator. He found her two weeks ago in a place about three hours outside of town, and she was hanging out with people widely described as 'weird' and 'creepy'. The investigator had also done some research and found people associated with them have gone missing."

"Alright."

"It gets worse." He swallowed nervously. "He says there are rumors they meet in remote places and do..." he fumbled for a word. "Things. Rituals."

"So you want some insight."

"I'd be grateful for literally any help at all. The PI is good, but he lost them. Said they just up and vanished without a trace."

"And here you are."

"And here I am." He nodded. "I'm Alec, by the way."

"Isla." I reached out and shook his hand. Alec's grip was firm, but gentle. Then I stood up from where I'd been leaning over the counter and looked him in the eye. "Well Alec, the first thing to remember is that a ritual means different things to different people. The term ritual has an inherently ominous connotation in many cultures, but anything can be a ritual. Opening presents on Christmas morning after you eat a breakfast of pancakes is a ritual. Like most things, everyone and everything has rituals, it's just a question of how far some people take it."

"Fair enough. I just," he struggled for a moment to get the words out. "I'm scared. We all are. We've noticed people following us. Lurking outside the house. Nothing serious or overtly scary. Or enough to call the police. But it's just enough to let us know they're there."

"Right."

"But I did manage to get a picture of some of them one night. Here it is." Alec took out his phone, swiped through it, and held the screen up to me after a moment.

The picture was of a group of people who were dressed casually, but in ways that took care to hide their faces, be it with baseball hats, knit caps, or the odd hood up. I was almost done with the photo when something in it caught my eye. One of the figures in the middle of the frame looked vaguely familiar. So I took a closer look and noticed that despite the baseball cap on his head, I could still make out his face from the angle. My stomach sank when I recognized it immediately.

"Oh my God. One of the people in it is my ex-boyfriend Cameron."

"You're kidding me?"

"No. That's him." I jabbed my finger at the picture while the floor felt like it was tilting beneath me.

At some point we ended up calling Vivian, the store owner and a good friend of mine who knew Cameron. She didn't hesitate to come in when I explained what was going on. Despite arriving on short notice, Vivian looked great as always. She's one of those people who always looks great no matter what's going on or what she wears.

"So where do we go from here?" Vivian asked when Alec had finally finished explaining things.

"Well, everything we've been told says that unless an actual crime has been committed, there's no reason to call the cops. But regular people like us? We're free to do our own legwork. Although I'm not sure how much good that would do. We tried that before and got nothing. The group Kelly is with constantly moves and leaves false trails."

"But we know they remain in the general area," Vivian brushed a strand of auburn hair out of her face. "Which means they must have a place to go where they do, well, whatever it is they do. And if there's one thing I know, it must be well hidden. Because everyone notices a group of people."

"That's exactly what the PI my family hired said. It's what drove him so crazy. That a large group of people would be so hard to keep track of."

"The island." I blurted out without warning.

"The island?" Alec asked.

"It's the name for a stretch of land that's been in Cameron's family for generations. It's been his ever since his father died. There used to be a cabin there, but it's been long since demolished."

"Is it a good place to hide?" For the first time since he walked in, Alec was looking at me with something that resembled hope.

"You have no idea. It's out in the middle of nowhere, and unless you know what you're looking for, you'd never find it."

"Well then, what are we waiting for? It's field trip time." Vivian clapped her hands together.

It took Vivian no time at all to close up and flip the sign to 'closed' on the shop door. Then we piled into her black SUV and headed for the island. Vivian drove, Alec took the passenger seat, and I was in the back. We drove there in complete silence, and while the radio was on, I couldn't tell you what was playing if you paid me. The whole thing had a surreal, dreamlike atmosphere to it.

Eventually the city faded away in the rearview mirror, and we were the only ones on the road. I'm not sure how I felt about that. It was fitting for sure.

"I can't believe Cameron is mixed up in this," I said eventually. "I just can't."

"Why?" Alec turned around in his seat to face me.

"He was always so normal and intelligent. The last person you'd expect to get involved in something like this."

"My sister was like that, too. That's what makes it so terrifying."

"They wanted his land," Vivian said from the driver's seat.

"What?" I asked.

"His land. They wanted it. Whoever is the ringleader probably saw Cameron had something useful and then did whatever was necessary to recruit him. Made him feel included. Important even. Same reason people get involved in gangs or organized crime. From what you told me, Cameron always felt like he was an outsider and excluded. Being made to feel part of something when you have that feeling is incredibly powerful."

"I think you're onto something there." Alec whispered. It was a sentiment I agreed with.

It didn't take long to arrive at our destination after that. The Sun had gone down by then and the area came to life at night like only a swamp can. The air hummed with the sounds of splashes in the water and of things whizzing through the air. I never did particularly like coming out here with Cameron. The island was a massive bit of land situated deep in the swamp that was surrounded by water on almost all sides, and the only way I knew how to get there was through a narrow path that wound around the swamp. So with my phone in hand as a flashlight, I lead the way.

We all trooped silently on the worn dirt path, with only the frogs, crickets, and other swamp dwellers to keep us company. But it didn't take long to find out we had the right idea. Because after walking for about 20 minutes, I could see through the trees that there was a massive bonfire sitting right in the middle of Cameron's land. And as is often the case with massive bonfires, there were plenty of people surrounding it.

They were dressed casually enough, but that was the only remotely normal thing about the situation. The people moved and danced around the fire in ways that can only be described as unnatural. I love to dance, and I love the freedom and the fun that comes from dancing to one of your favorite songs. You can always tell if someone is truly happy while they're dancing because no matter what the tune is, they move in a way that's inherently calming to watch. This was anything but. The movements I was witnessing now were manic and intense. If you didn't know better, you'd suspect them of having a bad reaction to some kind of drug, which was entirely possible. Which was why, despite the dense humidity, which was already making sweat drip down my arms, a shiver ran through my body at the sight.

But I did my best to stifle the feeling as we slowly crept around and settled in a spot that gave us a perfect view of the area. It was a sliver of land with several trees that was raised above the island, so it allowed all three of us to look down at the group without them having a clue. So all that was left was for us to sit there silently and watch until Vivian took out her phone and began recording what the group was doing.

"In case there's something we can use." She explained when the two of us looked at her.

"Good idea." Alec nodded.

Whatever we were witnessing went on for a few minutes until a loud popping sound rumbled through the dense swamp air.

It was obvious that something was up, because the group immediately stopped what they were doing and looked around in what I could tell was total confusion. There were no deliberate, unnatural movements here; it was all good old-fashioned surprise.

Moments later, more popping sounds penetrated the air, and it was obvious that it was gunfire, and someone was shooting at the group. One of them on the far-right side had been hit and went down immediately. As several more shots rang out in the air, more people around the fire went down and didn't get up.

The group was in full confusion now; they were trying to run for cover, but there was nowhere to run to, and they had no clue what they were even running from. The three of us sat there spellbound as the sight unfolded before us.

After several more moments of haphazard gunfire, it was silent. But not for long, because from far across the swamp, several figures emerged from the shadows and approached the roughly two dozen group members still remaining. In the flickering light from the massive bonfire, I could see there were four figures. They were all armed with machetes and wearing cheap, costume store masks.

It didn't take me long to realize what would happen next. But nothing could've prepared me for the raw brutality of the four masked strangers and how they raised their machetes and hacked through the group one at a time. They were methodical, taking care to surround them and pick them off at odd intervals like a pack of lions going after a herd of prey. The screams were without a doubt the worst sound I've ever heard. The assailants' blood-soaked machetes gleamed in the fire light as Vivian silently recorded it all.

But eventually the area fell silent again and the masked assailants left soon after. Then it was just the three of us, what was left of the group, and the bonfire. Once a few moments had passed, Vivian used her phone to call the police and tell them what happened. Then we were left with nothing but the hum of bugs and frogs to keep us company.

Vivian, Alec, and I didn't talk much as we waited. There wasn't much you could say after something like that unfolds right in front of you. And the longer we were there, the more the massacre we had just witnessed chilled me to the bone. This wasn't some random act of violence by people who were just out for a thrill. The assailants knew exactly what they were doing, knew that the group was there, picked off just enough of them to cause a panic, then methodically set about executing the rest of them in a way that suggested they'd done this all before.

It was late at night when help finally arrived, and by then the bonfire was little more than smoldering ash and glowing coals. No one was prepared for what the paramedics found when they arrived. As they were cataloging bodies, they stumbled onto Alec's sister Kelly, and she was still alive. Unconscious, but alive. And she was the only one. She'd been hit with gunfire, but it was in the right shoulder and the leg. Then she immediately went down and was knocked unconscious when her head hit the ground at an odd angle. Which was how the paramedics found her.

The surgery went fine, but it's a long road to recovery, and that's just the physical part. The mental therapy involved will be even more grueling. But Alec and his family got what they wanted, as Kelly was finally free of those people and whatever they had planned.

Cameron wasn't so lucky. He'd fallen victim to one of the machetes and there was nothing to be done. I felt sad at his demise, but worse about how his family would take it. They were such nice people. That's the real tragedy of the situation; all the people who were nothing but collateral damage.

But somewhere along the line, you make ties that even if they don't replace broken ones, they help ease the pain. Which is why it was no surprise Alec stayed in contact with Vivian and I after what we saw in the swamp. He's told me a million times I'm the only reason Kelly had a shot at making it out. Vivian agrees. The one thing that bothers us the most is the assailants who massacred the group. There was absolutely no way to identify them, which means their motive was unknown and they were still out there. The theory is that the group messed with them in some way, and this was their way to get even. If that's the case, then mission accomplished.

The Buttered Roll Buffet

ONE NIGHT MY FRIEND Taylor and I were driving around town looking for someplace to eat. Living in a big city with literally a thousand places to eat is a lot like having a TV with a thousand channels at times. There's no limit to the possibilities, but sometimes you still can't make up your mind about what sounds good. We were tired of all our usual places and wanted something new, but couldn't figure out what that should be. I was just about to turn around and order a pizza when I saw it.

Inside a massive strip mall was a large restaurant with a sign over the top saying it was the Buttered Roll Buffet. The place looked brand new, and the parking lot was packed, which was saying something because the parking lot was big.

"Shall we give it a try?" I asked Taylor.

"Sounds good to me."

We parked in the first spot we could find and went inside. Once we walked through the glass entryway which was lined with paintings I barely glanced at, we arrived at the hostess's station. The restaurant was massive, and the floor was packed with tables while wooden booths lined the walls.

As the hostess seated us, I was hit with a thousand different smells at once. The minute we both gave our drink order we were free to head up to the buffet and grab a plate. The place was filled with activity because the restaurant's patrons were all circling each buffet section and examining the potential items to try. I didn't blame them one bit, because the buffet was a sight to see.

The salad station was filled with romaine and iceberg lettuce, spinach, and arugula all sitting on a massive pile of ice. There were also large dishes of Caesar salad and a huge bowl of coleslaw made with vinegar dressing. Alongside that sat shimmering piles of dressing and further down was a huge bowl of ambrosia salad and a colorful spread of melons and berries.

At the front was a station filled with appetizers. Deviled eggs, crab wontons, jalapeno poppers, fried mushrooms, mozzarella sticks, potato skins, and potato and tortilla chips fresh from the fryer sat beside queso dip, salsa, and guacamole,

The next row was filled with meat dishes; spare ribs, fried chicken, pulled pork, several flavors of chicken wings including buffalo, meatloaf, hamburgers, ham, roast beef, pork chops, and chicken fingers. Behind that was a station dedicated to Italian food. Pizza with varying types of toppings, lasagna, penne, fettuccine alfredo, rigatoni, spaghetti with meatballs, and calzones were perched next to heaping piles of garlic bread and breadsticks that glistened in the intense heat lamps.

Seafood was located next to the salad, one half was filled with hot entries, and the other was chilled. The chilled section was filled with smoked salmon, shrimp cocktail, tuna salad, and oysters, while the hot section was loaded with crab legs, coconut shrimp, clam chowder, fried clams, calamari, fried perch, tuna casserole, and crab cakes. A station dedicated to side dishes was filled with mashed potatoes, fried potatoes in several forms, cheesy potatoes, macaroni and potato salad, baked beans, macaroni and cheese, pasta salad, and onion rings.

But the most impressive spread of all was the desserts. It was massive. A self-serve ice cream machine that offered vanilla, chocolate, and strawberry was beside a spot to make your own strawberry shortcake. Farther down a chocolate cake with icing that gleamed in the light sat beside baklava, massive slabs of cheesecake, tiramisu, chocolate chip cookies, apple turnovers, fresh baked blueberry and cinnamon muffins, donuts, peach cobbler, banana pudding, and coffee cake.

Taylor and I eventually each loaded up a plate and returned to our table. Neither of us said a word as we chowed down. It was all delicious and in no time at all, we'd finished what we got and went back for a second plate, taking care to get what we'd been unable to try last time simply because we didn't have big enough plates.

It didn't take long for us to get full and before long we asked for the check, paid and left a good-sized tip, and slowly walked out of the buffet.

"That was the best buffet I've ever been to in my life, no question." Taylor said once we were back in the car.

"Me too." I nodded as I started the car. "It's no wonder that place is packed."

"We'll have to come back."

"Absolutely. For all I ate, I still didn't get to try everything I wanted."

"Me either."

I dropped Taylor off at his condo before I went back to my own place. In the morning I was still so full I could barely manage a bagel. But by lunchtime, I was slowly starting to feel like I could eat normally again. Which was good because that evening I was expected at a dinner party at my cousin Jocelyn's house on the west side of town.

I arrived right on schedule at 6 and after some appetizers of buffalo chicken dip and stuffed artichokes, the seven of us all gathered around for some roasted chicken, mashed potatoes, baked carrots, and spinach salad. While everyone was having some pineapple upside down cake for dessert and chatting, Howard, my cousin's husband, looked up at everyone.

"Did everyone hear about that apartment building that caught fire last week?"

Everyone around the table murmured a yes.

"The sister-in-law of one of the people who died is my coworker. She said that night she had gone out with her brother-in-law at that new Buttered Roll Buffet place."

"I just went there for the first time," I said.

"How was it?" Josh, another dinner party guest, asked.

"Tasty."

"Jocelyn and I went there the other day for the first time." Howard said. "It was delicious."

"I've heard it's amazing." Josh said." I'll have to try it."

"You'll enjoy it." Howard added, before taking a sip of coffee.

The rest of the week passed without anything interesting happening. Time went on until it had been some time since Taylor and I had our first meal at the buffet. It wasn't until the next month we decided to go back. The experience walking in was the same as the first time, with the competing smells of food greeting you. And just like last time, we ate a wide variety of food until we were full. The place was even fuller than last time, with each table full so we sat in a booth. On one trip up to the buffet I noticed the people at the booth next to us. The man had closely cropped black hair, and the woman had thick blond curls. I politely nodded my head and said hello when I made eye contact with them, and they did the same.

Taylor and I left just as full as last time, and we went our separate ways to go home to relax. But I still felt full as I went to bed. The following morning I was beginning to feel something resembling an appetite again, so I made my way to the kitchen to make myself some oatmeal for breakfast. I was waiting for the microwave to finish when I saw on my phone that there had been a nasty car accident last night on a highway about 15 minutes away. A truck had lost control and absolutely totaled an SUV.

My jaw dropped when I saw the couple involved were the people we'd sat next to at the buffet last night. Ignoring my oatmeal for the moment, I texted Taylor.

"That's terrible." He texted back quickly. "But that buffet is most definitely last meal worthy."

"It certainly is."

I eventually finished my oatmeal and went on with my day. It was another month before I was remotely ready to go back to the Buttered Roll Buffet, but after Taylor and I went out hiking with some friends, we were ready. And just like before, the buffet was more than ready for us. Cody and Justin, the two friends we'd gone hiking with, had never been to the place before, and they were just in awe of it as we'd been.

This time they had a station for waffles and crepes with toppings you could choose from. I went with banana, peanut butter, and chocolate, while Taylor went with strawberries and cream. Then it was off to get some chicken parmesan, baked ziti, and antipasto salad. Meanwhile, Cody and Justin were waiting at the panini station, where a smiling chef was customizing sandwiches for patrons. Cody got a ham and cheddar, while Justin got a turkey and gouda.

We all ate plenty and once our bill was paid, we strolled out at a leisurely pace. Once we got in Taylor's car, he turned on the radio and we sat in a peaceful silence as we drove to Justin's where our cars were all parked.

We were almost to his house when there was a detour sign blocking off the main road, so we had to take a route that added 15 minutes to the drive. It took us to a part of town that was quiet with houses spaced far apart from each other. The area had been bought by a bunch of companies for development. But for what, I had no idea.

Taylor eventually turned right onto a stretch of road near an abandoned warehouse. By now it was pitch dark out and the few street lights the area did have cast a sickly glow onto the pavement. I would not want to be one of the few houses on this street.

When we were halfway down the street, Taylor slammed on the brakes. The road was obstructed by a massive SUV that was parked in the middle of the road with its doors ajar. I looked around and there was no one in sight, nor was there any sign of an accident. Something about the situation gave me a bad feeling. Something was up, I just didn't know what.

"What's going on?" Taylor asked everyone in the car.

"I don't know, but I don't like it." Cody muttered. "Let's go back the way we came."

"Especially because that's the only way we can go." I added. "You can't go around it."

Taylor nodded briefly and made a deft turn-around. But just as he was about to start back down the way we came, I saw a flash of movement come out of a nearby alley, and a bunch of men in dark clothing emerged into the clearing. We weren't close enough to see their faces or make out their features, but the minute they saw us I heard angry yelling, and Taylor floored it out of there.

I did my best to ignore the sickening lurch in my stomach as I looked in the passenger side mirror and saw the group of strangers pile into their SUV and immediately start to follow us. My chest felt uncomfortably tight as I clenched my hands into fists and tried to stay calm. From behind me, I saw Cody and Justin had begun to notice we were being followed. Taylor also did, but to his credit all he did was take a deep breath and try to focus. No small feat considering the car following us seemed to be gaining on us. If they caught us or we wrecked out here we were in serious trouble. But after a moment, I saw Taylor's eyes light up.

"Cody, can you see that box there on the floor by your feet?" He asked.

"Yeah, what about it?"

"I've been helping my uncle with some maintenance work at his loft. That box is full of nails. I want you or Justin to roll down the window and dump them all in the road behind us."

"I'll do it." Cody quickly nodded and picked up the box. As I looked in the backseat, I saw that it was stuffed to the top with nails in various sizes.

"Slowly shake them out so they're spread everywhere on the road," Taylor instructed.

Cody nodded and looked a bit pale as he rolled down the window and a chilly breeze filled the air, but he slowly tipped the box in our wake, and all the nails began to scatter on the road. In the dim lights they cast a silver gleam as they spread and rolled across the blacktop in every direction.

The SUV behind us took notice of that after a moment and tried to swerve to avoid the nails, but since they were everywhere, it was impossible. In an instant they drove over some and I saw the vehicle swerve unsteadily and go off the road, only to collide with a signpost.

We all cheered and patted Taylor on the back while he got us out of there and drove to my house, which was the closest one. On the way, I called the police and told them what happened. They agreed to check out the road and meet us at my place. When I hung up, I was on edge for the rest of the drive, as I was afraid there were more of them out there or they'd find some way to come back and follow us. I sighed with relief when we finally got to my duplex where the police were indeed waiting for us.

They found the crashed car that had spun out because of the nails. All four people in it had suffered some kind of injury. It turns out all four of them were well known to law enforcement from past incidents. Only this time they got caught, as they had been up to no good in that part of town when the four of us stumbled upon them.

The next bit of information they gave us made my blood run cold. When the authorities searched the area, they discovered the business the four men had been up to when we found them. The four strangers had kidnapped a man, but he'd managed to escape on that stretch of road, and he ran far enough away that the four men followed him until they gave up and he stayed hidden until he saw the police sirens. That was why the car had been pulled over so randomly. I don't even want to imagine what they would've done to him had they caught him. Or us, had they caught up with Taylor's car.

The cops eventually thanked us for our quick thinking and left. The four of us were exhausted, but we knew there was no way we were gonna be able to sleep after that, so we hung around. At some point, a thought in my head clicked and I remembered something. We had almost encountered disaster after eating at that buffet, like several other people around town.

I took out my phone and after some searching, I found there were many other cases of people encountering disaster or near disaster after eating at that buffet. The incidents ranged from accidents to events like ours. It was uncanny to see. I told the other three what I thought, and they sat there silently.

"I know what you mean Craig, and I can't explain it," Taylor eventually said. "Sometimes there are just things you can't explain. Things that are beyond coincidence. I don't know what to call it, but I don't disagree with you."

"Remember how you said that place was last meal worthy?" I asked.

"I do. I can't stop thinking about that either. But one thing I know for sure is that I'm not exactly keen on going to that buffet ever again."

"Me either." I agreed.

We eventually went our separate ways and spent the next few days trying to get some sense of normalcy back. Part of that included avoiding the buffet at all costs. I didn't even want to drive past it.

But even I wasn't prepared for a news headline I saw about two weeks later. I'd just finished my morning coffee when I saw that the buffet had been the victim of a terrible fire late the previous evening. According to the fire department, the fire had taken place when the buffet was closed, and no one was there. But then things got weirder, because virtually all the damage was limited to the entryway and the buffet's front, with the glass entryway and the walls lining it sustaining most of the damage. As if to cap off the weirdness, the fire chief said that there was a pending investigation but didn't flat out say the fire was intentional. Not that he needed to.

I sat there with my coffee in one hand, my phone in another. Someone had set fire to the buffet, but focused on the entryway? That was oddly specific. But then I remembered something. Those weird paintings lining the walls as diners walked past on their way in and out. Was that what the fire was supposed to destroy?

A quick search turned up an article about the buffet's opening. I skimmed through the usual stuff and went straight to the pictures of the restaurant and stopped when I saw a photo of the entryway. I'd never really taken a good look at it before, but now I was, and the paintings were downright creepy looking to me. In the restaurant's regular lighting they were indecipherable, but in the sharp light from photography they were unsettling. Some paintings showed vague humanoid shapes crawling on the ground and scratching for what looked like food, while others showed similar looking shapes gathered together with sick grins on their faces.

I had no desire to look further. All I know is that my friends and I will never go back to that buffet again, if it ever reopens. There are plenty of other options, and plenty more new places will come. That's what I love most about a big city. It's ceaseless change. There's always something new to see, try, or experience.

ABOUT THE AUTHOR

G RANT BUTLER IS THE author of the novel *The Heroin Heiress*. His short fiction has been published in *Sick Cruising*, *Close to the Bone*, *Mardi Gras Mysteries*, *Punk Noir Magazine*, *Horror Bites Magazine*, and *The Siren's Call*. His nonfiction has been featured in *Interstellar Flight Magazine*, *The Daily Drunk*, *Film Cred*, *Hear Us Scream*, *Certified Forgotten*, and *The Best New True Crime Stories*.

MORE CHILLS FROM VELOX BOOKS

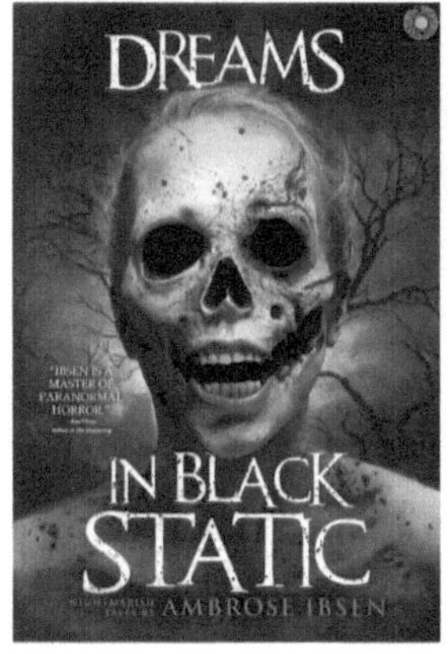

MORE CHILLS FROM VELOX BOOKS

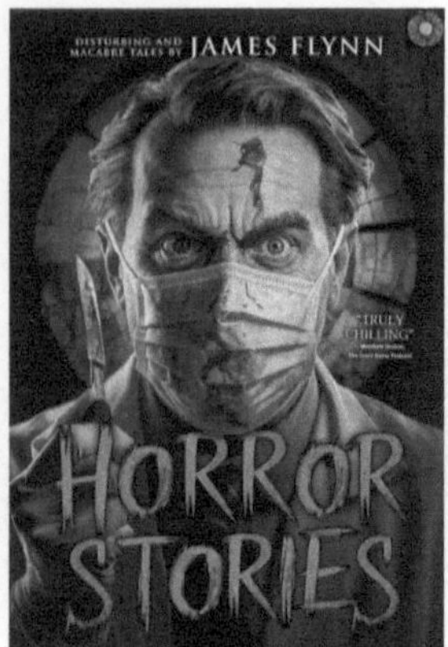

MORE CHILLS FROM VELOX BOOKS

MORE CHILLS FROM VELOX BOOKS

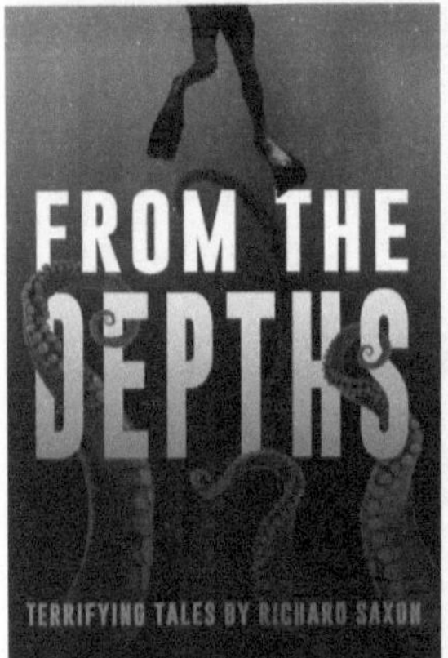

MORE CHILLS FROM VELOX BOOKS

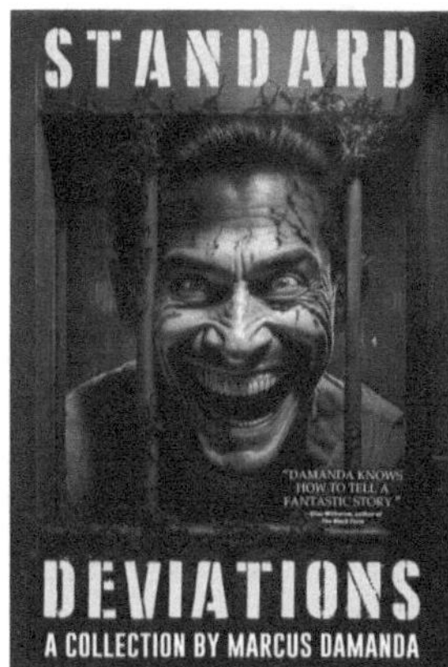

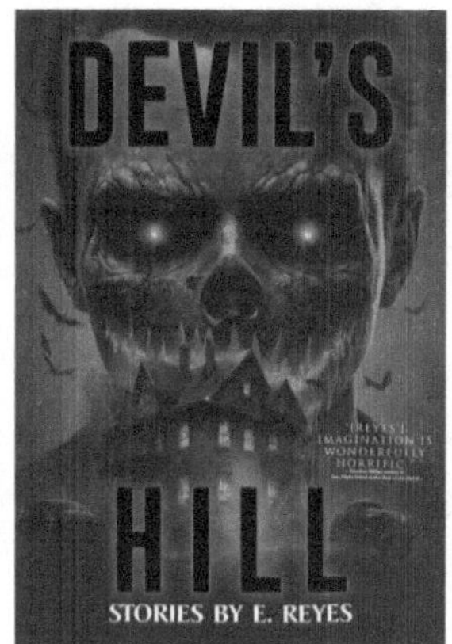

MORE CHILLS FROM VELOX BOOKS

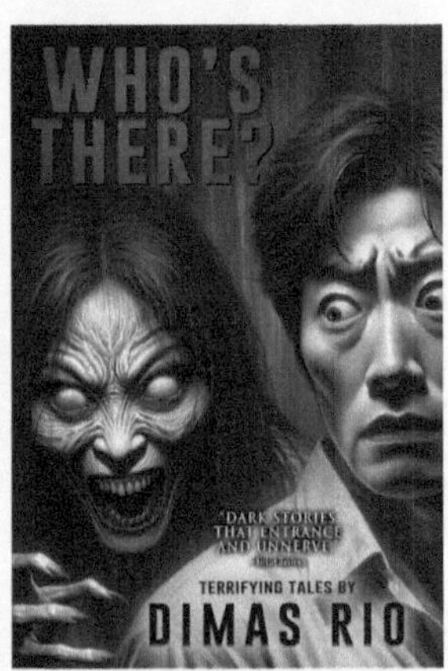

www.ingramcontent.com/pod-product-compliance
Lightning Source LLC
Chambersburg PA
CBHW061248310726
48971CB00007B/2277